HOW TO
TAIL A CAT

Center Point
Large Print

Also by Rebecca M. Hale and available from
Center Point Large Print:

The Cats and Curios Mysteries
How to Wash a Cat
Nine Lives Last Forever
How to Moon a Cat

**This Large Print Book carries the
Seal of Approval of N.A.V.H.**

HOW TO
TAIL A CAT

REBECCA M. HALE

CENTER POINT LARGE PRINT
THORNDIKE, MAINE

For Ashley

This Center Point Large Print edition
is published in the year 2012 by arrangement with
The Berkley Publishing Group,
a member of Penguin Group (USA) Inc.

This is a work of fiction. Names, characters, places,
and incidents either are the product of the author's
imagination or are used fictitiously, and any resemblance to
actual persons, living or dead, business establishments,
events, or locales is entirely coincidental.
The text of this Large Print edition is unabridged.
In other aspects, this book may vary
from the original edition.
Printed in the United States of America
on permanent paper.
Set in 16-point Times New Roman type.

ISBN: 978-1-61173-521-5

Library of Congress Cataloging-in-Publication Data

Hale, Rebecca M.
 How to tail a cat : a Cats and Curios mystery / Rebecca M. Hale. —
Center Point large print ed.
 p. cm.
 ISBN 978-1-61173-521-5 (lib. bdg. : alk. paper)
 1. Cats—Fiction. 2. Treasure—Fiction. 3. Investigations—Fiction.
 4. San Francisco (Calif.)—Fiction. 5. Large type books. I. Title.
PS3608.A54576H67 2012
813′.6—dc23
                                                    2012024572

Introduction

A VELVET FOG draped over San Francisco's steep hills, the blank canvas forming the curtained backdrop to a theater's stage.

November had begun with a few short days of Indian summer, but the opening act had been whisked away by the month's main attraction, a mysterious gray character who skulked through the shrouded streets, erasing the sky and blurring the edges of the city's pastel-colored buildings.

Off in the distance, a foghorn bellowed out a warning to a ship approaching the Golden Gate Bridge. The low hooting *honk* echoed through the bay, floating up into the mist-masked hills that housed the Presidio's former military post before sinking into the murky depths of Mountain Lake.

A slender white cat with orange-tipped ears and tail sat on a bench near the lake's southern rim, staring intently through the soupy haze at an object floating in the water about twenty feet from the shoreline.

The tip end of Isabella's long pipelike tail strummed the bench, an outer sign of her inner contemplation. Her slim shoulders hunched forward; her front claws dug into the seat's worn wooden planks. Blue eyes glittering, she tilted her head inquisitively.

There was something decidedly unnatural about the ghostly creature inhabiting the lake.

ON THE BENCH beside Isabella, a fluffy feline of similar coloring and far greater girth let out a satisfied *burp* as he rolled himself into an upright position. Rupert smacked his lips and let loose a wide, sloppy yawn. His belly was still digesting the fried-chicken dinner he'd devoured a few hours earlier.

Isabella issued a disparaging glance at her brother's bulging stomach; then she resumed her surveillance of the lake.

On a short rise above the far embankment, a streetlight lit a jungle gym's shiny metal bars and, in the parking lot beyond, gave a dim glow to the large white van that had carried the cats, their person, and the vehicle's owner to this isolated spot at the heart of the crowded city.

The moist, pink padding on Isabella's nose quivered as she sniffed the scents of the surrounding wildlife. Her ears widened, taking in the sounds of the night.

A pair of squirrels rustled in the leaves beneath a wooly grove of cypress . . . a raccoon rummaged through a nearby Dumpster . . . a homeless man asleep on the grass let out a whiffling snore . . . and a tall, skinny fellow in a rubber wet suit and flippers clomped through the brush at the edge of the lake.

"Are you sure this is a good idea?" Isabella heard her person ask as Montgomery Carmichael stopped to fit a snorkel mask over his narrow face.

Isabella glanced up at the vacant sky and pondered the question.

Would it be such a terrible thing if their pesky neighbor was devoured by a hungry albino alligator?

Isabella's whiskers twitched skeptically as Monty turned toward the bench, stretched his arms out in front of his chest, and flexed his meager muscles. In her opinion, he didn't stand much of a chance against the ravenous reptile awaiting him in the water.

Her tiny face crimped into a dubious expression.

Eh, she concluded indifferently.

After a moment's consideration, however, Isabella appeared to take a different view on the matter. Pawing the air, she opened her mouth to form a series of sharp clicking sounds that terminated in an instructive *"Mrao."*

Her person glanced down at the bench and sighed ruefully.

"I suppose you're right," she said with a grimace. "The gator might choke on his snorkel."

The woman placed her hands on her hips and pursed her lips, as if considering.

Finally, she called out, "Monty, wait!"

7

• • •

A PALE, LUMINOUS beast with colorless eyes and a snaggletoothed grin swam through the muddy water near Mountain Lake's southern shoreline. The twelve-foot-long, torpedo-shaped body looked like a moldy, bump-ridden log—until you focused in on its sharp claws and prominent jawline.

Clive, San Francisco's reigning celebrity albino alligator, floated comfortably in the darkness, humming to himself as he bobbed in the water. His pointed snout beamed a radiant, if somewhat menacing, smile.

He had enjoyed his short stay at Mountain Lake. Other than the occasional stray golf ball bouncing into the pond from the nearby course and a few distant shrieks from the children at the playground, his visit had been blissfully undisturbed.

Of course, the recent change in diet had left his insides feeling a tad unsettled, and the sudden onset of cooler weather had made him long for his heated rock back at the aquarium's Swamp Exhibit. But, overall, he had welcomed the rest and relaxation at this idyllic retreat. He would have to see about booking these accommodations again next year.

A hungry growl rumbled through Clive's midsection, and his thoughts turned to more immediate issues. It was time for his late-night snack.

With a paddling stroke of his front legs, the yellow nodes of his nostrils rose from the water,

8

prompting a pair of ducks to squawk out a warning. The alligator's gray eyes rotated halfheartedly toward the skittish birds. They were hardly worth the effort, he thought, remembering the digestive complications he'd suffered after his last avian meal. And besides, he generally preferred fish to feathers.

Clive flicked his tail, rotating his body in a reluctant pursuit of the ducks—but a rippling in the surface of the lake caused him to stop, mid-motion. A commotion near the beach had generated the telltale disturbance of a creature unaccustomed to maneuvering in the water.

He focused his eardrums on the stilted splashing movements emanating from the reeds, his sense of hearing being far keener than his albino-diminished vision. After honing in on his target, he optimistically reversed course and began gliding in the direction of the noise.

His jagged mouth cracked open with eager anticipation. The animal who had just entered the lake promised a far more substantial and easier-to-catch meal than that of the elusive ducks.

Even better, Clive thought, squinting at the creature's smooth silhouette—it appeared to be completely free of feathers.

MONTGOMERY CARMICHAEL FLOUNDERED through the reeds in his wet suit and flippers, anxiously fiddling with his snorkel mask as he scanned the water for Clive's waxy white skin. He stepped awkwardly into the lake, struggling to keep his balance as the water seeped up to his knees.

"Nothing to worry about," he hollered, an effort to assure the bystanders on the shore as well as himself. "This critter's been all over San Francisco the last couple of days. He's perfectly harmless."

Surely, the future mayor of San Francisco could handle a meek, domesticated alligator, Monty thought brashly. Heck, he could probably carry the beast back to the van using nothing but his bare hands.

Monty turned toward the beach and flexed his muscles, a show of bravado for his doubting observers. Then, he returned his attention to the lake and whispered coaxingly.

"*Cllliii-iive.* Over here, *ally-gator, ally-gator.*"

A pair of ducks squawked to his left, drowning out the concerned voice of the woman standing next to the cat-occupied bench.

"Just like a puppy dog," Monty muttered under his breath as he adjusted the snorkel and prepared to dive below the surface.

Awash in bolstered confidence, he failed to notice the neon glow stalking him in the reeds.

A single sound broke through the night, its sharp staccato ricocheting across the lake to the craning spectators at the water's edge.

Chomp.

Chapter 1
THE LAMP

A few days earlier . . .

IN A QUIET corner of San Francisco, on a secluded street in Jackson Square, the building that housed the Green Vase antiques shop shifted ever so slightly on its foundation, sending a low, creaking groan into the unusually warm, humid night.

The framing, brick, and mortar had been bound together since the mid-1800s, so a little architectural easing could be forgiven—after a hundred and fifty years, even a building feels the need to stretch its limbs.

The three-story structure rested on ground that had originally been covered by an inlet surge of the Pacific Ocean. The dirt beneath its basement had once looked up through fifteen feet of water to the undersides of small boats that ferried Gold Rush immigrants from ships moored in the bay to the rapidly growing city on the shore.

As California passed from Mexican to American rule and the settlement of Yerba Buena morphed into San Francisco, bucket loads of sand from nearby dunes were dumped along the marshy banks, raising this strategic location up out of the sea. The expanding shoreline immediately filled with new construction, creating the rough-and-tumble neighborhood that would become the Barbary Coast.

The Green Vase had a front-row seat to this historic transformation. Throughout the tumultuous Gold Rush years, a colorful parade of reckless, gold-crazed explorers passed by its iron columns and redbrick facing. The first-floor windows reflected an ever-changing collage of rich and poor, those about to discover their fortune and those on the verge of losing it. Characters of every stripe and color ventured into its saloon, swilled drinks at its bar, and swapped tall tales at its dining tables.

All of these many visitors left their imprint on the building. Shadowed footsteps seeped into the floor's deep hardwood grains; reflected images transferred into the metallic sheen of the bar's brass furnishings. Countless spirits soaked into the brickwork—quietly waiting for the day when their stories might be rediscovered.

Through the decades, San Francisco endured fires, earthquakes, and social upheaval. Forty-Niners gave way to flower power. Railroad magnates and sugar barons were replaced by search-engine entrepreneurs and dot-com millionaires.

The redbrick building on Jackson Street saw its own sequence of change. Over time, the saloon became an all-purpose mercantile, followed by a fine tailor and, later, a tobacco shop. Meanwhile, the Barbary Coast matured into the quiet, respectable neighborhood of Jackson Square.

Much of the area's history was gradually forgotten, subsumed by the layers of modern-day infrastructure, fragmented by the inevitable decay of archival records, buried beneath a landfill of lost memories—lost, that is, until a man named Oscar moved into the apartment above the Green Vase, opened a dusty antiques shop on the floor below, and began coaxing out the building's hidden secrets . . .

LONG PAST MIDNIGHT on the first Sunday of November, Isabella the cat lay near the foot of a twin-sized bed on the top level of the living quarters above the Green Vase antiques shop. Her furry chin rested on her front paws; her slender body curled protectively against that of her sleeping person.

The cat's sharp blue eyes kept a careful watch over the woman dozing fitfully beneath the sheets.

It had been more than a year since Oscar's niece had inherited the Green Vase from her mysterious Uncle Oscar. The Jackson Square apartment built into the two floors on top of the store was now a permanent home to Isabella, her brother Rupert, and their human owner.

The once demure accountant and her two feline

companions had explored many of the historic building's nooks and crannies, along with a sizable portion of the relics and antiques Oscar had left behind—but theirs was an ongoing investigative process.

That night, like many that had gone before, Isabella's person had fallen asleep while reading one of the many reference books she'd culled from the numerous boxes and crates stacked in the basement. The woman's bifocal eyeglasses were perched off-kilter on the tip of her nose; the threadbare book was spread open on her chest.

Isabella shifted her gaze toward the window and the Jackson Square neighborhood that slept beyond its blinds. The upper pane of glass had been cracked open, an invitation to whatever light breeze might be circulating in the warm night air.

The cat lifted her head, listening to the building's low, creaking groan. Her tail slowly tapped the surface of the bed, its orange tip moving like a thoughtful finger.

Her feline intuition had begun to tingle with the suspicion that their next adventure was about to begin.

IN THE DARKENED living room one floor below, near the front window overlooking the street, a small decorative lamp rested on a short end table. The base and stem of the fixture were made up of burnished brass; the curved metal edges bore the speckled tarnish of dust and time.

The lamp's design had been conceived in the early 1900s, at a time when a still young San Francisco was struggling to convince the rest of the world that it could grow beyond its brash Gold Rush beginnings. The earthquake-prone upstart was determined to show its detractors that it could provide the best in five-star entertainment and accommodations.

The fixture captured a critical moment in the city's development. The lamp's ceramic globe depicted one of the many efforts to transform San Francisco into a cultural cosmopolitan center.

THE LAMP'S ELECTRICAL circuit hadn't been switched on in well over a year, leaving its ceramic globe darkened and unlit. Without the glow of the interior light, the images depicted on the globe's outer surface were almost indistinguishable, and the murky gray shadows embedded in the glass had gone unnoticed by the current owner of the Green Vase antiques shop.

The lamp had rested, unused, on its end table, ever since the cat and human trio had moved into the apartment above the showroom. Oscar's niece had assumed that the bulb was burnt out, or, more likely, that the lamp's internal wiring had rusted beyond repair.

She was wrong.

The lamp had been carefully maintained by the shop's previous caretaker, and the bulb was only slightly loosened in its fittings. If tightened in the socket, the bulb would emit a bright light that shined through the globe's translucent surface, illuminating the scene depicted across its wide circumference.

Once lit, the front half of the globe displayed a large stone building in a peaceful, forested setting. Stately columns fronted the structure, which looked out over a landscaped courtyard that featured a series of sunken pools inhabited by a half-dozen frolicking sea lions. Human figures wandered through the courtyard, admiring the animals as they made their way toward the entrance.

The scene painted on the globe's opposite side provided an interior view of the columned building shown on its front.

A brass balcony framed a wet, swampish enclosure that contained a large banyan tree, several rocks, and a tank of water. The balcony's upper and lower railings were connected by a perpendicular row of seahorses, whose curved bodies had been flattened into slats.

In the tank below lay the principal feature of the painting, an intriguing creature who basked on a rock protruding from the water.

Resting peacefully on the rock, a gilded grin on his long, bumpy face, sprawled a pale, luminescent albino alligator.

Chapter 2
A CONSTANT CRAVING

THE NEXT AFTERNOON, Rupert sat on the floor at the front of the Green Vase showroom, staring impatiently through the glass panes of the iron-framed door to the street outside.

He shifted his weight from left to right, all the while craning his head, trying to see as far as he could up Jackson Street to the corner that led toward North Beach.

His person had been gone for several hours, and her return was long overdue.

Where is she? Rupert demanded internally as he raised himself up on his back haunches and propped his front feet against the lower panes of glass.

He'd been planted to this spot for the last thirty minutes, eagerly waiting for the moment when his person would appear around that corner. He was starting to wonder if she would ever get back.

This was her longest jog *ever*.

RUPERT BLAMED THE weather.

The last few days had been abnormally hot for the northern end of San Francisco's typically temperate peninsula. Thermometer readings had risen into the mid-nineties, unfamiliar measurements for the residents of these wind-buffeted hills.

Indian summer, Rupert had heard his person call it. He was familiar with the phenomenon, if not the actual terminology. The annual burst of subtropical warmth that swept over San Francisco before the start of the winter's rainy season was the subject of great anticipation—for most of its citizens.

Sometimes the heat wave came in late October; in other seasons, not until early November. Some years it never arrived at all. But when it did hit, San Francisco's fog-beleaguered populace would fill the streets from dawn until long after dusk, their pasty bodies soaking up the sun, a hedonistic last hurrah before the damp down-to-business drudgery of December.

Rupert sighed with frustration. He pressed his face against the door; his blue eyes searched for the first sweaty blur of his person's running clothes.

He didn't join with the majority on the joys of Indian summer. As far as he was concerned, the sooner it started raining, the better—his person didn't dally around on cold, wet, windy jogs.

THE SCROLLING WROUGHT iron frame of the Green Vase's front door rocked in its hinges as Rupert pressed his chunky body against the lower panes of glass. A four-by-eight placard hanging

18

from the tulip-embossed doorknob fluttered with each furry head-bump, but the side reading "CLOSED" remained facing toward the street.

It had been turned that direction for several months now, ever since late May, when the occupants of the apartment above the showroom had concluded their search for California's original Bear Flag.

Behind the Jackson Square antiques shop's redbrick facing and green-painted iron columns, there had been a subtle transformation, a slight shift in focus. For the woman who had inherited the Green Vase from her Uncle Oscar the previous year, something had changed.

Gone were the days she'd spent sitting behind the cashier counter, fretting about the store's financial prospects as she waited for antiques shoppers to wander inside, all the while speculating on what had really happened to her secretive uncle—whether he had passed into the irretrievable afterlife or merely transitioned to a murky, half-hidden existence under a new name and disguise.

The questions surrounding his death had finally been resolved, in her mind at least. That knowledge had given her a purpose, a sense of belief in her new profession.

THE NIECE'S TIME was now occupied with the many artifact-filled boxes and crates that her enigmatic uncle had left behind. Pile after pile of dusty papers, photos, newspaper clippings, and assorted memorabilia passed beneath her gaze as she rummaged through the contents, intent on creating an extensive catalogue of the inventory.

She'd been through portions of the collection before, but this time she had a road map, of sorts. She still struggled to identify the hidden significance behind many of the items, but now she had a much better idea of how to process the information.

Despite the unlikely sequence of events that had led the once shy, timid accountant to take over her uncle's business, she had put aside her doubts and embraced her new role—not as an antiques dealer, but as an investigator of history, a sleuth of bygone riches . . . a treasure hunter.

UNBEKNOWNST TO THE woman sifting through the Green Vase's historic trinkets, her next search would lead to something far more treacherous than hidden treasure. Despite the sunny, carefree sky hanging over Jackson Square, brooding black clouds were gathering just beyond the horizon.

A death—this one of unquestionable authenticity—loomed at the end of this trail of clues.

BUT, FOR NOW, the day's warm afternoon light playfully beamed into the Green Vase showroom, where the pudgy white cat plastered his body against the front door, urgently awaiting the jogger's return.

ALL OF THE recent archiving activity going on inside the Green Vase was of little interest to Rupert. He usually nodded off while watching his person pore over the heaps of Oscar's hoarded clutter, and he fell asleep completely whenever she began talking about the latest trinket whose secret meaning she'd decoded.

He was concerned with more important issues: his thoughts typically teetered between reminiscence over his last meal and anticipation for his next. He had adored Uncle Oscar—but that affection had had nothing to do with the man's vast knowledge of San Francisco history.

It was Oscar's culinary prowess that had captured Rupert's loyalty and devotion.

Rupert still fondly recalled the Saturday-night dinners Oscar had hosted in the apartment above the Green Vase. The menu had almost always been the same: fried chicken paired with coleslaw, lumpy mashed potatoes, green beans, and gravy. Rupert had spent many a decadent evening stuffing himself silly in the small upstairs kitchen where Oscar served his meals.

Rupert licked his lips, remembering the heavenly aroma that would rise from the massive iron skillet as the chicken's battered coating began to crisp. And the meat, he thought, swooning from the memory—those juicy morsels had been so tender.

The recollection of past poultry dishes brought Rupert back to the source of his present frustration. His furry, round stomach let out a loud rumble of protest, and he once more shoved his face against the glass portion of the door.

His feline brain focused on a single pressing thought.

"Where is that woman?"

A PEDESTRIAN ROUNDED the critical North Beach corner at the end of the block and turned onto Jackson Street. Rupert nearly flipped a somersault—before realizing that it wasn't Oscar's niece.

His hopes weren't completely dashed, however. The storklike man carrying a suit jacket slung over one shoulder, whistling as he strode briskly down the sidewalk, might just be able to assuage the cat's surging hunger.

Rupert's gaze quickly scanned over the man's curly brown hair and rolled-up shirtsleeves, past the frog-shaped cufflinks poking out his front pocket, to the paper bag he carried in his free hand.

Holding his breath, Rupert carefully studied the green and gold image printed on the side of the sack.

Come here, come here, come here, Rupert mentally pleaded, throwing himself once more against the glass, stretching up his front paws beseechingly.

But Montgomery Carmichael only waved to his furry friend as he stopped at the entrance to his art studio, fed a key into its lock, and stepped inside.

A stream of feline curses flew thick and furious through the door and across the street as Monty took a seat at the small desk beside his easel, slid a takeout box from the sack, and popped open the lid.

Rupert couldn't bear to watch. The torture was more than he could endure. He was about to abandon his post altogether when the slow *thump, thump* of approaching tennis shoes sounded in the distance.

With immense relief, he turned back toward the corner. This time there was no mistake; he immediately recognized his person's colorful running shorts.

She was now mere seconds away.

AFTER UNCLE OSCAR passed away, Rupert had feared the recipe for his special fried-chicken concoction had been lost for good. He had spent several nights worrying about a future devoid of his favorite meal. In recent months, however, Rupert's faith in fried chicken had been restored.

Hurry up! Rupert begged, bouncing up and

23

down like an overstuffed bunny rabbit, his eyes never leaving the paper bag gripped in the woman's left hand. *I can't wait a second longer.*

Isabella sauntered to the front of the store, joining her brother as their person fumbled with a tulip-shaped key, trying to align the ridges so that it fit into the lock.

Each day on her way home from her run, Oscar's niece made a quick stop in the nearby North Beach neighborhood at a homestyle restaurant that had opened a few months earlier. There, she picked up two cat-sized portions of the restaurant's popular entrée.

The daily treat had become Rupert's all-consuming fixation.

In his expert opinion, it tasted exactly the same as the fried chicken Uncle Oscar used to make.

Chapter 3
A DISTINGUISHED DINER

BRIGHT SUN SOAKED the hood of a pearl-colored Bentley as it slogged its way through the Monday afternoon rush-hour traffic clogging Columbus Avenue. The main artery for San Francisco's North Beach neighborhood, the road was crowded with orange and white Muni buses, beat-up taxis of myriad shapes and colors, and a wide assortment of privately owned vehicles, each one filled with frustrated commuters fleeing the financial district. Tourists packed the sidewalks, rounding out the chaotic scene.

The gentleman piloting the Bentley was instantly recognizable to many of those trapped in Columbus's knot of congestion. His immaculate dress, smooth mannerisms, and beaming smile were a familiar sight in downtown San Francisco. The city's residents had long grown accustomed to his glad-handing public appearances. The Previous Mayor of San Francisco—or PM, as he was referred to in certain circles—knew how to make an impression.

Today, however, the PM was intent on a more low-key outing. As the car inched to a stop at a red light, he slumped down in his seat, uncharacteristically avoiding eye contact with a group of pedestrians gawking from the crosswalk. He reached for the felt bowler perched jauntily on the crown of his balding brown head and tugged it forward to shield the upper portion of his face.

Generally speaking, he wasn't the type to shy away from recognition—truth be known, he was drawn like a moth to even the dimmest spotlight—but his next appointment was not one meant for public display.

AS THE PREVIOUS Mayor shrunk behind the wheel, wishing he'd commandeered a less conspicuous ride, a light wind funneled through his open driver's side window.

Given the day's unusually humid heat, the PM might have welcomed a refreshing breeze against his face. This gust, however, received a hostile reception.

The PM crinkled his nose as the protruding scent of roasted garlic permeated the car's interior. He had a keen sense of smell, one easily rankled by an off-putting odor.

"My luck," he grumbled, turning to look at the black-painted storefront of a nearby restaurant. "*This* is where I get stuck."

The PM shook his head as he counted a half-dozen out-of-town eaters seated by the front window, gorging themselves on a table full of garlic-laden entrées.

He remembered his one—and only—meal at the dining spot, which was a favorite of visiting tourists. He hadn't been able to stand the smell, much less the taste, of garlic ever since.

"I had that wretched stuff oozing from my pores for three days straight," he muttered with a shudder. His whole body cringed. "Spent an entire day at the sauna trying to sweat out the stench."

THE PM HAD described the unpleasant after-effects of his garlic-eating experience in his weekly op-ed piece for the San Francisco news-paper. The column was a free-ranging collection of his thoughts and opinions on various topics: local politics, culture, and current events—but his most frequent subject was that of culinary critique.

The PM ate out two, sometimes three times a day, and dutifully reported the details of each meal in his column. His name and photo were mounted on the interior walls of his favorite restaurants and bistros, next to tables that were on permanent reserve, awaiting his arrival.

Despite this preferential treatment, no eating establishment was above his reproach. If the PM felt that the service was too slow, the temperature of his food less than optimum, or the ambience of the dining experience in any way marred, he would call out this deficiency in his column. Suffice it to say, the garlic restaurant had received a lengthy and scathing condemnation.

The PM's face contorted into an unpleasant grimace as the garlic-infused air inside his vehicle intensified.

"Never again," he snapped, rolling up the window.

He took one last look at the exuberant eaters, their silverware flashing as they bent over their plates.

"Enjoy it now," he said with a wry pump of his eyebrows. "You'll pay for it later."

Deftly, the PM jerked his car into the opposing lane of traffic. Ignoring the resulting blare of horns, the Bentley surged forward and swerved around the vehicles blocking the intersection before dipping back onto its side of the road.

Turning the ventilation fan to its highest setting, the PM took in a deep breath of fresh garlic-free air and sighed ruefully.

"Trust me, *I know*."

A FEW BLOCKS later, the Bentley veered off Columbus and swung around a corner into a side alley. After a few sharp turns, the Previous Mayor squeezed the car into a narrow slot beside a Dumpster and killed the engine. Peeking over the steering wheel's upper rim, he stared out the front window at the rear entrance to a popular North Beach bistro.

JAMES LICK'S HOMESTYLE Chicken had only been open since late spring, but the fledgling diner had already become a mainstay in San Francisco's competitive culinary scene.

Lick's short menu consisted of fried chicken and a limited number of accompanying fixings: cole-slaw, mashed potatoes, green beans, and gravy. But the abbreviated offering had proved wildly popular with the young professionals who worked in the nearby financial district. The restaurant's green and gold takeout boxes had become a common sight in the high-rise office buildings that housed the city's many legal and financial firms.

Surprisingly, the diner's near-overnight success

had been achieved without the typical commercial enhancers of advertising or promotion. Praise of its food had spread solely by word of mouth.

Certainly, the storefront did more to discourage than entice patrons. A tattered green awning hung over the dusty windows; the peeling gold letters painted onto the fabric were almost impossible to decipher. From the sidewalk, it was difficult to tell if the place was even in operation.

The establishment's reclusive proprietor generally kept out of sight, leaving the front-counter operations to his business partner, Harold Wombler, a perpetually grumpy man with greasy black hair and sagging, wrinkled skin.

Mr. Wombler was rarely seen wearing anything other than a ragged T-shirt and threadbare over-alls, the latter of which showcased his bony knees and rather too much of his hairy white legs. Despite Wombler's unappetizing appearance and his tendency to growl at customers, the popularity of Lick's Homestyle Chicken continued to grow. The sumptuous meals kept eaters coming back for more.

THE PREVIOUS MAYOR glanced around his parking space, checking for observers, but his presence in the alley behind the restaurant appeared to have gone unnoticed. The car keys jingled in his hands as he studied the scene, trying to be sure.

The PM frequented North Beach on a regular basis, but Lick's was not the kind of establishment he typically patronized. After the notorious garlic incident, he had assured his readers that, henceforth, he would be steering clear of any eatery that failed to meet his exacting standards of dining and decorum—in particular, he had vowed to avoid restaurants with a kitschy one-item focus.

He'd never hear the end of it if anyone caught him walking into Lick's.

Checking his reflection in the rearview mirror, the PM shoved the bowler down over his brow, turned up his shirt collar, and stealthily stepped out of the car.

His leather shoes squeaked as he scurried across the alley, painfully pinching his toes, but he refused to slow his pace. The sound of a car backfiring echoed from a few blocks away, causing him to jump into the air and then swiftly crouch to the ground. After another quick look around, he resumed his course with intensified speed.

It was with a great deal of relief that he pulled open the rotting screen door at the rear of the restaurant and, slightly panting, ducked through its darkened doorway.

THE PREVIOUS MAYOR stood in a corridor next to a rack of cast iron skillets and waited for his eyes to adjust to the dim lighting. He reached

30

instinctively for his hat, his fingers fiddling with the feather tucked into its brim as he lifted it from his head and rotated it sideways to block his face from any potential onlookers.

A shadowed figure turned from a stool at a nearby kitchen counter and grunted out a greeting.

"Relax, Mayor," the man said with a derisive snort. "Your cover's safe. It's just me." He nodded at the empty dining room. "Evening service hasn't started yet."

The PM's face reddened as he dropped the bowler to his chest.

"Wombler," he replied in the sanguine tone of a practiced politician. "Nice to see you."

Harold wiped his palms on the flour-dusted apron tied loosely around the waist of his frayed overalls. He gummed his dentures, sliding them in and out of his mouth as his beady black eyes stared at the PM. After several seconds of surly deliberation, he gave a shrugging *hmnh* and tossed his head toward the ceiling.

"He's waiting for you upstairs," Harold said curtly. Gripping an ache in his left hip, he returned to the vegetables spread out across the counter.

The PM hurried to the stairwell, intent on vacating the dining area before a customer arrived.

When he reached the foot of the stairs, however, he stopped and looked back over his shoulder, smiling sheepishly at the counter.

Just because he didn't want to be *seen* eating at Lick's didn't mean he was immune to the kitchen's appetizing aroma.

Harold's flat lips curled into a sarcastic response. He waved a dismissive hand in the air, as if swatting a fly, and then grabbed a skillet from the rack by the door.

"I'll fix you a box on your way out."

Chapter 4

THE MILLIONAIRE TRAMP

GRINNING HUNGRILY, THE Previous Mayor began climbing the narrow ascent to the private offices on the restaurant's second floor. Halfway up, the vertical tunnel of ancient wood paneling turned a sharp corner. The PM paused on the landing, reflecting on the man he was hoping to find at the top of the stairs.

He had arranged this meeting mostly on conjecture, based on an educated guess of the proprietor's real identity. There was still a chance, he supposed, that James Lick was nothing more than your everyday restaurant entrepreneur, a regular guy with a special knack for frying chicken and an unusually strong aversion to publicity.

But the PM didn't think so. A long list of indicators had convinced him otherwise.

· · ·

THE FIRST INKLING had come a few weeks earlier, when the Previous Mayor had stopped in at City Hall to chat with the night-shift janitor. It was a routine visit, one he made several times a month, more frequently if circumstances required.

During the PM's many years of experience in local politics, he'd found City Hall's cleaning staff to be one of his most valuable sources of information. The janitors had full unfettered access to every corner, closet, and restricted stairwell of the domed building and could circulate, virtually unnoticed, within earshot of the most confidential of conversations.

Moreover, they had exclusive possession of an otherwise untapped source of intelligence. In the PM's view, you could often learn more from the trash a person left behind than you could from the unveiling of his most zealously guarded secrets.

And, in most instances, he thought with a grin, the trash was a lot easier to access.

THE PM KNEW a thing or two about the janitorial profession. When he'd arrived in San Francisco as a young man in his late teens, he'd taken a job cleaning the pews at one of the city's largest churches.

The PM smiled at the memory. He had picked up a lot of valuable information during that early period of employment, some of which was still useful to him today.

Granted, he'd come across a few odd individuals during his janitorial dealings over the years. A couple of the characters he'd encountered had been downright strange.

But after several decades of navigating the complex competing interests that sought to influence the power structure at City Hall, he'd never once been blindsided by a political opponent. The janitors had always come through for him—even though they generally remained oblivious to the significance of their contributions.

IT WAS ON a recent janitorial visit to City Hall that the PM discovered the fried-chicken clue.

He'd been accompanying one of his janitorial informants on the evening rounds through the building's basement. The janitor had just given the PM the details of the latest spat between the Current Mayor and the President of the Board of Supervisors.

Given the long-standing animosity between the two men, there was little surprising or newsworthy in this development, and the PM had yawned off the information. He had been in the midst of formulating a follow-up question that might steer the conversation toward more productive grounds when his sensitive nose latched onto a familiar smell.

Stopping short, the PM sucked in a full whiff of the distinctive scent.

"What's that . . . Who's that . . . Where's that coming from?" he stuttered with disbelief.

The amused janitor pointed toward an area housing overflow office space for the Current Mayor's junior staff.

His nasal senses fully engaged, the PM stepped into a narrow corridor of cubicles.

ALL OF THE desks were darkened and empty, save for the one at the far end of the row, where a bleary-eyed staffer bent over his desk, staring hypnotically into a computer monitor as he munched on a leg of fried chicken.

The young man wore a T-shirt, blue jeans, and high-top canvas sneakers—not unlike the outfit the PM had favored in his youth.

A well-worn bicycle painted the reddish orange color of the Golden Gate Bridge leaned against the corner of the cubicle, the chinstrap of a plastic helmet looped around its handlebars.

The PM paused, struck by another image from his past. He couldn't help remembering the beat-up bike he'd used to get around during his early days in San Francisco.

Still reflecting on the similarities, the PM surveyed the chicken-eating scene.

The staffer's desktop was stacked with note-filled tablets, scribbled-on sheets of paper, and several heavy binders containing drafts of pending city ordinances. A stained coffee cup perched atop one of the piles, its remaining liquid having long gone cold.

It was rare to find any showing of motivation in the lower ranks of an outgoing administration; most political staff spent the transition period angling for their next job. This fellow, however, was so surprisingly intent on his legislative project—and the fried chicken—that he hadn't noticed the PM and the janitor standing nearby.

The PM squinted at the name tag hanging from the staffer's neck. Beneath the cheery photo of a youthful dark-skinned man with a grinning smile read the words, "Spider Jones."

After a long moment of silent observation, the PM cleared his throat to draw the staffer's attention.

"Say, son," the PM had asked, pointing to the conspicuous green and gold takeout package discarded in the canister near the staffer's desk. "Where'd you get that meal?"

"New place . . . just opened up in North Beach. It's unbelievable," the man had replied between mouthfuls. "I'd offer you a bite but . . ." He'd smiled and looked greedily down at his remaining portion.

"No, no, that's all right," the PM had replied, holding his hands up in refusal, although his mouth had begun to water.

With difficulty, he'd meted out his oft-repeated mantra.

"I don't eat anything that comes in a box."

IT HADN'T TAKEN long for the Previous Mayor to track down the name and address of the new fried-chicken restaurant. That had been a relatively straightforward procedure.

Obtaining an audience with the camera-shy proprietor, however, had been a far more difficult task.

Despite the restaurant's unprecedented popularity, James Lick had declined all of the local news media's requests for interviews, directing their inquiries to his uncooperative and decidedly unphotogenic business associate, Harold Wombler.

As a result, little had been written in the culinary press about San Francisco's growing fixation with Lick's signature fried chicken. The man behind the addictive recipe remained a mystery.

ALTHOUGH FEW DETAILS were known about the restaurant's owner, the biography of its historical namesake was well documented.

A figure from San Francisco's Gold Rush past, the original James Lick was commemorated on freeway signs, placards at local schools, and as the primary benefactor to a prestigious observatory in the hills east of San Jose.

For those unfamiliar with Lick's life story, each

of the restaurant's takeout bags included a green paper insert providing brief anecdotes about the man's legacy and achievements.

Many saw the flyers as a convenient cover, another means of preserving the current Lick's anonymity. But for the PM, the historical references had been a further hint to the elusive proprietor's identity.

The story of James Lick seemed tailor-made for the man the PM suspected had now taken on the moniker.

MANY INSTANT MILLIONAIRES emerged in the years following the California Gold Rush. One the richest of that group was James Lick.

A piano maker from Pennsylvania, Lick traveled throughout South America before finding his way to California's then Spanish-held territory. Upon arrival at the isolated backwater of Yerba Buena (the predecessor to San Francisco), Lick surveyed the town's peninsular landscape and predicted that its route of future growth would likely extend out into the bay. Betting on this hunch, he proceeded to invest his entire life's savings on water lots located along the shoreline—parcels of land that were then physically underwater.

Prior to the spring of 1848, most thought Lick a fool. The real-estate transactions left him cash poor, and, for several years, he lived in extreme poverty. He reportedly slept on the street and was frequently seen in his ragged suit, begging for food.

With the onset of the Gold Rush, however, the keen foresight of Lick's land purchases became clear. As the city began scraping sand from nearby dunes to fill in those once-worthless water lots, Lick's net worth skyrocketed.

Strangely, the sudden onset of enormous wealth did little to change Lick's pauper lifestyle. Even after his dramatic reversal of fortune, he continued to dress in the same shabby clothes; his gaunt figure still reflected a diet of malnutrition.

Despite the influence and power he'd wielded as a real-estate mogul, Lick's miserly mannerisms had been mocked throughout San Francisco. He was known by his nickname, the "Millionaire Tramp."

"THE MILLIONAIRE TRAMP," the PM had mused when he'd read the short story printed on the green restaurant flyer he'd salvaged from the young staffer's trash bin.

He could think of no better alias for the hermitic old man who had once cooked his fried chicken in a kitchen above a Jackson Square antiques shop.

And so he had persisted.

AFTER THE MODERN-DAY Lick failed to return the PM's phone calls or reply to the messages his new unofficial intern couriered to the downstairs kitchen counter, the PM took the matter to an expert—one who resided most days at a tiny flower shop in the city's financial district.

In all outer aspects, Wang's flower stall appeared similar to countless others scattered throughout the downtown area. The low one-story structure was packed with bright racks of blooming vegetation and multi-colored bouquets.

Each day, the racks were rolled out onto the sidewalk, an attempt to catch the eye of the well-heeled office workers strolling past during their lunch and coffee breaks. A demure young Asian woman with long, shiny hair manned the cashier register, greeting each customer with a serene smile.

But there were a few subtle differences, not visible from the street-side view, that set Wang's flower shop apart from the rest.

Behind the racks of petaled plumage, in the dark recesses of the store's back room, the farthest inner wall contained a door leading to a broom closet—the floor of which opened to a tunnel system that ran beneath the city's financial district.

Near the broom closet's tunnel entrance, a wizened Asian man sat in a wheelchair, peacefully smoking his pipe as he monitored the comings and goings both in his shop and in the passageway below.

If there was anyone who could arrange an

audience with the fried-chicken connoisseur—previously the enigmatic shopkeeper of the Green Vase and, even farther back, the most fascinating janitor the PM had ever met—it was the Montgomery Street flower-stall owner, Mr. Wang.

Sure enough, a few days after seeking Wang's intervention, the PM had been granted the invitation for today's meeting.

THE PREVIOUS MAYOR stroked his gray-flecked, neatly trimmed mustache as he stared up the darkened stairwell toward the second-floor living quarters above the fried-chicken restaurant.

He hoped his perseverance had been worth it.

Gripping the railing, he smiled with confidence.

It had to be Oscar, he concluded wryly.

No one else could have convinced Harold Wombler to don a chef's apron.

A MOMENT LATER, the Previous Mayor reached the summit of the stairs, clapped his hands together triumphantly, and stepped into a large, open room.

Light streamed through a pair of bulging bay windows that looked down on Columbus Avenue. To the left, the outskirts of Chinatown crept up against the spiked tower of the Transamerica Pyramid; North Beach's cluster of Italian restaurants filled in the view to the right.

41

Behind the restaurant and around the corner, the PM added in a mental aside, Jackson Square and the Green Vase antiques shop resided in secluded obscurity.

Against the far wall, a tiny hairless mouse played happily in a wire cage filled with a maze of plastic tunnels and several wire-rimmed exercise wheels. In a corner of the cage, a doll-sized wardrobe held a colorful collection of mouse-sized jackets, each one neatly wrapped around a miniature clothes hanger.

In the next slot over, a low table held a glass terrarium filled with mounds of natural greenery. Inside, two frogs lounged beside a small pool equipped with a tiny pump to circulate its water.

The amphibian pair looked up as the PM crossed the threshold. Both blinked a demure welcome; then their froggy gazes shifted toward a spot in the middle of the room.

The PM turned toward the dusty piles of papers, deteriorating cardboard boxes, and roughly hewn crates that took up much of the center floor space. Crouched over one particularly disorganized-looking heap was an elderly man with thinning white hair, short rounded shoulders, and a middling paunch.

The old man stood with a stiff, painful movement and gripped the small of his back as the PM strode forward, offering his hand enthusiastically.

"James Lick, I presume," the PM said with a

grin. "I have to say, you look a lot like a man I used to know . . . a fellow who ran an antiques shop around the corner from here . . . a place called the Green Vase. I hear his niece is running it now."

The man dusted his palms on the front of his navy blue collared shirt. After a slight hesitation, his rough, calloused hand met the PM's firm grip.

"Good to see you, Mayor," Lick said as they completed the shake. He tilted his head conspiratorially. "You came in through the back?"

Nodding, the PM glanced at the tottering pile at their feet. "No offense, but I'm not sure my reputation could survive me being seen in this joint."

Lick threw up his arms in mock affront. "It was *our* reputation *I* was worried about."

Chuckling, the PM strolled over to the nearest window and looked out onto the busy street.

"It's a nice setup you've got here," he said casually. He shoved his hands into the pockets of his dress slacks and leaned back on his heels. "Right in the middle of things, and yet—neatly tucked away."

The PM cleared his throat anxiously. Lick's reemergence on the San Francisco scene could mean only one thing.

"I assume you're following the situation at City Hall? The Mayor will be shipping out for Sacramento any day now."

He paused as Lick joined him at the window. Then he added tentatively, "The board's holding a special session on Thursday to select his replacement. Are you backing one of the contenders?"

Lick's pale, worn face creased with a knowing smile. "Oh, I have a candidate in mind . . ." He paused and pumped his wild flyaway eyebrows. "An unconventional nominee."

"You have to let me in on this," the PM said, barely containing his excitement. "Who's your man?"

Stroking his stubbled chin, Lick issued a cryptic reply.

"Patience, Mayor. The show's about to start."

Chapter 5

THE FROG WHISPERER

TUESDAY ARRIVED WITH another rare showing of Indian summer's warmth. A glorious linen blue sky stretched over the San Francisco Bay, causing its cold, numbing water to look almost inviting. Vibrant colors bloomed in temporarily unshaded courtyards. Plants across the peninsula took on a verdant green glow.

It was a deceptive, seductive lure—one that threatened to disrupt the efficiency of the entire workweek.

In the financial district's high-rise office

buildings, the lazy afternoon seeped into the endless rows of dungeonlike cubicles, taunting the poor souls trapped within. Those who didn't pause to gaze dreamily out the nearest window began to twist and squirm in their seats, tugging at the constricting confines of their suits, ties, high heels, and skirts.

As the clock ticked slowly toward its five o'clock release, the antsy army of young professionals grew more and more restive, and a palpable tension began to build. Several hundred minds coalesced around a single pulsing thought.

If only I could be outside.

ACROSS TOWN, A far more relaxed and contented individual strolled through the thousand-acre green space of Golden Gate Park.

The bright sun sparkled across the sky-high tops of a stand of ancient redwoods, splashing down through the needled canopy to the ruffled red head of a burly man with a freckled face, a gap-toothed grin, and a beefy lumberjack's build.

A trail of dried mud crumbled from the man's thick-soled hiking boots as he ambled along a sidewalk cutting across the middle of the park. He threw his shoulders back, taking in a deep, chest-filling breath of redwood-scented air.

Sam Eckles preferred rural living to city life, but in this part of San Francisco, he felt completely at home.

• • •

HUMMING HAPPILY TO himself, Sam continued down the path to a fork, where the trees parted for a wide field.

On his left lay the Music Concourse, a multiuse amphitheater filled with a number of open-air stages along with several small elms whose branches had been pruned down to short, knobby limbs. To his right stretched the sprawling complex that housed the California Academy of Sciences.

Recently reopened after a lengthy renovation, the Academy's new structure featured an eco-friendly grass-covered roof, a planetarium, a flock of webcam-mugging penguins, and a four-story rain forest exhibit, all seamlessly integrated with a vast aquarium. The establishment drew thousands of visitors each year, the majority enraptured schoolchildren.

A nonstop roster of activities took place in and around this busy enclave—concerts, festivals, school field trips, and the like. Despite all this bustle, the area retained the quiet tranquility of the surrounding park, a surprising oasis in the center of the busy city.

AT THE FORK, Sam directed his dirt-caked hiking boots toward the Academy of Sciences. He soon reached a row of metal bike racks flanking the turnoff for the front entrance. Hooking a right, he strode purposefully up the walkway toward the ticket booth.

As he reached a short flight of concrete steps, Sam paused to look up at several banners attached to the building's eaves. The sheets, which stretched three-fourths of the way down the concrete and glass walls, were printed with adverts promoting the Academy's special time-limited exhibits.

One of the banners, Sam noted with approval, highlighted the rare amphibian species he had been summoned there to inspect.

DESPITE HIS HEFTY size and intimidating physique, Sam was a tender, inquisitive soul—one who saw the world through a unique frog-fascinated prism.

He had spent much of the last year tromping through the lower hills of the Sierra Nevada, communing with his beloved amphibians as he took notes on their numbers, movements, and habitat preferences for a research team based out of UC Davis.

During that time, word of Sam's uncanny insights into his slimy-skinned brethren had spread far and wide. Among the state's wildlife biologists, his stature had rapidly risen to near-legendary status.

So when the Academy became concerned about the stars of its latest showcase amphibian exhibit, a call had gone out urgently requesting Sam's consultation.

THE ECCENTRIC FROG-MAN certainly looked the part. His broad shoulders were clothed in a grubby T-shirt that hadn't been washed in several wearings. The shirt was, in any case, fresher than Sam, who had gone even longer since his last shower.

Over the T-shirt, Sam wore a frayed green vest with a circular patch sewn onto its right chest pocket. He beamed with pride as a passerby squinted to read the writing embroidered beneath the caricatured image of a smiling frog.

The first line of text bore his formal title: Samuel T. Eckles, Amphibian Consultant.

But he was known throughout the wildlife biology community by his more informal designation, the tagline that had been inscribed just beneath.

The Frog Whisperer.

CONFIDENTLY, SAM APPROACHED the glass-fronted entrance and presented his credentials to the attendant seated inside the ticket booth.

"Welcome, Mr. Eckles." The man greeted him with a smile of recognition. He'd been told to be on the lookout for the grubby mountain man. He slid a laminated visitor's pass through the opening at the bottom of the window and motioned for Sam to clip it to his vest.

"Dr. Kline will meet you inside by the dinosaur," he shouted in an effort to be heard over the noisy group of schoolchildren who had just approached the booth.

"Thanks," Sam replied with a wary glance at the hyperactive youngsters. He swiftly scooped up the visitor's pass and hurried inside.

THE DINOSAUR WAS easy to locate. The creature's bony head almost touched the atrium's twenty-foot-high glass ceiling; its long, curving tail swept down to just a foot off the ground.

With a nervous tug at his vest, Sam parked himself beneath the skeleton.

So far, everything was going according to plan. His cover was working perfectly.

After several successful consults with Academy scientists out in the field, he had finally been brought into the main headquarters—the mother ship, so to speak.

No one had any reason to suspect that he was there to do anything other than diagnose the illness of a pair of seemingly off-color amphibians; no one could possibly guess the real purpose of his mission.

JUST AS SAM was starting to relax into his undercover role, an eerie sensation swept over his psyche. The sunlit room took on a cooling shadow, and an anxious tension crept over his body.

He turned a slow circle, his eyes warily scanning the room. With all the time he'd spent outdoors, observing both predator and prey, his finely tuned naturalist's skills were quick to discern when he was the one being watched.

After a minute of careful surveillance, he shook his head, trying to dismiss the unsettled feeling.

"Probably just my imagination," he tried to assure himself.

He glared sharply up at the empty eye sockets in the dinosaur's skull and added an admonishment.

"But I'd appreciate it if you'd stop looking at me."

SAM WAS STILL trying to calm his nerves when a boy of about three bounced across the atrium toward the dinosaur. The tyke's shoes lit up each time his soles hit the floor.

"Dangerously unpredictable creature," Sam muttered as he began to fret over this unforeseen complication.

Of course, he had known there would be children at the Academy. They were a naturally occurring species in this type of environment.

He just hadn't realized how *many* of them would be running about the facility, untethered to any supervising adult.

FROM SAM'S POINT of view, there was nothing wrong with children, per se. He found them a bit difficult to relate to and their tendency toward loud shrieking noises horribly off-putting, but, generally, they weren't any more of a bother to him than their adult counterparts.

The problem with children, at least for purposes of today's operation, was their keen sense of perception, Sam thought with growing unease. They had a way of picking up on things. They saw right through even the whitest of lies.

He shuddered with apprehension. He couldn't escape the sense that someone was tracking his every movement.

One of the little people, he feared, had seen through the ruse.

SAM TOOK A wide step to the side to avoid the approaching child, but the action only served to draw the boy's interest.

"Shoo," Sam whispered hoarsely as the battery-powered shoes stomped ever closer. "Get lost."

Sam eased backward toward the exhibit space behind the central atrium, his thick boots scraping against the concrete floor as he kept his eyes fixed on the tiny, inquisitive human.

"Run along now," Sam urged again, waving his hands in the air.

The boy only giggled and continued to trot toward him, his face lighting up as brightly as his shoes.

Sam had backed halfway across the room when

his attention was diverted to a second short-statured interrogator moving in on his left flank, a little girl with a high-pitched voice and long pigtails that whipped through the air like samurai swords.

"Little buggers are everywhere," he muttered under his breath as the girl raced toward him.

A nervous sweat broke across his brow. They were all onto him. He just knew it.

"Dr. Kline?" he called out desperately as a swarming mass of the Academy's younger clientele rushed in from one of the side corridors.

For a few tenuous seconds, Sam struggled to maintain his composure, but after a short hesitation, he turned and ran the remaining length of the atrium, his fleeing figure trailed by a squealing line of children who thought they were participating in an impromptu game of tag.

STANDING JUST INSIDE a gift shop located on the far side of the atrium, an elderly man wearing the shabby clothes of a tramp watched as Sam sprinted headlong across the building.

The man wore several grimy shirts loosely draped over his upper half; each layer was riddled with holes and stained with smears of dirt. His ragged pants were two sizes too big, secured around his rotund middle with a worn piece of rope. The shoes on his feet had been reinforced with used duct tape, the frayed strapping wrapped around the arch of each foot.

A ray of sun fell across the man's pale, wrinkled face as he stepped into the atrium, illuminating his bristly gray eyebrows, thinning white hair, and scruffy false beard.

He lifted his right sleeve to his mouth and whispered into a hidden microphone that relayed his voice back to the kitchen of a North Beach fried-chicken restaurant.

"Wombler, this is Lick."

He paused and stared at the far side of the atrium, where he'd last seen the fugitive frog-man.

"We might have a problem."

Chapter 6
A CONTENTED CAT

BACK IN JACKSON Square, a woman with long brown hair tied up in a messy ponytail collapsed onto a worn couch in the apartment above the Green Vase antiques shop.

Her face was flushed, and she still wore the sweaty exercise clothes from her late-afternoon run. It had been a fantastic jog, out and back through the Presidio's Crissy Field to Fort Point at the southern foot of the Golden Gate Bridge. But after the second lengthy route in as many days, she was too tired, as yet, to move toward the shower.

Oscar's niece had landed on the couch's right

side, closest to the kitchen, farthest from the window overlooking the street, the section where the cushions still retained the majority of their stuffing.

The seating on the couch's opposite side cratered down into its wooden framework and what was left of the furniture's inner springs. The upholstery and the support beneath it had been molded into their bouldered-out shape by her uncle, the couch's previous owner.

It had been over a year since the woman and her two cats, Rupert and Isabella, moved into the apartment above the Green Vase showroom. During that time, Oscar's niece had assumed almost every aspect of her uncle's previous life.

For some reason, however, she still didn't feel quite right about taking over his long-established place on the couch.

Besides, given the inoperative lamp on the opposite end table, the lighting on the firmer side of the couch was far better for reading.

THE WOMAN GUZZLED down a glass of water as she glanced across the sofa's length to the windows overlooking the street. The glass panes were propped open, letting in a hot, balmy breeze through the slats of the blinds.

The sudden arrival of Indian summer had inspired anyone who was able to head for the waterfront; the Embarcadero as well as the wide path cutting through Crissy Field had been packed with both people and pets.

Despite the sunny weather, Oscar's niece had left her animals at home.

She had a special cat-adapted stroller, fitted with a net covering to secure its occupants, that she occasionally used to take Rupert and Isabella for walks, but it had been folded up in a closet for several weeks. Also packed away was a set of cat-sized harnesses, one slightly larger than the other, each with leash hooks sewn onto the back straps.

The woman hadn't been tempted to try either of these contraptions during that day's outing. Her cats, she'd found, simply weren't the best jogging or walking companions.

First off, Isabella had a tendency to hiss at any dogs they came across. As canines made up the majority of the pet population on San Francisco's running trails and beaches, this habit led to several uncomfortable altercations—Isabella was unintimidated by size or breed.

For his part, Rupert would have spent the entire trip howling his demands for a stop at the fried-chicken restaurant.

The woman knew from past experience; the pair was better off staying at home in the Green Vase.

THIS WAS NOT to say that the cats didn't express any concerns regarding their person's earlier whereabouts.

As Oscar's niece wiped the sweat from her brow, Isabella leapt primly onto the nearest armrest and issued a disapproving glare. She assumed a haughty sphinx pose, daintily crossing her front feet one over the other.

The cat knew her person had been out mingling with the canine species. The unmistakable trace of doggy odor on the woman's clothes indicated she had stopped to pet a number of the offensive beasts.

"You never know, Issy," the woman said teasingly. "One day, I might just bring one of those dogs home with me."

Isabella turned her head, ever so slightly, and stared icily down at her person.

THE NIECE SPOTTED a crumb hanging from one of Isabella's white whiskers, likely a remnant of her afternoon snack.

"Issy," she said, pointing between gulps of water. "You've got something . . . right near your mouth."

Isabella's orange ears swiveled sideways, expressing regal affront—as if someone had peeked under the princess's mattress and pointed out the pea.

"It's just right . . . there," the woman continued, reaching toward the cat's face.

Before the finger could touch the encumbered whisker, Isabella shook her head, triggering a violent vibration that removed the offending crumb without acknowledging its presence. Then she immediately resumed her imperial pose, settling onto her perch as her brother's fluffy form padded into the living room.

RUPERT PROCEEDED DIRECTLY to the couch and, despite the open seat to his person's left, hopped straight into her lap.

A flurry of white cat hair floated into the air as Rupert nuzzled the woman's face. Purring loudly, he began turning in a tight circle, kneading his front feet into her stomach, each prodding poke digging a little deeper into her gut.

"I was here first," she protested. A feathery clump of cat hair floated past the tip of her nose, triggering a loud sneeze.

Rupert paused for a moment and turned his wobbly blue eyes to gaze into her hazel ones.

"All right, all right," she relented with a sigh.

Lifting the large cat over her lap, she slid herself sideways and dropped down into the scalloped-out cushion.

Rupert immediately flopped onto his back in the preferred seat. The plump of his distended stomach swelled upward as his legs splayed out on either side.

It wasn't a very dignified position, but Rupert didn't care. After gobbling down his serving of fried chicken—and checking Isabella's bowl for any leftovers—he was the most contented cat in the universe. On top of all that, he'd just secured one of his favorite places to sleep.

Scooping up the day's newspaper, the niece settled into her spot. With a sigh, she propped the heels of her running shoes on the edge of the long wooden trunk positioned in front of the couch. Her hand drifted over to rub Rupert's belly as her feet slid into the same scuffed divots her Uncle Oscar had worn into the trunk's top planking.

This had become their regular end-of-day routine. The niece, scanning the headlines as she recuperated from her run; Rupert, crashed out on the firmer side of the couch as he digested his afternoon chicken snack; and Isabella, lording over them both with noble disdain.

ALL THE WHILE, the brass lamp sat on its end table, within arm's reach of the niece's seat on the couch. The image of the Steinhart Aquarium's original alligator Swamp Exhibit remained darkened and unseen, stoically waiting to be discovered.

Chapter 7
THE MISSION

NEAR THE ACADEMY of Science's rear entrance, Sam Eckles ducked behind a stone column to catch his breath. After gathering his wits and calming his pulse, he slowly peeked around the edge of his hiding place.

His eyes slid back and forth, studying the near perimeter. He didn't see any of his tiny tormentors lurking in the wings, but he couldn't be sure.

Of this, he felt certain: he was still on *someone's* radar.

Crouching near the column's base, he waited, listening for the telltale *thud* of little feet, but the area had fallen silent. The afternoon penguin-feeding session at the opposite end of the building had created a momentary lull in the rush of pedia-traffic.

After several seconds of ambient noise and more than a few concerned stares from nearby adults, Sam pushed out a steadying sigh. He couldn't stay hidden forever. Perhaps, if he moved into the open, he could draw out the spy.

All of his senses on high alert, Sam stepped from behind the column and took stock of his surroundings.

His eyes widened when he realized where he'd ended up.

As luck would have it, he found himself near the aquarium's signature Swamp Exhibit, a multilevel feature that spanned the width of the Academy's rear entranceway and sank two levels down into the basement below.

This was, after all, the reason his team had concocted the frog diversion in the first place.

This was the target of his covert operation.

PAUSING SEVERAL TIMES to look over his shoulder, Sam cautiously crept up to the Swamp Exhibit.

A brass balcony surrounded an opening in the floor, providing a vertical support for patrons looking down on the occupants of the open-roofed tank below.

Still wary of potential spies, Sam began a visual sweep of the exhibit. He turned his attention to an artificial tree with a ribbed banyanlike trunk that rose from the base of the tank all the way up to the first floor's elevated ceiling.

His eyes searched through the reams of fake moss that hung from the limbs, but he found nothing more than the Academy's regular arsenal of artificial greenery.

No one hid behind the tree's thick trunk; no eyes peeped through its branches.

His gaze slid down toward the brass balcony

that surrounded the upper ring of the sunken exhibit. The balcony's facing was made up of a row of vertically aligned seahorses. The flattened bodies had been artfully arranged in close parallel alignment to prevent any of the Academy's smaller visitors from slipping through the slats.

A few foreign tourists leaned against the railing on the opposite side of the tank, and a homeless man rested, half asleep, on a nearby bench. But no one unusual appeared to be lurking about the exhibit's top floor, Sam quickly concluded. He could find nothing to explain the persistent and unsettling sensation that he was being watched.

Satisfied that he had cleared the upper level, Sam leaned over the railing to look into the tank.

A trimming of decorative ceramic tiles, each one depicting an aquatic image, ran just beneath the balcony's footings.

In the water below, a boulder-sized snapping turtle climbed clumsily over a half-submerged log. The awkward, lumbering creature had a wart-covered head that looked as bony as its shell. A second turtle floated, motionless, a few feet away, its short, stumpy appendages pulled inward as if it were impersonating a rock.

Sam lingered briefly on the turtles before shifting his focus to the exhibit's main attraction, an albino alligator that, according to a plaque posted by the brass balcony, was named Clive.

He stared down at the creature, intrigued by its

unusual coloring. He'd never seen anything quite like its scaly, segmented skin, which held just enough pigment to give off a yellowish, almost neon glow. Creamy leather squares filled in the flat length of the animal's back; the center of each segment of skin tufted up like the baked whipped topping on a meringue pie.

Mist began pumping out of spigots mounted onto the sides of the tank, a mechanism used to increase the humidity at the water's surface. As the tiny droplets coated the gator's body, the corners of his mouth curved gently upward, giving the impression of a smile.

Slowly, Sam met the alligator's bleary gaze, and one of the gray-pupiled, red-tinged eyeballs blinked back. For a moment, Sam forgot the paranoid fear that had gripped him minutes before.

This was a peaceful, gentle beast—Sam could tell. He felt an instant kinship with the reptilian misfit.

JUST THEN, A stampede of pounding feet emanated from a distant corridor. The accompanying chorus of high-pitched screams signaled the end of the penguin-feeding session in the building's opposite wing.

Sam flinched, and his hands instinctively clenched the brass railing. He watched the gator's lids sink down over its eyeballs, as if he were trying to shut out the irksome noise.

Standing there, pressed against the seahorse balcony, staring down into the alligator's tank, Sam felt a renewed commitment to the day's mission.

His voice whispered his thoughts, his tone soft but resolute.

"Don't worry, Clive. We're going to get you out of here."

ON THE OPPOSITE side of the Swamp Exhibit, the old man in tramp's clothes stood up from his bench. He watched as one of the Academy's frog scientists hurried across the atrium to greet her amphibian expert. Still bent over the seahorse balcony and staring into the tank, Sam didn't appear to hear the woman call out to him.

Seemingly satisfied with the turn of events, the hobo transmitted an update into the microphone tucked into his sleeve. Then, he skirted the edge of the exhibit area and crossed to the atrium.

Thoughtfully stroking his stubbled chin, he took one last glance back at the seahorse balcony before heading toward the Academy's front entrance.

A little girl looked up at her mother as the old man passed by the dinosaur skeleton.

"Mommy," she said, lifting her tiny nose into the air. "I think I smell fried chicken."

Chapter 8
A PENDING VACANCY

OSCAR'S NIECE TILTED the newspaper, angling it to catch the rays of the setting sun coming in through the window overlooking Jackson Street. Gripping the paper's edges, she straightened the top sheet to read the headlines on the front page's upper fold.

The main story, predictably, focused on the recent election of San Francisco's mayor to lieutenant governor and the speculation about who would succeed him at City Hall.

The Mayor had won the race with a comfortable margin—despite his penchant for hiring questionable life coaches, his well-documented frog phobia, and his two emotional breakdowns while in office (the first after the infamous frog invasion of City Hall, the second after a less publicized frog sighting on his office balcony).

Though not overly popular with the state's voters, the Mayor had benefited from the sweeping coattails of the incoming governor. Soon, he would be headed to Sacramento to begin his new job.

If pressed, few, including the Mayor, could say for sure exactly what duties were required of the lieutenant's post—other than maintaining his status as a living human being so that he could step in, should the governor become incapacitated or otherwise unavailable.

For a man who had once been seen as a potential candidate for national office, it was a marked step down in prestige and stature. Regardless, after two tumultuous, frog-plagued terms in San Francisco, the Mayor appeared eager to leave his troubles—and the city's pesky amphibians—behind.

ALL THAT REMAINED was the tricky matter of naming the Mayor's replacement. It was a year until the next citywide election, so a temporary appointment would be needed to fill the intervening void.

Under the city's constitution and bylaws, the exiting Mayor had no formal role to play in the selection of his successor. Procedurally, that issue was left solely to the board of supervisors.

The Mayor was, however, receiving a great deal of pressure from his political party to exert whatever influence he had left on the board members' decision. Conventional wisdom assumed that whoever became the temporary nominee would have an edge over the other contenders at the next election.

The process promised to be contentious. The number of candidates vying for consideration grew by the day. Anyone and everyone who had ever dreamed of running the city had begun lobbying the board for votes.

With a special board session to decide the matter scheduled to be held later that week, San Francisco was abuzz with speculation over which of the contenders might succeed.

Pushing her bifocal glasses farther up the bridge of her nose, Oscar's niece adjusted the newsprint so she could read the full story.

As usual, Hoxton Fin, San Francisco's longtime political reporter, had the latest scoop.

Chapter 9
HOXTON FIN

HOXTON FIN STRODE into City Hall's marbled foyer, a man on the prowl. He jerked a nod to the security guard, who waved him through without screening.

Hox, as he was known throughout San Francisco, had been covering local politics on and off for more than twenty-five years. The veteran reporter was a near-permanent fixture in the building, and the guards had long since bored of inspecting the contents of the backpack he carried slung over the shoulder of his rumpled tweed jacket.

Other than the pack, Hox's regular reporter's ensemble included a collared shirt, typically unbuttoned at the neck; denim blue jeans, neatly belted around the waist; and a pair of sensible brown walking shoes.

His once jet-black hair had started to pepper with gray, but the lightening color around his temples had done little to soften his dark, brooding expression. He spoke quietly, sparingly, and with a seething intensity. He was prone to outbreaks of temper, for which he rarely apologized, and an obsession with facts, in which he took great pride.

Many were put off by the reporter's direct questioning; his sharp probing stare and often sarcastic remarks tended to rankle those with sensitive dispositions.

Hox was unsympathetic to criticisms of his investigative approach; such complaints merely caused him to probe further.

Only a few trusted colleagues had managed to penetrate the man's stiff outer shell. Most of those would say that an even harder surface lay beneath.

Somewhere within that dry emotional desert, however, Hox carried a wry sense of humor and a fondness for practical jokes—so long as he wasn't the butt of them.

"Howdy-ho, Hox," the guard called out as the reporter shifted his pack to the opposite shoulder and marched through the scanner.

The greeting earned the guard a silent but withering look.

"I mean, hello, Hox . . . Hox . . . Mr. Hoxton,

sir," the guard stuttered, before stuffing a half-eaten sandwich into his mouth as a means of deflecting attention.

With a last iron stare, Hox turned and walked out of the security area. As he turned from the still-blushing guard, the thin crease of a smile appeared on his rugged face.

In a voice that was barely audible to the sandwich-munching guard, he replied, "Hox is fine, thanks."

THERE WAS A slight hitch to Hox's gait as he crossed beneath the dome of City Hall's ornate rotunda and headed toward the central marble staircase leading to the building's second floor. The hobble was due to an injury he'd sustained several years earlier while visiting the Los Angeles Zoo with his then movie-star wife.

Because of the zoo administrator's fondness for one of his wife's films, the couple had been invited to a behind-the-scenes visit with a rare komodo dragon. Prior to entering the cage, the reporter had been cautioned by zoo personnel to remove his white tennis shoes, lest they be confused for the mice that were routinely included in the dragon's meals.

Unfortunately, removal of Hox's shoes had done little to deter the dragon from the tempting morsels at the end of his feet. No sooner had the couple stepped into the beast's enclosure than the wily lizard nipped off the end of Hox's left big toe.

There were conflicting reports about the melee that followed the attack. Some sources alleged that the terrified movie star fled the cage, leaving her husband alone to wrestle the komodo for his missing digit. Others, primarily associated with the starlet's publicist, claimed that she fiercely defended her husband against the rampaging lizard and had to be forcibly dragged from the cage by the zoo-keeping staff.

This much was certain. After the unsuccessful reattachment surgery and the couple's subsequent divorce, Hox's already brash demeanor had become far more abrasive.

The only thing that made him crankier than standing for long periods of time on the ampu-toed foot was the sight of an advertisement for his former wife's next movie.

A WINCE TWITCHED the corners of Hox's face as he continued to climb City Hall's central marble staircase. Halfway up the steps, he pulled a small, tablet-sized notebook from his inside jacket pocket and whacked it against his left thigh.

The action was primarily meant to be a distraction from the piercing pain in his foot, but it also served a second, more aesthetic purpose.

Hox preferred the old-fashioned way of reporting. The scratching sound of a pencil scribbling on paper, the sight of coded notes scrawled across a page, the pride of reading his byline laid out on traditional broadsheet newsprint—this was what he lived for. But the most satisfying sensation of his trade, bar none, was the smarting *pop* of a notepad slapping across his leg.

Sadly, these physical embodiments of his life's work were quickly disappearing. Whether he liked it or not, he was slowly but surely being dragged into the new age of digital media. His City Hall beat now included blogs, tweets, chat rooms, and, the most onerous on the list, television appearances.

Hox groaned, thinking of the last item.

The paper had recently formed an unorthodox—and, in his view, ungodly—alliance with one of the local television news stations. Touted as a means for streamlining and efficiency, the end result had been the creation of a regular "man about town" video feature in which he, unfortunately, played a starring role.

During his long and prestigious journalism career, Hox had won several awards and commendations. In addition to his local political beat, he had covered military conflicts in overseas war zones, political races at the state and national level, and critical public policy issues such as health care, education, and the justice system.

The newspaper's joint media venture was only a

few days old, but already he had been forced, under vigorous protest, to do a fluff piece on San Francisco's local albino alligator—along with a sourdough replica that a bakery by the wharf had cooked up as a tribute.

"Sourdough Clive," Hox muttered with an extra forceful *whap* of the notepad. "Lowest point of my career."

AT THE TOP of the stairs, Hox veered left toward the supervisors' hall of offices. A few steps later, he paused to glance at his reflection on a glass wall outside the main corridor. Groaning, he ran his hand over the top of his head.

To add insult to injury, the station had recently assigned him a stylist, a wispy little man named Humphrey whose first order of business had been to give the reporter a haircut.

Hox was still bitter with the results.

Humphrey had somehow convinced Hox that a new hairstyle would help cover the growing bald patch at the back of his head. Hox hadn't really understood how combing his hair toward the center of his head would accomplish this feat, but he had, begrudgingly, allowed Humphrey to proceed.

"What a disaster," Hox grumbled under his breath as he gingerly poked at the quarter-inch spike running down the middle of his scalp.

The new hairstyle had disrupted his entire

71

morning routine. It had taken him half an hour to comb it into place, and he still wasn't sure he'd performed the maneuver correctly. Not once in his entire life had he been coiffed in such a ridiculous fashion.

With a sigh, he stepped away from the glass.

Instinctively, he dropped his hand to the thick mustache that covered his upper lip, taking comfort in its familiar coarse stubble. So far, he'd managed to fend off Humphrey's efforts to trim his thick eyebrows and overgrown mustache, but that, he sensed, wouldn't last much longer.

"I'm too old for this nonsense," he muttered as he prepared for the inevitable round of gibes he was about to receive in the next room.

Gritting his teeth, Hox pushed open the door to the first office on the right and stepped inside.

The man seated behind the desk took one look at him and nearly fell off his chair.

"Wait, wait. Don't say a word," the President of the Board of Supervisors chortled as he yanked open one of the desk drawers and thrust his hand inside.

"Where's my camera?"

Chapter 10
A SPIDER'S INTUITION

"OKAY, JIM. OKAY," Hox pleaded gruffly after several minutes of teasing commentary about his new haircut. "That's enough, already."

The President of the Board of Supervisors wiped several tears from his cheeks, which had pinkened from his laughter.

"Be sure to let me know when this Humphrey fellow starts working on your mustache," he replied. "Maybe I can e-mail the station some suggestions."

Hox rolled his eyes at the ceiling as yet another round of jokes commenced.

A WELL-KNOWN ENVIRONMENTALIST, formally associated with the Green party, James Hernandez—Jim to his numerous friends—had served as the president of the San Francisco Board of Supervisors for the last seven years.

An attorney by trade, Jim had a closet full of expensive suits, silk neckties, and fancy footwear—an extravagance expended for naught. Despite the diligent efforts of his tailor and the constant niggling adjustments of his wife, he routinely gave the impression of being wrinkled. His poor posture and lumpy physique negated all attempts to professionalize his rumpled appearance. The matter wasn't helped by the floppy hair that he wore just long enough to cover what he self-consciously perceived to be elephant-sized ears.

Jim shrugged this off with a good-natured grin. He was a perpetually happy man, and a smile was never far from his lips.

All of these features combined with his soft baby face to complete a roguish image, one that allowed him to charm the toughest of opponents—save the Current Mayor, with whom he'd been feuding for the better part of the last decade.

PRIOR TO HIS last two terms as supervisor, Jim Hernandez had dallied in national politics, serving as the running mate for a fringe presidential candidate. There had never been any question of the pair winning the election, but the stint had served to elevate his profile in local San Francisco politics.

It was no secret around City Hall that the board president desperately wanted to be awarded the pending mayoral appointment. Few odds makers, however, put any stock in that happening.

As a likely front-runner in the mayoral election next fall, Hernandez was unlikely to garner enough support from his fellow board members to obtain the caretaker slot. Although a majority of the supervisors had voted to make him the board president, those allegiances only went so far. Substantively, the mayor of San Francisco was a less powerful position than that of the president of the board of supervisors, but the former was a much more glamorous title than the latter.

The interim-mayor appointment would require a great deal more clout than Hernandez could possibly muster, leaving a chaos of would-be contenders seeking to fill the void.

Regardless, Hox still viewed the supervisor as a valid source for predicting what the board might decide at their upcoming meeting. Hernandez knew his fellow supervisors better than anyone else. Moreover, as board president, he controlled the gavel and, with it, the agenda. Given the unique circumstances of the vote, Hernandez could still influence the voting process, if not the eventual outcome.

This was the only reason Hox had suffered through the supervisor's twenty-minute monologue on his new haircut, but he was fast running out of patience.

HOX GROANED AS he deflected yet another hair comment. He glanced around the room, searching for anything that might facilitate a change of subject. Jim Hernandez could keep this up for hours.

The reporter's eyes latched onto a black plastic

picture frame resting on a bookcase behind the supervisor's desk.

"Still driving that shoe box, I see," Hox said sourly, pointing to the vehicle captured in the picture.

Jim turned in his chair to beam proudly at the photo.

The supervisor was religiously devoted to public transportation and rode one of the city's Muni trains to work each day. When necessity forced him off the public grid, he got around in a neon green hybrid-electric compact car.

Hox had once tried to squeeze his burly frame into the vehicle's front passenger seat—he had been complaining about the cramped experience ever since.

"Hamster-mobile," Hox grumbled as Jim spun back around.

Before the supervisor could get off his next retort, Hox leaned forward and, with a grunt, rested an elbow on his right knee. Bending toward the desk, he carefully opened his reporter's notebook and pulled a pencil from its spiral.

"Can we talk about something other than my hair?"

Jim smirked impishly. "I can't imagine another topic that would be anywhere near as interesting."

Hox glared testily and then intoned in a low voice, "The Mayor's replacement?"

The supervisor sat back in his chair and looked

thoughtfully up at the ceiling. "Hmm, yes, I suppose that issue has been getting some airtime of late."

Hox licked the pencil's lead point. Holding it poised over the paper, he prodded, "Of course, you'll be throwing *your* hat into the ring?"

Jim shrugged his shoulders, an unconvincing display of indifference. "I will if I'm asked."

Hox pushed away from the edge of the desk and stroked his grizzly mustache. "How many of the other supervisors are angling for the job?"

Jim brought his hands together in front of his chest. Wiggling his fingers in the air, he replied, "All of them."

Hox pumped his thick brows inquisitively. "All of them?"

The supervisor nodded, his floppy bangs emphasizing his response.

"Well then," Hox said, popping his notebook against the top of his thigh. "We're in for quite a circus."

AS HOX CONTINUED his hushed discussion with the board president, the glass wall around the corner from the supervisors' office corridor took on a new reflection.

A young man in gray-striped coveralls and high-top canvas sneakers shuffled past the glass, casually pushing the handle of a dust mop. Although he kept his head tilted downward, he paid little attention to the mop's path across the polished marble floor, frequently sweeping over the same spot multiple times while leaving other portions untouched.

A blue baseball cap pulled down over the young man's forehead hid the upper portion of his dark-skinned face, shadowing his eyes as they darted furtively to the left and right.

During his six months of employment at City Hall, he'd rarely ventured to the second floor. As one of the Current Mayor's low-level staffers, he spent most of his time sequestered in a basement cubicle.

Still, he thought apprehensively, surely someone up here would recognize him.

Suddenly, he heard the sharp *click* of a woman's high-heeled shoes approaching him from the rear. It was the unmistakable step of Mabel, the Mayor's administrative assistant. He saw the woman almost every day—she was the one who delivered the staffer assignments to the basement. She was bound to see through this disguise.

As the footsteps drew nearer, he felt his cheeks begin to blush. The palms of his hands started to sweat against the dust mop's worn wooden handle. The Previous Mayor had assured him this would work. Why had he believed him? He looked ridiculous in this janitor's outfit. How could he have been so foolish?

Cringing, the young staffer caught a whiff of

Mabel's distinctive perfume, a sweet lemony scent she sprayed each morning against the sides of her neck.

Any second now, he would be exposed. He would probably lose his job over this silly prank.

Mabel clipped to a stop next to the edge of the dust mop as the sweat spread to the man's brow, dampening the brim of his baseball cap. Flushed with embarrassment, he kept his face turned to the floor. He could just imagine the confusion in her voice as she spoke his name.

"Spider Jones?"

But those words never came.

"Excuse me, sir," she said smartly, tapping him lightly on the shoulder. "I think you missed a spot."

Then she pulled open the door to the supervisors' offices and strode off down the hallway.

SPIDER STOOD WATCHING Mabel's departing figure, his mop frozen to the floor as he shook his head. He couldn't believe it.

His gaze dropped to his gray-striped coveralls. He couldn't possibly be that invisible . . . or could he?

Slowly, he began to slide the mop forward. Calmly concentrating, he focused on making regular, even sweeping movements.

His confidence growing with each gliding step, he felt himself falling more and more into character. He wasn't a junior staffer *posing* as a janitor, he told himself. He actually *was* a janitor.

ANOTHER SET OF footsteps sounded against the marble floor—a man's heavier stride in flat-soled dress shoes.

Spider risked a quick glance at the incoming figure. It was one of the supervisors, returning from an off-site meeting.

Amazed at his own brazenness, Spider swept himself into the supervisor's path. Tilting his head at a slight angle, his eyes tracked the man as he passed.

Even when the supervisor had to skip sideways to avoid the mop, he never gave Spider a second glance.

FILLED WITH A renewed respect for the Previous Mayor, Spider pushed the dust mop toward the hallway that held the supervisors' offices.

Not far down the corridor, he spied the closed door to President Hernandez's office. He could just make out the heads of the two men sitting at the desk inside. The PM had told him to be on the lookout for something like this—a shut door was the sure sign of an attempt to cloak a confidential conversation.

Proceeding cautiously but deliberately, Spider sidled up to the door and pretended to discover a particularly resistant piece of dirt stuck to the floor. He pushed the dust mop vigorously back and forth, trying to decipher the murmur of the hushed voices inside the office. His young face twisted with concentration as he strained to hear the words.

Finally, after checking up and down the empty hallway, he cupped his hand around his ear and pushed the edge of his palm against the door to amplify the sounds from the opposite side.

As the junior-staffer-turned-fake-janitor processed the details being discussed inside the president's office, his demeanor became more and more animated.

After listening for several minutes, Spider issued a vigorous fist pump and then took off down the hallway, the dust mop now zooming across the floor with no regard for the appearance of cleaning efficacy or discreet janitorial conduct.

Out past the glass wall, he ditched the dust mop, leaving its handle propped against a marble column. Nearly losing his baseball cap from the top of his head, he sped around a corner and dove into one of the building's enclosed stairwells. The rubber soles of his sneakers squeaked against the slick marble stairs as he sprinted to the first floor, clearing the last three steps in a single leap.

After flying down one of the main hallways flanking the building's center rotunda, Spider spun into a granite-walled vestibule located beneath the central staircase.

A light flickered on, illuminating a row of empty pay-phone stations.

Fingers trembling, he pulled a crumpled piece of paper from his chest pocket and read the number scrawled on its front. He punched in the digits and waited anxiously as the phone began to ring.

"I've got something for you," he whispered excitedly when the PM answered.

"No," he added with a confident *pshaw*. "Of course no one saw me."

Chapter 11

THE DOCTOR IS IN

DR. KIMBERLY KLINE scanned the Academy of Sciences' front entrance, searching for her missing frog expert.

Not five minutes earlier, the attendant at the front ticket booth had called down to her office, alerting her to Sam's arrival. Kimberly had proceeded directly to their meeting spot beneath the dinosaur skeleton, but the burly frog aficionado was nowhere to be found.

A petite woman in blue jeans, sneakers, and a dark blue Academy T-shirt, Dr. Kline wasn't much taller than many of the schoolchildren exploring the museum that day. Her light blond hair was cut in a short bob that bounced when she walked. A nonstop bundle of energy, she fit in well with the Academy's youthful patrons.

She had joined the aquarium's cadre of herpetologists—or, to use Sam's terminology, *frogologists*—just a few months earlier, but she was already acquainted with the eccentric Frog Whisperer from their previous consults at his field camp. She knew he was prone to distraction, along with several other odd behaviors.

Perhaps, she mused, he had wandered off.

Turning a slow circle, Dr. Kline studied the front atrium area once more before reaching for a walkie-talkie hooked to a belt around her waist. Pushing a plastic button on the side of the device, she brought its mike to her mouth.

"Has anyone seen Sam?"

WITH A LITTLE help from a curator who happened to be walking past the Academy's Swamp Exhibit, Dr. Kline quickly honed in on the location of her wayward frog expert.

She found Sam bent over the brass seahorse balcony, staring down into the tank at Clive, the Academy's famous albino alligator, who was resting comfortably on his heated rock.

"There you are, Sam," she called out with relief.

He didn't appear to hear her greeting; his attention remained focused on the colorless creature in the tank below.

She approached the balcony and tried again.

"Hello there, Sam."

Still receiving no reply, she leaned over the railing, trying to intercept his gaze.

"Sam?" she repeated, aiming the full volume of her voice at the big man's left ear—to no effect. His shoulders dropped another inch or so over the side of the balcony.

Standing on her tiptoes, she reached up and tentatively tapped him on the shoulder.

"Sam?"

At her touch, Sam's whole body convulsed. The scientist ducked as he jumped and spun around, a startled, wild-eyed expression on his freckled face.

"Hey there, Mister Frog Whisperer," she said, grabbing hold of his vest to keep him from flipping backward over the balcony. "Thanks so much for coming."

"It's my pleasure . . . ahem . . . Dr. Kline," Sam mumbled with an awkward grin as he straightened his shoulders, centering his weight on the concrete floor.

"I'm so glad you're here." She sighed, taking a short step away from the railing. "I've tried everything. I just can't figure out what's wrong with them."

"Mm-hmm," Sam nodded, absentmindedly fiddling with the green button sewn onto his vest as he glanced over his shoulder at the Swamp Exhibit.

"They won't touch their food," she persisted. "And their color is off. They seem a little pale."

"Mm-hmm," he repeated, still preoccupied by the alligator.

Dr. Kline paused, perplexed. It was unusual for Sam to act so disinterested in an important frog-related matter.

"Would you like to take a look at them?" she asked hopefully. "They're downstairs on the aquarium level."

Immediately, Sam turned to face her. "Why didn't you say so?" he replied briskly. "Let's go."

Without further hesitation, he set off toward a large stairwell leading to the basement.

Brow furrowed, Dr. Kline chased after him.

Moments later the pair disappeared through an entrance bearing the label "Steinhart Aquarium."

DR. KLINE STRUGGLED to keep up as Sam clomped down the concrete stairs, his long legs taking two and three steps at a time.

"They're just off to the right," she panted as they entered the basement level.

Abruptly halting, Sam swung his arm out in front of his chest.

"After you."

Dr. Kline hurried off down a tank-filled corridor. Sam took two strides to follow and then veered sharply off course. By the time the scientist looked back to check on him, he had disappeared into the maze of exhibits.

He had one more thing to do before visiting the frogs.

SAM CROUCHED IN front of the nearest display to get his bearings, and a pair of ten-year-olds soon packed in around him. The boys were captivated by the neon-striped ribbon eels in the display's tank. Sam briefly joined them in staring up at the eels—their thick, wiggling arms of clothlike skin looked for all the world like sock puppets. Then he pulled an exhibit map from his pocket and held it up to the tank's light to search for his location.

He was now in a dramatically different environment than the Academy's upstairs level. The floor above had been a light, airy place with high ceilings, numerous open water features, and an abundance of live plants.

In contrast, the aquarium's underground domain was a dark, cavelike theater, a network of narrow passageways with blanketed walls that absorbed all sound, dampening even the most excited of young voices to a hushed murmur.

Tanks lit by strategically placed track lighting featured a dazzling array of exotic sea life. Delicate creatures with intricate spines and elaborately painted fins inhabited alien landscapes. Black velveteen backdrops behind each display further enhanced the illusion of an underwater grotto with an endless supply of nooks and crannies to explore.

After a quick study of the exhibit map, Sam stood up from the ribbon eels display and set off down the nearest hallway.

Somewhere within this dank labyrinth, he knew, was the viewing station for the lowest level of Clive's Swamp Exhibit.

HALFWAY TO HIS destination, Sam caught a glimpse of Dr. Kline's blond-headed blur passing to his right.

"Oops," he whispered guiltily.

Pulse racing, he ducked behind the closest available cover: a wide partition wall at the junction of two narrow hallways. A pair of oval-shaped reliefs hung on the nonstructural wall, the large ceramic discs depicting the heads and shoulders of the aquarium's original benefactors, Bavarian brothers Ignatz and Sigmund Steinhart.

Sam hunched behind one side of the display while Dr. Kline circled the other. Holding his breath, he watched the blond halo of her reflection in an enormous glass tank on an angled wall a few feet away.

When at last she trotted off down another corridor, he was once more on the move.

A FEW MINUTES later, Sam entered a glass-roofed tunnel that provided a view through the bottom of the aquarium's largest water exhibit. Craning his neck, he glanced up at the passing undersides of several large tarpon.

"Whoa," he murmured as the layers of streaming fish parted to give him a glimpse of the tropical rain forest that spanned several stories above the tank.

But a flash of white at the far end of the tunnel soon captured his attention. He rushed through the remaining glass-roofed passage and hurried over to the basement level of Clive's Swamp Exhibit.

THE LOWER VIEWING station provided a window into the submerged portion of the alligator's tank. From this position, Sam could see the moss-covered pilings that Clive used to heave his long body up onto his heated rock. The nearest supporting post was missing a large, triangular-shaped chunk from its side, as if Clive or one of his alligator predecessors had taken a huge bite from the wood.

Sam watched as one of the turtles sank to the exhibit's sandy bottom. The creature's bony head, nearly indistinguishable from its boulderlike shell, turned toward the crowds looking into the tank. The turtle's face was expressionless, the eyes those of a living fossil.

As the turtle came to rest on the tank's floor, a plump catfish curled past the foot of the pier and sneaked into the shadows beneath. Its long, tubular whiskers trailed across the sandy bottom, causing small puffs of debris to float up in its wake.

Slowly taking in every detail, Sam raised his eyes toward the upper portion of the glass window. The alligator had apparently decided to take a short break from his rock. His albino body now floated just below the water's surface, all but the tip of his nose submerged. His front and rear legs hung limply, passively, while his thick tail drooped downward.

"Just hang tight, Clive," Sam said as his eyes focused on a service door on the lower side of the tank. "We've got a plan."

AS SAM CONTINUED to study the service door's details, Dr. Kline's exasperated voice sharply pierced his eardrums.

"Sam! Where have you been?"

Wincing, he turned to find the blond-headed woman standing, hands on her hips, directly behind him.

"Oh, there you are, Dr. Kline," he replied with a sheepish grin. He shrugged apologetically. "I got a little lost."

Throwing her hands up, she sighed and pointed toward the glass-ceilinged tunnel. "It's right this way."

She gave him a stern sideways glance.

"This time, I'll follow *you*."

KEEPING A FIRM grip on his sleeve, Dr. Kline guided the Frog Whisperer, who was acting far more eccentric than usual, away from the basement-level view of the Swamp Exhibit. A few minutes later, she ushered him toward a prominently marked glass terrarium mounted into a wall next to a hands-on experimental station for young children.

"Here we are," she said with exhausted relief. "As you can see, the little guys just don't look right . . ."

Sam leaned in toward the glass, his green eyes squinting.

"Do you have the keys?" he asked, holding out his hand. "To the rear of the tank," he added in response to her questioning expression.

She eyed the children congregated around the display. "Are you sure that's necessary?"

Sam straightened to his full commanding height. "Absolutely," he pronounced, deepening his voice with as much authority as he could muster.

"We'll have to go in by the shark exhibit," she said pensively, pulling out a large set of keys.

Glancing back several times to check on Sam, Dr. Kline led the way down a short hallway to a black-painted wall. Triggering a penlight attached to the key chain, she waved the beam across the dark surface until she illuminated a small handle. A second later, she had unlocked a black door, beyond which lay a narrow opening that ran behind the rear of the exhibits.

Motioning for Sam to follow, she proceeded into the walkway. A line of removable placards hung from the back side of each exhibit, identifying the species occupying the adjacent tanks. Halfway down the line, she inserted a second key into a slot in the wall and removed the rear paneling from the large glass terrarium.

Dr. Kline stepped aside as Sam stared at a trio of tiny frogs sitting beneath the fronds of an artificial fern. He rubbed the red scruff on his chin, sucked in his breath, and then rotated his head toward her.

"We'll need a little privacy," he said, knitting his brow. "Doctor-patient confidentiality. I'm sure you understand."

Her face flushed with confusion. "Well, ah . . . I don't . . ."

Somberly, Sam arched his red eyebrows.

"Yes, of course," she replied dubiously, tentatively stepping away from the terrarium. "I'll be at the other end of the hall."

Sam waited until she had disappeared down the walkway before bending back into the exhibit.

A group of children crowded past on the opposite side, their eyes widening at the sight of the man behind the glass. He gave them a short wave, and then motioned as if to encourage them to move along.

"Do you ever get the sense you're being

watched?" he asked as the frogs waddled toward him.

The nearest one blinked its eyes, conveying its agreement.

Sam's mouth flattened into an understanding grimace. Then he flipped through the key chain Dr. Kline had left hanging from the terrarium's rear facing, found the set that would unlock the Academy's main doors, and unhooked them.

Sliding the pilfered keys into his vest pocket, he whispered conspiratorially into the tank.

"You guys are doing a great job. Keep it up."

Chapter 12
MORE THAN CHICKEN

IN THE APARTMENT above the Green Vase antiques shop, Isabella watched as her person's face slowly disappeared behind the newspaper. She listened for the sharp *snap* of the woman's hands tugging the sides of the printed sheet to smooth out the portion containing the main article, signaling that a lengthy reading spell was about to commence.

The slender cat yawned, as if bored by the proceedings, but in actuality, she was performing a close surveillance.

Isabella waited until she was sure her person was fully engrossed in Hoxton Fin's latest City

Hall report. Then she silently hopped off the couch's armrest and stealthily crept out of the room.

It was time for Isabella to give her person a nudge toward the clue to her next treasure hunt. Oscar's niece had missed something important when she came in from her run.

A MOMENT LATER, Isabella crossed the threshold into the kitchen.

Her toenails clicked softly against the tile floor as she circled a worn wooden table and sniffed at the now-empty food bowls positioned beneath. She could still pick out a faint whiff of fried chicken from the earlier afternoon snack.

Whiskers twitching, Isabella gazed up at the kitchen walls. The sheets of tulip-covered wall-paper that Oscar had tacked to the framing were now gone. New plasterboard had been installed and the surface covered with light purple paint.

Dark green hand towels hung from a rack near the sink; several green figurines cast in the shape of frogs adorned the open shelves secured to the walls.

The purple and green color scheme was a tribute to the green vase that rested on the downstairs cashier counter and the fresh-cut purple tulips that Oscar's niece purchased every week from a flower shop in the nearby financial district.

The tulips, Isabella reflected, had a singular

meaning in and of themselves—both to her person and to the mysterious Uncle Oscar. Their use in combination with a rare paralysis-inducing spider venom had played a central role in Oscar's transition from the Green Vase antiques shop to his new enterprise at the North Beach chicken restaurant.

APPROACHING THE CABINETRY below the sink, Isabella trained her focus on the counter above. She took her time studying the distance, carefully sizing it up as her pipelike tail rose into a contemplative curve.

She needed to make sure she executed the jump perfectly. The slightest skidding scrape of claws across the countertop would give her away.

After a thorough analysis of the counter height and a last check through the doorway to confirm her person was still fixated on the newspaper article, she was ready to proceed.

GATHERING HER FEET beneath her body, Isabella leapt gracefully onto the counter. Now properly elevated, she tilted her head in a pleased manner, appreciative of the height's change in perspective. She didn't mind a ground-level view—a cat could pick up several important details from that angle—but she generally preferred the advantage of a little altitude.

In her not-so-modest opinion, a cat's proper role was at the highest point in the room, where she could look down on her minions. But because her person did not share these beliefs, most of Isabella's counter surfing took place late at night, when the potential objector was tucked in bed, fast asleep.

This was a tribute to Isabella's heartfelt devotion to Oscar's niece. Even though her human was a lesser being, Isabella didn't like to upset her. A daytime visit, such as this one, was a rarity. It required a great deal more finesse and the right distraction.

Isabella paused and listened to the reassuring crinkle of newsprint emanating from the living room. A confident expression crossed her pixie-like face.

She had plenty of time to complete her task.

GINGERLY STEPPING OVER a rack filled with drying dishes, Isabella skimmed nimbly across the kitchen countertop. With skill honed from a year's worth of experimentation, she quietly maneuvered around a small toaster oven and a stand-alone rack of coffee cups.

A few steps took Isabella to the stovetop, whose burners she took extra care to avoid. She had learned the hard way that the raised metal ridges sometimes contained residual heat from their last use.

Her last hurdle was a wooden cutting board. Its uneven surface would rattle against the counter if she stepped on top of it, so after a short pause, she hopped neatly over. Having cleared the last impediment, she had finally reached the far side of the room.

Isabella turned to glance back at her starting point.

She supposed she could have leapt onto the counter at this location instead, but what would have been the challenge in *that?*

HAVING SUCCESSFULLY NAVIGATED across the kitchen counter, Isabella was ready to get down to business.

Her blue eyes honed in on her target—the trash bin. The lid of the tall cylindrical-shaped container rose just flush to the counter where she now stood.

Crouching down, Isabella leaned toward the canister's metal lid and prepared to perform yet another of her well-practiced moves. After wedging the flat portion of her nose against the edge of the lid, she quickly jerked her head upward, flipping it open.

Balancing precariously, she anchored her paws on the top edge of the oval rim and slowly eased her weight from the counter to the canister. Her toenails gripped the slippery plastic-covered rim as she positioned herself over the bin's opening and bent her head to retrieve the last item deposited inside.

With her teeth, she nipped the folded top of a green paper bag. Still straddling the trash can, she tossed it onto the counter.

The maneuver was awkward, but effective.

Isabella quickly followed the bag back to the counter and set about the task of accessing its contents. Swatting at the folded-over opening, she managed to separate the two sheets of paper and slip her paw into the sack.

The process generated far more rustling than Isabella would have liked, but she continued to dig through the discarded chicken wrappings until she found the item for which she'd been searching: a green flyer with the restaurant's logo, followed by a brief historical excerpt about a man named James Lick.

Chapter 13
THE LONG SHOT

A FRIED-CHICKEN-SMELLING BURP bubbled up from the right side of the couch as Oscar's niece reached the end of Hoxton Fin's latest report on the increasing number of aspiring mayors crowding the corridors at City Hall.

According to Hox, the list of potential candidates included the current members of the board of supervisors, several local civic leaders, and even the city's Previous Mayor.

Hox's article had focused on the short list, the serious contenders. Of course, this being San Francisco, a large number of oddball applicants were also petitioning the board for consideration.

The expanded roster included the "Chicken Man," a person of unknown gender who had been appearing at the Current Mayor's public events for the last seven years, each time wearing a feathery chicken costume and clucking vociferously. Also seeking the nomination was a rather large, extremely hairy gentleman from the Castro, who boasted his credentials as a practicing nudist.

And then there was Monty.

DROPPING THE PAPER to her lap, the woman glanced through the living-room window to the art studio across the street. She could just make out the profile of the man sitting inside at his desk, wiping his hands with a wet paper towel after finishing his takeout meal from Lick's Homestyle Chicken.

In the months since it had become clear that the Current Mayor would be headed to Sacramento, Monty had talked of little other than the pending vacancy at City Hall. The mayor's job was his lifelong dream, as he'd tell anyone who would care to listen. The antics of the local newspaper's editorial board had only inflated those hopes.

• • •

IT HAD BEEN a slow summer, newswise. Other than the pending shake-up at City Hall, there had been few stories of interest on which to report.

That was the only explanation Oscar's niece could come up with for why a San Francisco television station had aired a lengthy interview with the outgoing Mayor's Life Coach. During the hour-long conversation, Monty had described in great detail his various life-coaching techniques, including the specific steps he had designed to alleviate the Mayor's debilitating fear of frogs.

The interview had generated a great deal of public interest, little of it positive.

For the local newspaper, the topic had been too tempting to resist. In the weeks since the spot aired, the editorial page had run numerous tongue-in-cheek advice columns purportedly written by Life Coach Carmichael.

Each article had been more over the top than the one that came before. Topics ranged from key elements in frog-aversion therapy to guidance on how San Franciscans could nurture their inner frog. One of the most popular pieces in the series had pretended to explore the depths of the Mayor's frog-addled psyche, speculating on the childhood cause of his phobia.

With the outcome of the selection process for the Current Mayor's replacement growing more unpredictable by the day, the newspaper had naturally lampooned a Monty-themed solution. Their mock endorsement had run in the most recent Sunday edition, generating chuckles across the political spectrum.

MONTY, UNFORTUNATELY, HAD failed to appreciate the joke. He'd seen the commentary as an indication of his growing prestige. Clippings of each of the columns graced a corkboard mounted on a wall in his studio. He quoted his favorite lines at every opportunity.

Oscar's niece shook her head as Monty stood up from his chair and began walking back and forth across the studio, his hands gesticulating as if he were practicing a speech.

Sighing, she folded the paper and set it on the side table next to the couch, tucking it beside a brass lamp covered by a ceramic globe.

With so many qualified candidates competing for the post, there was no way the board of supervisors would select a fruit loop like Monty.

Then again, she reasoned with a cynical grin, this *is* San Francisco. Stranger things have happened.

Chapter 14

A CULINARY CHALLENGE

STILL ENERGIZED FROM his earlier eaves-dropping operation, Spider Jones steered his bike onto Powell, quickly picking up speed as he approached San Francisco's Union Square.

Even in the falling dusk, the city retained the day's Indian summer heat. Above the front entrance to the venerable St. Francis hotel, a row of scarlet-colored flags hung limply from their poles, the brisk breeze that normally popped their sheets missing in the damp heat.

Generating his own wind, Spider zoomed past the hotel, swerving at the last minute to avoid a red-jacketed bellhop who had stepped off the curb to hail a cab. The bellhop's piercing whistle sent out a sharp rebuke, but the warning failed to slow the young man's pace.

A cable car clanged down the hill as Spider weaved his bike around a group of female shoppers headed for a shoe sale at the massive multi-story department store that dominated the bottom half of the square. Boutiques, billboards, and a jeweler's topped by an Atlas figure cradling a clock filled in the rest of the perimeter.

Buoyed by reckless confidence, Spider pedaled across the square's concrete-covered clearing. At the opposite corner, he bumped his tires down a short flight of steps, squeezed through the last blinking seconds of a crosswalk, and continued into the financial district.

The warm evening air rushed over his sweating cheeks as he raced along the emptying streets. His wheels spun past a blur of office buildings, the metal flashings on his bike flickering in the short clips of light between shadows.

Finally, brakes screeching, he arrived at his destination, a small French bistro not far from Chinatown's south gate.

SPIDER STARED UP at a line of neon tubing that spelled out the restaurant's name. He checked the wording against a scribble on a piece of paper from his pocket and confirmed he was at the right location.

"French," he murmured, somewhat perplexed as he looked for a pole near the yellow-and-red-painted storefront where he could secure his bike.

Across the street and up the block, he spied Chinatown's festive entrance. He stared longingly at the pair of serpentine dragons that crested its gate. Spicy Asian food would have been much more in his culinary wheelhouse. He wasn't exactly sure what to expect from French cuisine.

Brow furrowed, he turned his gaze toward the menu affixed to the bistro's front window, quickly noting a number of intimidating items on the list.

Then, he glanced down at his T-shirt and blue jeans. Even without the janitor coveralls, he wasn't anywhere close to being dressed appropriately for this occasion, but there had been no time for him to change clothes.

With a shrug, he tried to dismiss his wardrobe concerns. The Previous Mayor had assured him it would be fine.

Still hesitating, Spider gripped his handlebars. He couldn't believe the recent turn of events.

Just the other day, he'd been studying draft city ordinances in his basement-level cubicle. Now, he was meeting with one of the city's most powerful political kingpins. For a middle-class kid from a sleepy East Bay suburb who had taken a year off after high school so he could try another shot at getting into UC Berkeley, this was quite a turn of events.

"Gosh," was about all he could muster as a waiter in a black tie leaned out the bistro's front door.

"Mr. Jones?" the waiter asked as he motioned for Spider to bring the bike inside. "The Mayor is expecting you."

SPIDER HANDED HIS bicycle off to the waiter and watched as the man wheeled it down the bistro's long, narrow dining area toward a coatrack by the door to the kitchen. Lifting his baseball cap from his head, he smoothed a hand over the short hair that had been ruffled beneath and slowly took in his surroundings.

A wooden brass-rimmed bar dominated the left side of the room. On the front corner, a silver ice bucket held chilling bottles of wine that he was too young to legally drink. Beneath the counter-top, a shelf mounted onto the bar's facing contained several copies of the local newspaper's most recent edition. The top page prominently displayed Hoxton Fin's byline and his article about the upcoming board of supervisors' meeting and the contenders seeking to replace the Current Mayor.

Rows of upended wine glasses hung from a rack above the bar's long counter, the stemware's delicate round bulbs glinting in the bistro's dim light. Tiny shaded lamps affixed to the corners of the booths that lined the opposite redbrick wall gave a cozy glow to each table.

Spider's gaze traveled upward. A pair of intricate stained-glass skylights were positioned at the center of the ceiling; the rest of the roof was covered with pleated white sheets that had been starched the same crisp white as the tablecloths.

The bartender coughed to attract Spider's attention; then he nodded toward the front booth.

This section of seating was set aside for special commemorative tables. Three poster-sized portraits hung from the brick wall, each one signifying a different honoree. The first delegate was a local haberdasher—a portly but well-dressed man who ran a storefront in Union Square. The second was a beloved, but now deceased, newspaperman who had gained nationwide renown for columns that captured San Francisco's quirky oddball essence.

The last picture displayed a man in a black tux, top hat, and spats—the real life embodiment of which sat at the table beneath.

Beaming fondly, the Previous Mayor pointed to an empty chair.

"Take a seat, Spider."

AS SPIDER SLID into his seat, the waiter arrived carrying a large platter. With a flourish, the man set the dish on the white tablecloth and removed its metal cover, revealing the contents: an array of shucked oysters laid out on a bed of crushed ice.

Spider stared dubiously at the platter while the PM picked up a lemon half covered with a thin mesh netting. Turning the lemon upside down, he squeezed the juice out through the netting and dribbled it over the plate.

"Bon appétit," the PM said encouragingly.

"After you, sir," Spider replied with a nervous gulp.

"Oh, no, none for me," the PM said with a mischievous wink. "These are for you. My treat. I can't eat the things myself. Shellfish allergy."

Paling, Spider reached tentatively for the nearest

shell. Its outer surface felt like a rock in his fingers. The PM leaned back in his seat, amused, as the young man brought the oyster to his mouth.

Spider tilted the shell toward his face, trying desperately not to look at the squishy gray blob inside. Despite his best efforts to maintain a sophisticated composure, his nose instinctively crinkled from the fishy citrus aroma. Holding his breath, he scooped his tongue beneath the slimy mollusk and, drawing on every ounce of available willpower, swallowed it whole.

Eyes bulging, Spider reached for his water glass and drained half of its contents in one long gulp. With a relieved *thunk,* he set the glass down on the table, smacked his lips, and wiped a napkin across his mouth.

"Mmm . . . delicious," he said in a strangled voice.

The PM smiled with pleasure.

"Try the next one with a little sauce," he advised knowingly.

Before Spider could come up with a polite but demurring response, the PM interjected, "Now, about our next project . . ."

SPIDER MANAGED TO get down two more oysters while the PM discussed the upcoming board of supervisors' meeting where the interim mayor would be selected. The PM briefly summarized the procedure the board would use for making nominations and then outlined the list of candidates the local political punditry considered most likely to take the nomination.

"Of course, I'm certain that none of these blokes will be moving into the mayor's office suite—at least not anytime soon," the PM summed up with a sly grin. "So I need you to gather some intelligence on the true front-runner."

"I'm really getting the hang of sneaking around the second floor now," Spider boasted after stiffly swallowing yet another oyster. "That janitor trick worked like a charm . . ."

His voice trailed off as the PM waved his hand over the table, dismissing his comment.

"That was just a learning exercise," the PM said with a cryptic smile. "This assignment will require some sleuthing outside of City Hall."

The PM flagged the waiter with the flick of his index finger.

"Cup of coffee for me, Pierre," he said as the waiter rushed to his side. He gestured for the man to take his plate. "I've got another dinner engagement later this evening, but I wanted to give young Spider here an introduction to your fine cuisine."

Spider gave the remaining oysters a forlorn look as the waiter disappeared once more into the kitchen.

The PM pulled a small notepad from the front pocket of his suit jacket and handed it across the table.

"I've written the individual's details down on the first page. I'd like you to go to the address tomorrow and take a look around. Be sure to keep track of everything you see." He tapped a finger against the notepad. "Even if you think it's not important, write it all down."

Just then, the waiter arrived with a second tray containing a coffee setting and a large bowl steaming with a heavy butter sauce.

"You went light on the garlic, I presume," the PM said sternly. *"Very light,"* he added with a suspicious sniff of the dish.

"Of course," the waiter replied, stiffly polite. "As you requested."

The PM shifted his focus back to Spider. "Moderation is the key to a long and happy life," he said, cocking an eyebrow. "Especially in regards to garlic."

Spider stared down at the spiraling brown shells swimming in the sauce. A heaping amount of garlic was all that would have been able to get him through the next dish. Then he looked up at the waiter with despair.

"Escargot," the waiter supplied.

The PM flashed a gleaming smile and then translated.

"Snails."

Chapter 15

A LITTLE FELINE ASSISTANCE

OSCAR'S NIECE BEGAN folding the newspaper for her recycle bin, taking care not to disturb Rupert's snoring heap as she creased the folds. She had almost summoned enough energy to head for the shower when she noticed a rustling sound coming from the kitchen.

The instinctive response was out her lips before she could stop it.

"Rupert?" she called out sternly.

A yawn floated up from the next cushion over. The orange tip of Rupert's fluffy tail wiggled an "It's not me" response.

The woman's gaze immediately traveled from the furry mound sleeping beside her to the couch's now empty armrest.

"Issy?" she called out in disbelief as the rustling continued. It was rare for her female cat to get into trouble. "What's going on in there?"

Having cohabitated with the feline species for several years, the niece knew that a mysterious noise in an otherwise unoccupied room required immediate investigation. Few scenarios beginning with this fact pattern resulted in anything other than an enormous mess—although Rupert was usually the culprit of those crimes.

"Issy?" she repeated, her concern growing as the sound grew louder.

A garbled *mrrreow* brought the woman scrambling to her feet.

"Isabella . . ." the niece called out again as she heard the distinct sound of paws hitting the kitchen's tile floor.

From his spot on the couch, Rupert cracked open an exculpatory eyelid and yawned loudly, as if to say, "Told you it wasn't me." Then he heaved out a sleepy sigh and rolled over onto his side.

Just then Isabella entered the living room with a green piece of paper clenched in her teeth.

Head held high enough to keep the paper from tripping her front feet, Isabella marched purposefully toward her person, all the while issuing a stream of muffled cat commentary. A moment later, she dropped the paper on the floor and looked up expectantly.

Perplexed, the niece bent to pick up the green flyer. It appeared to be from the paper bag that had contained that day's fried-chicken cat treats. She had read the restaurant's standard blurb many times before, so she had tossed the greasy sheet from the earlier package into the trash bin without looking at it.

But as her eyes scanned the writing on the lower half of the paper, she realized the language had changed.

"Well, Issy," the woman murmured thoughtfully,

her mind immediately speculating on the clue's potential implications. "I believe someone's trying to send us a message."

Isabella gave her person a sarcastic look. *"Mrao."*

Chapter 16
THE STEINHART CONNECTION

HOLDING THE FLYER from the fried-chicken restaurant in one hand, stroking Isabella's silky head with the other, Oscar's niece sank back onto the couch. A few smears of chicken grease blotted the printing, but the text was still readable.

The flyer began with the familiar introduction to James Lick, the talented piano maker from Pennsylvania who had wandered the globe, taking a tour of South America before eventually landing in pre–Gold Rush San Francisco. Once there, Lick made several prescient land deals in water lots along the shoreline that he eventually converted into a substantial fortune.

Oscar's niece could recite the tale of the Millionaire Tramp from memory. She knew this portion of the restaurant's regular flyer by heart. It was unchanged from the previous printings.

A second paragraph, however, had been added to that day's edition.

• • •

THE NEW SECTION of the flyer highlighted Lick's many charitable contributions, including his sizable donations to the California Academy of Sciences.

Although Lick had eschewed the luxuries of fashion and fine food, he'd had no reservations about doling out funds for charitable organizations.

Lick had provided the fledgling Academy with an enormous multi-story building on Market Street. The Academy converted the structure, which had been used as a shopping emporium, into a museum, filling its open layout with its growing scientific collections.

The strategic location increased the new organization's visibility, and San Franciscans flocked to the site. The skeletons of a T. rex, a wooly mammoth, and an African elephant were particularly enticing draws.

An Academy expedition had just left for the Galapagos Islands to gather more specimens for the museum when the 1906 earthquake hit, destroying both the building and the bulk of its contents.

Fortunately, the Academy had had the foresight to insure the structure. Using the proceeds from the insurance payout, a new headquarters was quickly set up in Golden Gate Park. Soon after the move, the facilities were expanded with funds from the estate of the Bavarian-born Steinhart brothers, Ignatz and Sigmund, to include the world-class Steinhart Aquarium.

THE NIECE LEANED back into the couch, trying to imagine what kind of treasure her Uncle Oscar might have discovered that was associated with the Academy of Sciences.

She reread the selection, this time honing in on the last sentences.

"The Steinhart Aquarium," she murmured out loud as she recalled her last visit to the place just a few months earlier.

ALMOST A HUNDRED years after the Steinharts' bequest, the aquarium continued to attract thousands of visitors with its creative displays of fishes, frogs, and other water-related creatures. It was a well-known Bay Area attraction, an integral part of the Academy's Golden Gate Park facility.

The complex had recently reopened after an extensive renovation that had implemented much-needed improvements in earthquake stability as well as updated the overall design to give it a more modern feel.

If the niece remembered correctly, little of the aquarium's original structure remained. Anything the Steinhart brothers might have secreted away in the old building was unlikely to have survived the rebuild.

The green insert fell from the woman's fingers as her thoughts drifted inward and she wondered just what the proprietor of the fried-chicken restaurant was trying to tell her.

FROM HER PERCH on the couch's armrest, Isabella watched her person read the greasy piece of paper. Then the woman's head rotated toward the ceiling, deep in thought.

With a sigh, Isabella shifted her gaze to the end table beside the couch. Blue eyes glittering, she stared at the brass lamp and its still unlit ceramic globe.

Oscar's niece was going to need some additional feline assistance if she were ever going to get on the right track for this latest treasure hunt.

Chapter 17
THE SWAMP

AS ANOTHER DAY disappeared into the western horizon, the darkness of early evening descended onto the secluded confines of Golden Gate Park. Thick stands of redwoods reached up to cover the cloudless sky, spreading their needle-filled branches to blot out the scattering of artificial light from the surrounding city.

In the center of the park, the glass-fronted, grass-roofed Academy of Sciences complex grew silent and still. A walk up the front steps, past the foyer's fragile yet imposing dinosaur skeleton, revealed little in the way of activity. Most of the building's creature inhabitants had drifted off to sleep.

But in the rear wing, where a brass balcony surrounded a large hole in the floor, a slight splash could be heard as the Academy's showcase albino alligator hoisted his long, leathery body onto his heated rock.

Clive hummed happily to himself as the relaxing warmth radiated up through his spongy, wet belly.

THE STEINHART AQUARIUM had seen numerous changes since it first opened its doors in 1923: refurbishments to its water-filtration systems, exhibit modifications, wing additions, and, in the wake of the damage caused by the 1989 Loma Prieta earthquake, a complete retrofit and rebuild.

The Steinhart's original structure had been completely subsumed in the modern ecofriendly renovation. The aquarium section was now blended seamlessly into the planetarium, natural-history museum, and artificial rain forest that made up the rest of the complex.

The Swamp Exhibit, however, had remained a constant. It was one of the few features of the current building that carried back to the original design. The sunken tank ringed by its brass balcony of standing seahorses had stayed true to the Steinhart brothers' early conception.

THE SEAHORSE BALCONY had guarded countless alligators over the years, garden-variety green ones and rare albinos, but in the Academy's long history, no alligator had captured the public's imagination quite like Clive.

Due in part to the creativity of the Academy's promotions department, Clive had achieved a local celebrity the likes of which San Francisco had never seen. Beloved by children from across the city, his fame had surpassed that of all other public figures, entertainers, athletes, and politicians.

CLIVE SNUGGLED SLEEPILY against his rock, enjoying the evening's peace and quiet. After a busy day of receiving the public's admiration, he was ready for a good night's rest.

As he drifted off to sleep, he thought fondly of his little fans, their faces filled with awe and wonder, their curious minds abounding with questions. The slack-jawed expression he wore throughout much of the day—which some mistook for malaise—was really the reflection of his inner pride and satisfaction.

Every time he heard a docent describing his unique features to a fresh set of youngsters, he felt a pleasant glow swell in his chest. He truly relished his role as alligator ambassador.

The children's jarring shrieks, of course, Clive could do without. Although it was impossible for him to imagine life without his youthful visitors, he felt a small modicum of relief at the end of each day when the last one had been escorted out the Academy's front doors.

CLIVE WIGGLED HIS lengthy frame, spreading his legs to maximize his body's contact with the rock. He sighed contentedly as the warmth spread through his joints.

Given the limited options available to an albino alligator, he knew he'd scored the jackpot.

Gators of his kind were unable to survive in the wild. The albino's white skin stood out against the dark background of its natural swampland habitat, making young hatchlings an easy target for prey. Any newborn albinos that managed to escape being eaten soon suffered from their depigmented skin's sensitivity to direct sunlight.

In addition to these handicaps, most albinos had very poor eyesight, hindering their ability to hunt or scavenge for food. Clive, himself, was very nearly blind.

As a practical matter, timely discovery by one of the alligator farmers who routinely inspected the many nests scattered across the coastal wetlands was an albino's only opportunity for survival. A long-term gig in a well-stocked aquarium was a one-in-a-million shot.

CLIVE CAST HIS droopy eyes proudly around the perimeter of the Swamp Exhibit. The California Academy of Sciences was one of the most coveted albino alligator placements in the country. Despite the exhibit's relatively small confines, he couldn't help thinking he had the finest digs in town.

Beyond the heated rock, which was by far his favorite feature, he also appreciated the mist makers built into the tank walls just above the waterline that kept his delicate skin soft and moist. The artificial tree that stretched high above the tank cast enough shadow to mitigate any harsh sunlight that might permeate the skylights in the elevated roof. And, of course, the Swamp was stocked with plenty of turtles to keep him company.

Last but not least, there were the Academy alligator specialists, a busy team of scientists who catered to his every need. How many alligators, he wondered, had an entire crew of humans at their beck and call to keep them well furbished with floating fish pellets?

Clive's stomach rumbled with the thought. He turned his head toward the far corner of the tank, where he'd stashed a pile of pellets from the last batch the scientists had thrown in before leaving for the night, but his legs didn't move. He wasn't quite hungry enough yet to go dig them up.

With another contented sigh, his chin dropped once more to the rock's heated surface.

EMITTING A GRINDING gator grunt, Clive shifted his weight so that he could wedge his right elbow against a hot spot near the rock's center.

Having lived his entire life in a protected enclosure, his skin was generally clear of blemishes, scars, or scratches—with one exception. His right front paw was missing its outermost digit, leaving an exposed joint that occasionally twinged with arthritis.

Perhaps the main downside to living on display like this, Clive reflected with a painful wince, was your inability to choose your tank companions.

CLIVE'S TOE INJURY was the result of a love match gone horribly wrong. Several months back, the aquarium had introduced a non-albino female alligator to the Swamp Exhibit in the hopes she and Clive might strike up a romance.

He had been open to the idea at first, but he had quickly changed his mind.

Mariah, he thought bitterly. That was one temperamental alligator.

No sooner had the new alligator entered the swamp's enclosure than she had proceeded to take over the place. After taking a massive bite out of one of the underwater supporting posts, she had mounted the heated rock—not to share, but to occupy completely. She hadn't been the least bit amenable to his cordial attempts to discuss the matter or any of his offers of compromise.

In the ensuing territorial dispute, Mariah had snapped at Clive's right front paw, causing it to bleed.

Immediately concerned, the Academy staff members swooped in and quickly transported Clive to a behind-the-scenes operating room. The next thing he remembered, he was waking up from anesthesia, minus one digit.

By the time Clive returned to the Swamp Exhibit, Mariah had been dispatched to a zoo. Since then, he had been content in his bachelor-hood, socializing with the swamp's amiable and nonthreatening turtles when he needed companionship.

Women, he thought as he carefully rotated his right front leg to flatten his pared-down appendage against the hot spot.

STILL MUTTERING TO himself about the moody Mariah, Clive's eyelids fluttered to half-mast, and the first wheeze of a dozing snore buzzed through his snout.

He was on the verge of falling fast asleep when a movement at the balcony caught his attention.

Slowly, Clive roused his senses and focused his diminished vision at the swamp's top rim. To Clive, the rocks and tree trunks inside his swamp were fuzzy images. He even had difficulty telling his turtles apart.

He could barely make out the blurry shadow creeping behind the row of standing seahorses, but the figure struck him as slightly different from those of the security guards that roamed the Academy at night.

Just then, a man's husky voice whispered over the edge of the enclosure.

"Psst, Clive."

This was followed by the familiar *splatting* sound of a fish pellet hitting the water.

"Over here."

Clive needed no further encouragement. His stomach had awoken, this time roaring with hunger.

The alligator's snapping jaw quickly found the disc floating near him.

Chomp.

Chapter 18

OFF THE EMBARCADERO

HOXTON FIN STRODE along a nearly empty sidewalk, heading down Market Street toward the Ferry Building. The bulk of the financial district's traffic had retired for the evening. Only a few Muni buses and the occasional taxicab bumped along the pothole-strewn roadway.

Despite the late hour, the day's heat had yet to dissipate. The air was unusually heavy and clogged with exhaust. San Francisco's signature breeze had temporarily vacated the city, leaving it to suffer in sweltering stagnation.

Hox wiped the back of his hand across his sweating forehead. Then he reached for his collar to loosen an extra button at the neck of his shirt. He'd already removed his jacket, tucking it into the top of his backpack.

The weather was beginning to wear on him. He found it difficult to think under these conditions and, worse, impossible to write.

He, like his city, depended on the wind.

THE CLEANSING BLAST cleared out all the toxins, both environmental and emotional, that were constantly created by the crowded metropolis.

Yes, in other parts of the world, people managed to live in cramped quarters without the aid of a clearing wind. Some of those spots were even more densely packed than San Francisco, with citizens crammed inside tiny beehive cubicles stacked, row upon row, into honeycombed towers of uniformity.

Hox had visited such places, and he had come away from each experience with a certain amount of incomprehension.

The average San Franciscan was not amenable

to the conforming rigidness that kind of lifestyle necessitated. The Western heart was not so easily tamed.

A WALK OVER any of the city's residential hills proved the point. Houses, though tightly knit together, were painted with a distinguishing array of colors. Garish gables overdecorated many front facades. Each living space, no matter how small, was an important creative outlet. You'd be hard-pressed to find any two buildings that looked exactly the same.

In a city made up of such ardent free spirits, the cooling ventilation of the Pacific kept the excesses of all that individualism in check.

The wild whipping force ripped at hair, clothes, and makeup, defeating all but the most rigid styling mechanisms. It was a great equalizer, giving everyone, no matter his or her race or social stature, a uniformly windblown look, channeling the area's boundless creativity into matters beyond an individual's physical appearance.

In Hox's view, it was the wind that had developed San Francisco's laid-back, easygoing acceptance as well as its entrepreneurial spirit.

WITHOUT THE WIND'S tempering release, conflicts quickly began to build.

Everywhere, it seemed, petty squabbles were breaking out. Hox couldn't step foot inside the newspaper's offices without encountering some senseless argument raging at full red-faced volume.

As Hox neared the Ferry Building, he cast a hooded glance at an elaborately coiffed woman, who was painting her lips with a colored gloss as she hurried to catch the next boat.

He led out a gruff snort. This stagnant air led to far too much primping.

Then he caught a glimpse of his own reflection in the glass wall of a nearby storefront. The image elicited a groan.

The painstakingly prepared spike down the center of his scalp was still perfectly in place.

HOX FOLLOWED MARKET Street's bottom hook past the trolley turnaround outside the Ferry Building and set off down a sidewalk lining the inner lane of the Embarcadero.

He soon reached the restaurant where he was to meet his late-night appointment, but he was in no hurry to step inside.

Hox stood staring at the palm trees planted in the roadway's median. The tropical plants—that in the typical San Francisco fog looked so improbable—suddenly seemed far more appropriate. Their crown of fronds was better suited to the sizzling heat still radiating off the pavement than November's more typical drizzling rain.

He lifted his gaze to the western span of the Bay

Bridge. A row of antlike vehicles sped across the lower deck, their antennaed headlights shining against the bridge's metal rigging.

Hox desperately wished he were riding in one of those cars. He would rather be headed anywhere else than inside this restaurant.

WITH A BELLIGERENT sigh, Hox reluctantly turned his back on the water to face a multi-story gray stone building.

Located in the middle of a block, the structure housed a high-end hotel on its upper floors and, at street level, the restaurant that was the scheduled meeting place for his evening appointment.

His source had insisted that the rendezvous take place in secret. The man had made him promise that the information received would be treated on a strictly off-the-record basis.

Hox rolled his eyes, remembering the phone call. He knew the conversation held only the pretense of being confidential.

When the Previous Mayor penned his next op-ed for the newspaper, the column would no doubt include enough details for those in the know to piece together not only with whom he had been dining and what they had discussed, but also what they had both eaten.

HIS SQUARE JAW clenched with resignation, Hox shuffled through the restaurant's front doors, past the unmanned station for the seating hostess, and into the dining room.

The building's interior was appointed with dark wooden flooring, matched by a wainscoting of similar texture that covered the lower half of the walls. Plantation shutters blocked out the windows, completing the sense of being closed off from the Embarcadero's often bustling thoroughfare.

The tables were covered with blue-and-white-checkered cloths, lending a small amount of brightness to the space. Each setting was ringed with white ceramic tubs filled to the rim with hardened butter and beer glasses holding bundles of long, slender breadsticks.

The restaurant primarily served clientele from the nearby financial district. A few hours earlier, the dining area and adjacent bar would have been packed to capacity with lawyers, stockbrokers, and financial analysts who had just left their offices for the day. This late in the evening, however, most of those patrons had shifted to dining establishments located closer to home.

Hox glanced around. Other than a handful of out-of-town conventioneers, the place had emptied out. As he had expected, the Previous Mayor was nowhere to be seen.

He shuffled over to the table held on permanent reserve for the PM, pulled out one of its heavy oak chairs, set his backpack on the floor, and dropped into the seat.

To the anxious waitress who immediately hurried up, he waved a thick hand and said gruffly, "He's expecting me."

Before the woman could disappear, he added, "I'll take a Guinness."

FORTY-FIVE MINUTES LATER, Hox stared sulkily at the wall, absentmindedly twirling a breadstick in his fingers as he sipped his second beer of the night.

His meetings with the Previous Mayor were always lengthy, drawn-out affairs. Half the time, the old man didn't have anything worthwhile to share. *All* of the time, he was late.

Hox knew the PM loved to torment him. He, in turn, hated playing the stooge. But with an important story brewing at City Hall, Hox couldn't afford to mutter anything but "I'll be there" when the PM called to set up a meeting.

It had been almost eight years since the PM left his elected office, but somehow the man still managed to know everything that was going on in San Francisco's local government. Hox had tried for years to replicate the PM's sources—and failed.

It put a serious dent in his journalistic pride, but he had finally concluded he had no choice. He had to submit himself to the humiliation of these meetings.

Sucking down the Guinness's dark, bitter liquid,

Hox tilted his head to peek through the wide slats of the nearest blinds. The lights on the Bay Bridge twinkled against the dusky night sky.

There was no telling what time the PM might finally show up.

He'd better order an appetizer.

HOX HAD EATEN halfway through a plate of fried calamari when a gray felt bowler slid across the table in front of his plate.

The Previous Mayor's gravelly voice greeted him with feigned surprise.

"Hox—man, what have they done to your hair?"

"Hello, Mayor," Hox replied, raising his glass with a surly grimace. He suspected the PM had already been thoroughly briefed on his unfortunate run-in with the television station's stylist.

As the PM took his seat, the waitress rushed up with his regular cocktail. Hox arched his eyebrows in annoyance. The woman had taken far more time servicing his orders.

"Good evening, Eleanor," the PM intoned smoothly. "What's the fish special tonight?"

Hox listened impatiently through a tedious discussion of the menu, which involved numerous questions about ingredients and possible modifications—the answers to which Hox felt certain the PM already knew.

At last, the PM stroked the short gray mustache over his upper lip and voiced his selection.

"I'll take the fish," he said with a certainty that suggested he had made up his mind long before hearing all the other options.

THE PM TOOK a measured sip of his cocktail. Then he carefully set the dainty glass on the checkered cloth, rested his wrists on the table's edge, and folded his fingers together.

"Thank you for meeting me, Hox. I have some news to pass on about the business at City Hall."

Cautiously, Hox pulled out his notebook and leaned forward.

The PM raised his hands above the table, palms outward, a rebuffing gesture meant only to draw the reporter in.

"Of course, I don't pretend to be an expert on the matter. A man like *yourself* has many reliable sources."

Hox rolled his bottom lip inward, silently gritting his teeth.

The PM raised an index finger to his cheek and tapped it thoughtfully. "But—I do have an insight that might be slightly . . . ah . . . different from the other information you've been gathering."

Just then, the waitress approached carrying a plate piled high with greens. The PM smiled as she whipped out a pepper grinder from her apron pocket. Hovering the grinder over the dish, she gave the cylinder the PM's preset number of twists.

The PM inspected the plate and issued a gracious nod, signaling her to depart.

Hox drained the Guinness as he watched the PM reach for a side cup filled with dressing. Slowly, the PM poured the creamy substance over the mound of lettuce. Then he used his knife and fork to thoroughly mix the two together.

After munching down a mouthful of salad, touching his lips with a napkin, and loudly slurping from his water glass, the PM bent his head toward the impatient reporter.

"Obviously, each one of the supervisors would like to get the nomination for him- or herself . . ." The PM tilted his head to one side, as if dismissing the possibility. "But everyone knows that's not going to happen. They'll never settle on one of their own. There's too much infighting."

Hox licked his lips, hungrily anticipating the PM's revelation. Maybe the long wait here at the restaurant had been worth his time after all.

If he found out the identity of the dark-horse candidate the city's political elite were about to push for interim mayor, then he might just have to take back all of the vicious things he'd silently muttered about the PM over the course of the last two and a half hours.

"One of the outsiders, then?" Hox asked eagerly. "Come on, Mayor, give me a name."

The PM took another forkful of salad and repeated his ritual. Hox was about to leap across the table and strangle the man when at last he made his reply.

"I believe you're familiar with . . ." The PM paused, his brown eyes twinkling.

Hox held his breath, pencil at the ready.

The PM whispered conspiratorially, "The Current Mayor's Life Coach."

Hox bored the pencil into the notepad, breaking the lead.

"You've got to be kidding me," he grumbled bitterly.

He reached into his rumpled coat pocket, pulled out a wad of cash to cover his drinks and appetizer, and threw it on the table. Screeching his chair back, he stormed out of the restaurant.

STILL CHUCKLING AT the hotheaded reporter, the Previous Mayor finished his salad.

The waitress took his plate and brought him a glass of wine while he waited for his main course.

After taking a sip, he pulled out a sleek black mobile device from his jacket pocket and texted an update to his colleagues at the North Beach Homestyle Chicken restaurant.

Chapter 19
THE BAVARIAN BROTHERS

ISABELLA SAT ON the edge of the bathroom sink in the apartment above the Green Vase antiques shop, guarding the shower while her person finally cleaned up from her run.

Steam rose from the other side of the curtain and began to fog the mirror. As her person's wet shadow started lathering shampoo into her hair, Isabella quickly calculated the remaining shower time. Then, she gently hopped down from her perch and treaded softly into the bedroom.

Shower surveillance was one of Isabella's many duties—one she took quite seriously—but tonight, she had other priorities.

She set off into the apartment, looking for Rupert.

It was time to put that brother of hers to some use.

ISABELLA WAS WAITING on the edge of the bed when her person emerged from the bathroom, one towel wrapped around her head, a second around her body.

The cat could tell the shower had helped loosen the woman's thinking. Her lips murmured "Steinhart" as she slid on her bifocal glasses and picked up the green restaurant flyer from her dresser.

Isabella silently observed while her person reread the added paragraph regarding the Steinhart brothers and their contribution to the Academy of Science's flagship aquarium.

"Steinhart," the woman repeated, still gripping the towel as she skimmed the fingers of her free hand across the spines of a nearby bookcase.

Here in this shelving unit, the niece had gathered the bulk of Oscar's reference books on California history. In the entire three stories of the redbrick building that housed the Green Vase, this spot contained the highest concentration of biographical information on the Bay Area's early movers and shakers: from the explorers who had inhabited San Francisco's precursor, Yerba Buena, through the masses who had flooded Northern California with the onset of the Gold Rush. Other volumes focused on the city's later development, covering the bankers and financiers who had helped to construct its initial infrastructure—and those who had rebuilt it from scratch after the 1906 earthquake.

The woman considered this bookshelf to be the most comprehensive source of historical data from her uncle's vast collections. If there was anything to be known about the Steinharts—particularly a hidden Steinhart treasure—this was the place to start.

• • •

AFTER A MOMENT'S perusal, the niece selected a book and pulled it from the shelf. Taking a seat on the bed next to Isabella, she flipped through the index to the *S*s.

There was no listing for Steinhart.

"Hmm," she mused, dropping the book on the bed as she returned to the bookcase for another try.

This time, she picked out a larger, denser text on Northern California's early history.

"Surely, this will have something," she said confidently.

But, after a few minutes' search, she discarded that one as well.

She scanned the rows of books, refusing to accept defeat. The Steinharts were prominently named benefactors of one of the city's most popular public venues. The influential brothers had to be mentioned in one of Oscar's references.

As the niece stared down at the bookshelf, a cat-sized ripple appeared in the spines along the bottom row.

Thump.

Rupert's fluffy white body darted out from the space at the back of the shelf, knocking several books onto the floor at the woman's feet.

With a sigh, she bent to pick them up. As she began to slide the books back into place, she noticed a clump of white cat hair lying in the exposed portion of the shelf.

"Oh, Rupert," she muttered. "I'm always cleaning up after your . . ."

And then she stopped, puzzled. In the cavity behind the row of books, she spied a slim paperback with a blue cover depicting an underwater scene. Reaching into the slot, she pulled out *The History of the Steinhart Aquarium.*

From her perch on the edge of the bed, Isabella issued a satisfied *chirp.*

AN HOUR LATER, Oscar's niece was both reclothed and fully up-to-date on what little there was to be known about the biographical profiles of the Steinhart brothers. The aquarium book had provided more information than all the other research materials combined, but the details were still sketchy.

Bavarian-born Sigmund and Ignatz immigrated to America in the 1850s. Seizing on the Gold Rush's moneymaking opportunities, the brothers built a thriving mercantile business that soon expanded into a mining and finance empire.

Ignatz, the younger Steinhart, married and, by all accounts, was a devoted husband to his lovely wife, showering her with expensive presents and trips to exotic locations.

Sigmund, in contrast, lived the life of a swinging bachelor. A man with substantial means, he was on the guest list to the finest gatherings the growing city had to offer. He was a gregarious fellow and joined several of San Francisco's exclusive social societies, the most notable being the all-male Bohemian Club.

ESTABLISHED IN 1872, the Bohemian Club started out as a meager gathering of artists, writers, and journalists. Over the years, however, it grew into an ultra-exclusive fraternity of the rich and powerful.

Although the actual membership rolls remained shrouded in secrecy, rumor had it that participants included California luminaries such as publisher William Randolph Hearst, sugar baron Claus Spreckels, architects James Flood and Bernard Maybeck, vintner Robert Mondavi, and actor, movie director, and former mayor of Carmel, Clint Eastwood. Several U.S. presidents were also believed to have joined the ranks.

But back in the late 1800s, when Sigmund Steinhart attended his first meeting, the club was still an association of the original Bohemians. Likely, Sigmund would have made the acquaintance of one of the group's founding members, San Francisco writer Mark Twain.

AS OSCAR'S NIECE digested this last piece of information, she shifted the book away from her bifocal glasses and collapsed backward onto the bed, her head whirling with possibilities.

In her mind's eye, she imagined the private

property where the club had held its secretive meetings. The Bohemian Grove, as it was aptly named, was located in the forested coastlands near the Russian River on the western edge of Sonoma County.

It was probably at one of these retreats, she reasoned, deep within the Sonoma woods, that Sigmund came up with the idea of funding an aquarium for the growing city of San Francisco.

Instantly, she pictured the elder Steinhart brother, contemplating his future endowment as he sat on a log next to his fellow Bohemian, a character from San Francisco's past on whom her uncle had focused a great deal of his research: Mark Twain.

The woman lay there on the bed, pondering. Was this a clue to the Steinharts—or something more?

Information about the Bohemian Club would have been difficult to obtain, even for someone with her uncle's unique resources.

Had Oscar been a member of the secret club?

Force of habit had driven her to use the past tense. She revised her last thought.

Was Oscar a member?

Chapter 20
THE FRIED-CHICKEN ENTREPRENEUR

ABOUT A HUNDRED yards off the heavily trafficked tourist trail of Columbus Avenue, a safe distance from the catcalls of the maître'd's prowling the sidewalks outside the busy lineup of Italian restaurants, San Francisco's North Beach neighborhood slipped into a more relaxed scene. The steeply sloping streets that wrapped around the south side of Telegraph Hill discouraged casual wanderers.

It was mostly locals who congregated outside a vintage coffee shop at the corner of Vallejo and Grant. The Italian tricolor hung proudly from the front awning. Opera floated out of an antiquated sound system to the sidewalk, where many of the shop's patrons sat at rickety tables, enjoying the warm night.

Ragged scarves and multi-colored wool socks had been discarded, revealing bare white feet, unmanicured toenails, and wind-smoothed faces. A game of canasta started up as drinks transitioned from coffee to Chianti.

The café's front door had been propped open, exposing an interior that was clean but not antiseptically so; care had been taken not to wipe the aura off the place.

At one of the front tables, next to a knee-to-ceiling window, a serious-looking man in his mid-thirties sat nervously typing at his laptop. The would-be writer sucked in on his hollow cheeks, trying to capture the spirit of the famous local authors whose pictures were featured in a mural on the opposite interior wall. Many of the commemorated storytellers had honed their craft while sitting in this very café; some had likely scribbled at this same wobbly table.

After each word, the man looked up at the painting and took a deep breath. Every keystroke represented an epic commitment to a phrase.

The pressure of the previous authors soon took its toll. Sucking down the last dregs of his coffee, the man left his computer for a quick smoke on the curb outside.

AT THE CORNER, the aspiring novelist held a shaky lighter beneath his self-rolled cigarette as a man with a rolling paunch, a few day's gray stubble, and wild flyaway eyebrows strolled slowly past.

The elderly fellow had recently immigrated to North Beach's Italian neighborhood—although his trip had involved only a few blocks, not an entire ocean.

He wore a navy blue shirt and pants, both of which were dotted with grease stains and a light dusting of flour. In his arms, he carried a large paper bag he'd picked up at an exotic pet store up the hill.

Hobbling down the uneven sidewalk toward Columbus, the man nodded a gruff recognition to the members of the canasta set, but he didn't stop, at least not on that evening, to join the game.

A FEW MINUTES later, the old man reached the darkened storefront of James Lick's Homestyle Chicken.

He muttered a curse at the pigeons patrolling the entrance—threatening to add a new appetizer to the next day's menu—but his face softened as he reached into his pocket for a small plastic bag.

Flapping wings and satisfied cooing filled the air as the man pulled out a handful of bread-crumbs from the bag and scattered them across the sidewalk.

Still grumbling about pigeon recipes, he pushed open the restaurant's front door and stepped inside.

THE SPARSELY FURNISHED eating area con-tained several tables suited for family-style dining. Mismatched chairs lined the tables, and a few extra seats had been pushed up against the walls, which were otherwise mostly bare.

The only decoration of note was a portrait of an elderly gentleman with a long, straight nose and otherwise flat face. A thick, messy beard grew down from the man's jawline, giving the appearance of a ruffled collar. The rest of his torso was clad in a threadbare collared shirt and jacket. The fabric's worn, scruffy condition was evident even in the black-and-white depiction.

The portrait clearly conveyed the sense of an earlier era. A brass plate mounted on the wall beneath confirmed the image to be the restaurant's namesake, the miserly millionaire James Lick.

THE MODERN-DAY LICK—whose financial status remained as much a mystery as his real identity—shuffled across the dining room to the kitchen.

He slid the large paper bag from the pet store across the counter to his business partner, who was manning a sink of dirty dishes, the last cleanup task remaining from that evening's dinner service.

Harold Wombler looked up from the sink and wiped his wrinkled wet hands on a dishtowel. No words were needed; neither man was the type for unnecessary verbal communication.

Harold dug around inside the paper bag, nodded a grunting acknowledgment, and, carrying it with him, headed for the restaurant's front door. The items in the sink could wait until he returned.

AFTER HAROLD LEFT, Lick ambled to the rear of the kitchen and out the building's back exit. In the alley behind the restaurant, not far from a large

Dumpster, he stopped in front of a shed whose door was secured with a heavy iron lock.

After a cautious glance over his shoulder, he pulled the plastic sack of breadcrumbs from his pants pocket, dug around inside it, and fished out a metal key, one end of which was formed in the shape of a three-petaled tulip.

With a heavy puff, he blew a light coating of crumbs from the tooled iron surface; then he fed the key into the lock and pulled open the shed's door.

A neon tube suspended from the ceiling flickered on, illuminating rows of dusty shelving. Boxes and crates of all sizes, shapes, and conditions of wear had been stuffed into the cramped space.

Lick rummaged through several half-open containers, occasionally taking an item out and holding it up to the dim light. After a few minutes of casual sorting, he turned his attention to the outfit he'd worn at the Academy of Sciences earlier that afternoon. Carefully, he repacked the pile of ragged beggar's clothes in its box.

As he prepared to leave the shed, Lick glanced up at a clothing rod mounted along the back wall. The bar held the hangers for a number of costumes, each one covered in a clear plastic bag.

A rumpled linen suit hung from the near end of the rack. Leather lace-up boots rested on the floor beneath.

In a small kit attached to this outfit lay a bristly white mustache—one meant to emulate a writer who had spent several years in San Francisco—the modern-day Lick's favorite character from the time period: Mark Twain.

Chapter 21
THE GATOR-NAPPING

A WHITE CARGO van pulled away from the rear loading dock outside the California Academy of Sciences, leaving behind a Swamp Exhibit with several confused turtles and a heated rock that was missing its regular reptilian occupant.

After a few winding curves, the vehicle picked up Highway One and headed north into the sleeping city.

It would be several hours before the Academy's alligator staff discovered that their prized specimen had disappeared.

CLIVE BLINKED HIS large gray eyes, trying to adjust his albino-diminished vision to the dim lighting in the van's rear cargo area.

Even if he'd had crystal clear eyesight, there wouldn't have been much for him to see. He was surrounded on three sides by the van's metal walls. A stiff cloth-covered barrier separated the cargo hold from the front seating area.

Clive stared forlornly at the dark ceiling. He had only himself to blame for this predicament, he thought miserably.

He had followed the trail of tasty fish pellets right up the ramp into the back of the van. No sooner had he gulped down the last pellet than the rear door had swung shut behind him. The subsequent grinding *cinch* of metal had indicated the securing of a lock.

It was at that moment he realized his stomach might have led him into trouble.

CLIVE SHIFTED HIS weight, testing the slick surface beneath his feet. His front claws—all five plus four of them—gripped the metal brackets bolted onto the floor as the van careened around a sharp corner.

Who were these scheming bandits? he thought with worry. And where were they taking him?

He couldn't make out much beyond the nefarious pair's shadowed heads.

The driver was a small bald man. Clive squinted in frustration at the tiny frame hunched over the van's steering wheel, but the man's silhouette was unknown to him.

The gator did recognize the fellow in the right front passenger seat. He was the one who had called out to him from the seahorse balcony. The voice had been strangely familiar, but Clive couldn't quite place the man's rugged physique.

He sensed, however, that he had seen this scoundrel before.

Every day, thousands of humans peered over the Swamp Exhibit's balcony. It was impossible for Clive to keep track of all those onlookers. Even if he had recognized the criminal, he reasoned, that knowledge was of little use to him now.

His panic growing by the second, Clive's head swam with grim possibilities.

Were these men poachers? Thieves? Was he about to be featured in a new line of designer handbags?

Or worse, he thought with a shudder, *cowboy boots?*

The last time Clive left the confines of the Swamp Exhibit, he'd wound up on an operating room table with a front digit sawed off. At the end of this journey, he feared, he might be missing more than just a toe.

Only hours earlier, he remembered ruefully, he had been touting his life story's remarkable success, his great fortune among the ranks of albino alligators.

His luck had apparently just run out.

A FEW MINUTES later, the van slowed and, after a short pause, made a wide turn. Gravel crunched beneath the tires as the vehicle pulled to a stop in a secluded wooded area.

Clive watched as his captor in the front passenger

seat turned to look over the front partition. A light mounted onto the van's roof clicked on, illuminating the man's face.

A burly bloke with scruffy red hair and a chin full of rough stubble smiled down at him.

"How're you doing back there, Clive?" the man asked kindly. "Are you ready for your vacation?"

Clive seized on the word. *Vacation?* Was that crude slang for euthanasia—or did he dare hope that he might survive this abduction after all?

The van doors swung open, letting in the warm nighttime air. Crickets hummed in the bushes, a calm, soothing sound.

Clive hesitated at the doorway and looked down the ramp that the men had propped up against the van's bumper.

A third conspirator emerged from the bushes and growled out a welcome.

"Well, go ahead, then. Make yourself at home."

The alligator heard the familiar sound of a fish pellet skipping along the ground, and his stomach once more took the lead.

Trundling down the ramp, he followed the trail of pellets, gobbling up each one as he eagerly waited for the next signal.

The ground grew soft beneath his feet. Mud oozed up between his splayed toes. He found himself at the edge of a body of water—one far larger than that of his Swamp Exhibit.

He held back, unsure if he should enter, but the

soft *plunk* of a pellet dropping into the shallows convinced him to proceed.

As Clive disappeared beneath the surface, a last sound echoed into the night.

Chomp.

Chapter 22

A CRUEL CHICKEN

NEAR MIDNIGHT IN the apartment above the Green Vase showroom, Isabella stood in the doorway to the third-floor bedroom, assessing the scene.

Once more, her person had drifted off to sleep with a book laid open on her chest. Her glasses were tipped sideways on her face, and the light over the bed remained on.

Isabella sighed her disapproval. This was not a healthy routine.

She turned her attention to the bed's other sleeper.

Rupert lay stretched out on the covers beside the woman, his length sprawled across the bed's width, his tail hanging over the side. Every so often, the tail's fluffy orange tip twitched, the indication of much larger action occurring in Rupert's dream.

Knowing her brother, the dream involved eating. Not much to work with, Isabella summed up, momentarily stymied.

Isabella's small, pixielike face pinched with thought. Her person wasn't yet ready for the next day's events. There was still one more clue inside the Green Vase for the woman to sort out, and it was Isabella's job to nudge her down the right track.

Isabella's gaze shifted from the tail's latest gyration to the green chicken-restaurant flyer resting on the bedroom dresser.

Hmm, she mused cannily. That might just work.

RUPERT NUZZLED THE soft comforter beneath his head, flattening the side of his face into the blankets. His left front leg was tucked beneath his chest, while his right one stretched out with his paw turned up so that the tufts of white hair that grew between his toes poked into the air. Every so often, the exposed paw stretched, flexing to reveal the long curve of each claw.

It was a state of full and complete relaxation.

Rupert's furry eyelids fluttered at the single image that filled his sleeping brain. He had no need for complicated plotlines or a complex cast of characters. He was content with simple dreams.

All he could see was a plate piled high with fried chicken.

RUPERT WHEEZED CONTENTEDLY and rolled over onto his back, immediately transitioning into another loose, tension-free position. As his bulging stomach puffed out, he adjusted his imaginary plate, rotating the image in his head.

The chicken's crispy coating began to *pop* and *snap,* as if it had just been removed from a hot skillet. A purr rumbled through Rupert's chest, and he smacked his lips, savoring the illusion.

But as Rupert opened his mouth to take a bite from the top piece of meat, the sizzling sounds suddenly took on a more menacing tone. A low hissing growl spat out from the plate, challenging him to a duel.

Surprised, Rupert flipped over.

There were few situations in life where he took an aggressive stance. In most cases, he preferred flight over fight. He had been bested by his sister one too many times.

But not tonight. Not against a plate of chicken.

Emboldened by his dreamlike state, he gathered his feet beneath his body and summoned his sleeping muscles for a pounce. Then, with a mighty roar, he lunged toward the taunting chicken, swatting wildly, claws extended.

The chicken, it turned out, had far more manpower than Rupert had anticipated.

After a loud human shriek, he found himself soaring through the air. Still half-asleep, he landed with a *thunk* on the wooden floor.

A MOMENT LATER, Rupert's wobbly blue eyes peeked out from beneath the bed skirt. Tentatively, he scooted himself forward, his pudgy body hugging the floor as he slid out from under the bed, on the hunt for the dastardly fried chicken.

He glanced briefly up at the mattress as his person shifted her position. The bedsprings squeaked as she covered her head with a pillow. Still muttering about Rupert's unprovoked attack, she quickly drifted back to sleep.

The woman was obviously unaware, Rupert thought, of the dangerous plate of food rustling in the hallway just beyond the bedroom.

AS RUPERT SLUNK across the wooden floor and past the bathroom door, his quivering nose picked up on a distinctive fried-chicken scent. Stealthily, he followed the smell down the steps to the second floor.

At the bottom of the stairs, he lifted his head toward the kitchen, a logical location, he reasoned, for a rogue plate of food. But, after a thorough sniffing, he rejected this course of pursuit.

His prey had traveled instead to the living room. Stalking the renegade chicken, Rupert tracked the odor onto the couch. Rooting his head through the cushions, he traced the trail across the piece of furniture and over the opposite armrest to the end table near the window.

There, the aroma intensified. He sensed he had at last cornered his target—the frisky fried chicken was hiding inside a half-empty tissue box positioned on the end table next to a brass lamp.

His head hovered over the round hole at the top of the box for a long second and then plunged inside.

CRUEL CHICKEN, RUPERT thought a moment later as the tissue box clamped down around his head.

A LOUD *THUMP* provided the second jarring awakening of the night for Oscar's niece. Groggily, she propped herself up on an elbow. With a wide yawn, she straightened her eyeglasses and looked around the bedroom.

"What now?" she demanded, searching the room for the feline sleep disruptors.

But neither cat appeared to be present.

More bumps sounded from the floor below. Rubbing her eyes, the woman wandered into the hallway and down the stairs to the living room.

Taking in a deep breath, she crossed the threshold and flipped the light switch on the wall. "All right," she said sleepily. "What are you two . . ."

She didn't take time to finish the sentence. Sprinting on still half-asleep legs, she raced across the room to the end table on the far side of the couch where a large, fluffy cat with a tissue box stuck on his head was about to knock over a fragile brass lamp.

THE NIECE GRABBED the base of the lamp with one hand, the tissue box with the other. Giving the box a tug, she pulled it from Rupert's head.

The cat's expression was a strange mixture of gratitude and longing. He stared hungrily at the box and licked his lips.

"What's got into you?" the woman asked, perplexed.

Yawning, she peered into the box.

"How did this get in here?" she mumbled as she spied the green insert from the fried-chicken restaurant.

The niece stretched out her arm to set the lamp back on the end table so she could retrieve the insert from the tissue box. But as the lamp rotated in her hands, the bulb rattled in its socket.

The woman's face puzzled at the sound. Squinting at the bulb, she reached her hand beneath the ceramic globe to tighten it in its fittings.

"Hmm," she mused sleepily.

Meanwhile, Rupert began sniffing the tissue box, which, in the woman's distraction, had fallen onto the floor.

The niece bent to plug in the lamp's cord. As she did so, the bulb began to glow, and the once dull gray ceramic surface streamed with color.

"Would you look at that?" she said, her voice filled with wonder as she slowly spun the lamp's base.

"Issy, I think it's the Steinhart. The original aquarium." She pointed at the image depicting the aquarium's interior scene. "And that's the Swamp Exhibit."

Isabella turned for the stairs to the third-floor bedroom as Rupert's head, once more submerged in the tissue box, began to bump against the side of the coffee table.

Isabella paused at the bottom of the steps and issued a last summary comment.

"Mrao."

Chapter 23
PIER SEVEN

A FEW HOURS later, alarm clocks began to ring across the city. The shrill retort was accompanied by the weatherman's sad pronouncement: San Francisco's Indian summer would soon be coming to an end. A storm was gathering strength in the Pacific and would make landfall later that night.

In the cramped studio apartments that filled the neighborhoods surrounding the financial district, bleary-eyed law clerks, junior stockbrokers, and young financial analysts crawled out of their beds, pulled open their tiny closets, and stared morosely at the clear plastic bags of dry cleaner–wrapped clothing hanging inside. Then, slowly, their faces turned to look out the nearest window.

A bright sun spread across the bay, blooming the sky into a precious crystal blue.

For many, the siren's song was too tempting to ignore.

In several as yet unoccupied high-rise office buildings, suspiciously strained, frog-throated voice mails began to accumulate in the mailboxes designated for those calling in sick.

THE WIDE SIDEWALK lining the waterfront Embarcadero quickly filled with life. A number of healthy thirtysomethings converged on the sunny space, warily watching for potential office informants—lest they be forced to explain the miraculous curing of their earlier flulike symptoms.

Much of this growing crowd concentrated in and around the Ferry Building, queuing up for fresh-brewed coffee, munching on lox and cream cheese stuffed bagels, and browsing the area's numerous specialty markets—all while constantly texting and talking on their mobile devices.

A number surrounded the tables and benches set up on the ferry-receiving side of the building, while others ventured about a hundred yards away to Pier Seven, a long wooden walkway that angled off the Embarcadero into the bay.

BENEATH SAN FRANCISCO'S BUSTLING concrete shoreline lay a seawall whose origins went all the way back to the city's beginnings.

Constructed in the mid-1800s as part of the landfill operation that created the financial district, the wall ran in parallel with the length of the Ferry Building. Its base had been dug into the mud flats that once swamped the area.

The project took nearly fifty years to complete, but it forever changed the port, enhancing the fortunes of both the surrounding city and the owner of the surfacing water lots, James Lick.

A MODERN-DAY VERSION of that earlier vagabond millionaire hobbled slowly past the colorful scene outside the Ferry Building. With his ragged clothing and taped-together shoes, few paid him any attention, other than to step out of the way to avoid brushing up against his dingy-looking exterior.

Lick soon made his way to the entrance for Pier Seven. Rubbing a stitch in his lower back, he paused to look inland.

From this angle, the city spread out before him like a map, its layout easily discernible as the streets sloped gently upward. At the center of his view, the Transamerica Pyramid spiked the landscape, a radial point that matched up almost directly with the path of the pier.

The alignment was more than coincidence. Prior to the introduction of the seawall, wooden piers, similar to the one where Lick now stood, had pronged out into the water, linking the

Montgomery Street shoreline with ships moored in the bay.

As the landfill project progressed, those piers became the lower streets of the financial district and the raucous Barbary Coast.

Pier Seven, both its historic and contemporary versions, followed the track of Pacific Avenue, which ran two blocks north of the Transamerica Pyramid's wide base—only one block away from the Green Vase antiques shop.

LICK'S EYES SWEPT over the scene, lingering on the streets of Jackson Square, before he turned to face the water. With a short grunt of dismissal at the sharp pain in his back, he began the long walk across the rough wooden planks toward the end of the pier.

Iron railings flanked either side of the walkway, bulging out at regular intervals to accommodate the mounting of a light post. Every so often, Lick paused at a bench bolted into the wooden planking to rest an aching joint. Then, after a short break, he resumed his slow, methodical pace, resolutely plodding over the uneven boards.

Fishermen lined the railings near the walkway's end. These were serious, somber anglers, intently focused on their outflung lines. Buckets of ice waited optimistically at their feet, ready to store and preserve the day's catch.

A wide square formed the pier's terminus,

which was packed to capacity with fish-luring devices, everything from simple wooden poles to flexible high-tech fiberglass rods. Due to the fierce competition for spots over deep water, positions along this portion of the pier had been staked out for hours.

The location's success was evidenced by the rank stench emanating from its collection of buckets as well as the circling flock of seagulls eagerly waiting to pounce on any discarded scraps.

LICK SIDLED UP next to an elderly Asian man who, given the number of rods he had propped up against the railing, must have arrived on the pier at the crack of dawn.

Mr. Wang's bald, turtle-shaped head hid beneath a floppy canvas hat. His anemic body was almost lost in a pair of loose-hanging slacks and an oversized Windbreaker. His empty wheelchair waited close at hand, but he stood leaning over the railing, his wizened gaze never leaving the tiny red and white cork floating in the water about twenty yards away.

Lick picked up one of Wang's unmanned rigs. After digging around in Wang's toolbox, Lick pulled out a flashy lure and a jar of bright red fish eggs. Scooping out a half-dozen eggs, he expertly baited the hook.

Lick's calloused hands turned the handle's crank

to tighten the slack in the line. Then he flicked his wrist back, snapped the rod over his head, and swung it forward. The lure zinged through the air, landing on the water about thirty feet from the pier.

After Lick completed his toss, Wang gummed his thin lips and said cryptically, "Everyone's in place."

Lick nodded in agreement. His weary blue eyes remained focused on the floating line as he replied quietly, "Time to raise the curtain."

Wang's cork suddenly bobbed down into the water. With lightning-fast reflexes, the tiny man spun the reel's handle.

Lick stroked his chin as a fish flew out of the water and landed flopping on the pier. "Is Clive ready for his big debut?"

Deftly, Wang released the catch from his line and dropped it into a cooler by his feet. His narrow face cracked into a small grin as he turned to look at his coconspirator.

"I certainly hope so."

Chapter 24
THE SWORD

IN A THREE-BEDROOM penthouse apartment atop one of San Francisco's most prestigious residential hills, the Current Mayor stood in his living room, staring out the floor-to-ceiling windows at the city's shoreline.

The view swept across the bay, capturing the rock-faced island of Alcatraz and the towering red ladders of the Golden Gate Bridge. On a clear, cloudless morning like this one, he could see all the way to Sausalito.

It was going to be another gorgeous day in San Francisco, the kind of day that made him think he might almost miss this place when he left for Sacramento—almost.

"TIME TO GO, honey," his glowing wife said as he tugged anxiously at the narrow blue tie circling his neck. "Your driver will be downstairs with the car any minute now."

She ushered him into the foyer, brushing the back of his suit jacket to smooth out a wrinkle.

At the front door, he turned to kiss her on the cheek, nervously patting her growing baby bump as he checked his reflection in a mirror hanging on the entryway wall.

In the months since their wedding, his wife had gradually been scaling back his daily allocation of hair gel. She preferred a more natural look, she'd told him, not long after announcing her pregnancy. That, and she was worried about exposing their child to high concentrations of the gel's potentially toxic chemicals.

The Mayor had tried to accommodate her request, but he was growing more and more concerned about the stability of his swept-back, gel-anchored hairstyle.

After a quick peck on the cheek, he released his wife and, fretfully cupping his hands over his carefully coiffed crown, proceeded to the door.

As his hand wrapped around the knob, he glanced longingly at the umbrella stand by the entrance. It was packed with ten or more long, sharp-pointed, rain-repellent devices.

His wife noted the direction of his gaze.

"No need for an umbrella today," she trilled merrily, but with an unmistakable edge of sternness. "You'll be home long before the storm moves in tonight. There's not a drop of rain in the forecast until then."

"No, I suppose not," he replied briskly, trying to hide the disappointment in his voice. He pulled open the door, desperately wishing he could reach over to the stand and grab one of the handles.

• • •

STILL TRYING TO reassure himself, the Current Mayor strode onto the sunny sidewalk outside the apartment building.

His wife was right. (She was always right, he was beginning to understand.) There was no reason to carry an umbrella in weather like this.

He stepped to the curb, where a black town car waited, its engine humming expectantly. The driver, who doubled as the Mayor's bodyguard, extracted his enormous frame from behind the wheel, lumbered around the front of the car, and swung open the rear passenger-side door.

"Mornin', Gov," the man said in a powerful voice.

"Morning, Stanley," he replied back with his broad, bleached-tooth grin.

As the Mayor settled into the car's soft leather cushions, he fidgeted once more with the knot of his tie and asked, "Can we make a stop on the way in?"

The driver grunted, as if he had been expecting this request.

"I called ahead. They'll bring your package out to the car when I pull up."

"Thank you, Stanley. You're a good man."

The driver shook his head. "You must own more umbrellas than anyone else in the state of California."

· · ·

MINUTES LATER, THE Mayor gazed out the car window, watching as his sparkling city flashed by. Everywhere, it seemed, people were outside running, jogging, walking, sitting, and even lying on their backs, soaking up the last bit of sun. He tried to latch onto this exuberance, buoying himself as the town car approached City Hall's front steps.

Wrapping a pale hand around the polished wooden handle of his newly purchased umbrella, he stepped from the car's backseat and tentatively climbed the stairs to the building's entrance.

The security guards manning the scanner booth casually waved the Mayor through. As soon as his slim figure turned the corner for the rotunda, the youngest of the guards swallowed the last bite of his morning donut.

With a wink, he turned to his partner and whispered.

"Ribbit."

THE MAYOR SKITTERED across the marble floor beneath City Hall's ornate rotunda and started up the central staircase. His fingers clenched tighter and tighter around the umbrella's handle as he neared the second floor.

With an obligatory nod to the Harvey Milk bust in the alcove at the top of the stairs, the Mayor

162

raised the umbrella in front of his body, gripping it like a sword.

His office was located on this floor at the opposite side of the building. To reach it, he just had to traverse the outer hallway overlooking the central open space beneath the rotunda.

He had reached the least populated—and therefore most precarious—portion of his journey. He shuddered with foreboding, steeling his nerves for the long passageway. Frogs, in his experience, preferred quiet, isolated locales.

Despite this route's inherent risks, it was still preferable to the more direct path, which would have involved either the elevator or one of the inner staircases. Both of those options were far too closed in for his liking. There was too great a chance of amphibian attack.

CAREFULLY, THE MAYOR approached the first corner. Umbrella at the ready, he crept up to the nearest marble column and cautiously peeked around its polished curve.

The length of the empty corridor stretched out before him. On the plus side, it was well lit by the sunlight streaming in through the windows lining the exterior wall, and it was wide enough for evasive maneuvers, should the need arise.

And yet, the Mayor noted with a cringe, there were still a number of nooks and crannies where a sneaky amphibian might be lying in wait, ready to ambush him.

Summoning his last reserves of courage, the Mayor proceeded slowly down the corridor, his heart beating faster with each trembling step. On the lookout for the smallest sign of his slimy green enemy, he thrust the umbrella tip into every crevice he passed.

It was an exhausting, nerve-racking procedure, but at long last, he reached the south side of the building. He could see the entrance to the mayor's office suite up ahead. He had almost reached his destination.

He wiped a pale hand across his brow, pushing back a flop of hair that had swept forward during one of his overenthusiastic parrying maneuvers.

The hair's escape from the gel's goopy grasp momentarily distracted the Mayor from his anti-amphibian vigilance. Wetting his fingers, he began frantically trying to stick the wayward lock back into place.

It was at this moment that he heard a man's deep voice.

"Now, here we are on the second floor. That right there is where the mayor works. The supervisors have their get-togethers on the opposite end."

Must be a docent, the Mayor thought, relieved at the security extra foot traffic would bring. He's giving an early tour.

The Mayor sucked in his breath, straightened his posture, and eased out a polished, high-wattage smile. I'll give them a surprise meeting with the mayor, he thought brashly.

He ran his hand over the top of his head one last time to ensure that his hair had been returned to its proper alignment. His facade of confidence firmly in place, he rounded the corner.

The Mayor was unprepared for the sight that awaited him.

It wasn't a frog—of that, at least, he could be thankful.

One glance at the fearsome creature attached to a leash held by a burly red-haired man wearing a green vest achieved in an instant what hours of therapy had failed to accomplish.

Every last remnant of the Mayor's persistent frog phobia fled his fragile mental psyche when he took in the image of the albino alligator sprawled across the marble floor outside the south bank of elevators.

THE PRESIDENT OF the Board of Supervisors exited his office and strode briskly past the Harvey Milk bust at the top of the central marble staircase. The board would be voting soon on the Current Mayor's replacement, and he was getting desperate.

Jim Hernandez had decided to make one last attempt to convince the Mayor to support his bid to fill the temporary position.

The mere thought of asking that man for any favor—much less one of this magnitude—caused the typically sunny Hernandez to grit his teeth. Politics, however, sometimes made for strange bedfellows. This was his only shot left at winning the nomination.

Still grumbling about his unfortunate position, Hernandez turned onto the hallway leading toward the mayor's wing at the south side of the building. Halfway down the corridor, he noticed a crumpled form curled up on the floor near the hallway's opposite end.

Rushing to the Mayor's side, he bent over the man's unusually disheveled head of hair.

"You'll be all right, sir," Hernandez said as he pulled out his cell phone, but he stopped, mid-dial, at the faint words tumbling from the Mayor's thin lips.

"Alligator," the Mayor said fearfully, his eyes tightly shut. "There's an alligator on the loose in City Hall."

Hernandez sat back on his heels and shook his head. He cleared the emergency digits from his phone and punched in the number for the Mayor's administrative assistant.

"Mabel," he said grimly as the woman picked up on the other end. "I just found your man in the second-floor hallway."

With a sigh he added, "You'd better bring the straitjacket."

ON THE NORTH side of the second floor nearest the supervisors' offices, Spider Jones leaned his dust mop against a marble column. He'd just watched Supervisor Hernandez help Mabel carry the apparently incapacitated Mayor into his office.

Still puzzling on what he had seen, Spider whipped out a small notepad and pencil from the front pocket of his janitor's coveralls and scribbled a few notes. Then, he turned and ran down the central staircase to the phone cubby on the first floor to report the news to the Previous Mayor.

Chapter 25
THE JAPANESE TEA GARDENS

WHILE THE CURRENT Mayor continued to insist to anyone who would listen that he'd seen an albino alligator taking a guided tour of City Hall, the proprietor of James Lick's Homestyle Chicken left his fishing partner on Pier Seven and hobbled aboard a Muni streetcar headed toward the Inner Sunset district.

Half an hour later, Lick pulled the rope above his window, signaling his stop request to the conductor. At a street corner near the southern length of Golden Gate Park, Lick hobbled down the grated steps to the sidewalk.

As the Muni car rumbled off, continuing its winding caterpillar march to the coast, Lick slid his laminated senior pass into his back pocket, hefted a heavy canvas grocery bag over his left shoulder, and lumbered down the block toward the park.

CLOSER TO THE outside than the inside of the bay, beyond the protective mouth of the Golden Gate, the working-class neighborhoods in this part of the city bore a disproportionate share of the Pacific's cold, brooding fog.

The area's long, straight streets lacked the imaginative curves and elevation so prominent in other regions of San Francisco, allowing the weather to dominate the landscape. The fog's drab, color-leaching pallor settled in on these parallel rows of square, squatty buildings, often socking in residents for weeks at a time.

It was no surprise, then, that the recent stretch of sunny days had been greeted more joyfully in the Sunset than almost anywhere else in the city.

LICK THREADED HIS way through the unusually vibrant bustle, navigating around the tables of a local diner that had been dragged out onto the sidewalk for the morning's breakfast service.

After maneuvering past a group of previously pale, now pink-tinted eaters, Lick followed a line of joggers across a busy four-lane intersection and proceeded down a shady, tree-lined lane.

The layout inside Golden Gate Park broke with the uniformity of the surrounding streets. As the road entered the first of many sweeping turns, the sidewalk spun off a network of winding footpaths that quickly disappeared into the thick greenery.

Many found themselves disoriented by this labyrinth of trails, but Lick knew the route by heart.

Without hesitation, he veered off through a narrow opening in the bushes, taking a little-known shortcut to his destination.

A SHORT DISTANCE later, the pointed tips of the Japanese Tea Garden's painted pagodas began to peek through the trees. Emerging from a dense thicket, Lick made his way toward the swooping red and gold roof that marked the entrance.

The gardens were open, free of charge, for the next half hour, and he walked through the front gates without hindrance. Numbers of local Asian residents were already inside, some practicing their morning meditation while others sipped tea beneath the central pavilion, taking in the scenery.

Despite the growing crowd, a tranquil hush prevailed over the peaceful area. Only the occasional squawk of a duck or the call of a passing loon broke the silence.

An inviting path meandered through the

grounds, running alongside and over a rock-lined creek. Several plump goldfish floated in the shadows, waiting for their morning meal to drop into the water.

Lick paused at a wooden bench near the front entrance, gripping its railing for support as he rested a sore knee. While he waited for the pain to subside, he gazed thoughtfully at a collection of miniature shrubs. Each mound of branches had been painstakingly trimmed and trained into a sculpted, compact shape.

Yawning, he looked back toward the front gate, as if he were expecting someone, but after a moment's pause, he set off along the path.

NOT FAR DOWN the trail, Lick stopped and bent over the stream to stare at a particularly fat, languid fish. As he shifted the grocery bag to his opposite shoulder, an elderly woman with curly gray hair sidled up next to him.

"Tonight's special?" Dilla Eckles asked cheerily.

"I don't think this fellow would go with the rest of my menu," Lick replied dubiously.

He offered Dilla the crook of his elbow. As they began a slow stroll through the flowering grounds, he scratched his chin and added, "Now, a catfish, I might be tempted to squeeze onto the list . . ."

IN SOME RESPECTS, they looked like a typical retired couple out for a little morning air. Lick had adjusted his hobo garb so that he looked more scruffy than homeless. His walking partner wore sensible walking shoes, ankle-length capri pants, and a simple white shirt.

Any sense of normalcy, however, ended with Dilla's headpiece, a feather-topped creation with piles of plumage that hid most of her curly hair.

"I've been waiting for just the right weather to bring out this hat," she said proudly as she and Lick rounded a bridge fashioned into the shape of a waterwheel. "I thought this would be the perfect day to introduce it to San Francisco."

Lick gave Dilla's head a skeptical sideways glance.

"I got the design concept from England," she explained. "You should see the fashions *those* ladies wear, especially at the horse races."

She turned a pivot to show off an extra-long clump of feathers poking out of the hat's back brim. Lick had to duck to avoid being poked in the eye.

His companion didn't appear to hear his muttered comment as he returned his gaze to the path.

"I didn't know the English used piñatas."

LICK AND DILLA continued their casual walk through the gardens, Dilla chatting merrily about her new hat, Lick issuing an occasional grunt whenever she paused for his feedback.

171

At the far end of the grounds, they turned onto an extra loop that led into a secluded patch of redwoods.

Lick motioned to a shaded bench overlooking a manicured setting of bushes and raked gravel. As soon as his weight hit the seat, he reached to rub the soreness in his right knee.

"What did you need to see me about, Dilla?" he asked, his fingers working a knot in the portion of his thigh just above the kneecap.

Dilla pursed her lips, her soft face taking on a worried expression. The hat had been a cover for more than her head.

"It's about Sam," she said with a tense sigh. "I think he . . . well . . . he might be in a spot of trouble."

Lick slid the canvas shopping bag from his shoulder and asked casually, "What kind of trouble?"

Dilla fiddled nervously with the feathered fringe of her hat.

"You know my son," she replied nervously. "He takes up some strange notions. First it was the frogs, and now it's . . ."

Lick issued another noncommittal grunt, still apparently preoccupied with his knee.

Dilla's voice took on a deeper layer of strain.

"I'm afraid he may have *borrowed* something . . . something that I'll need your help to return to its proper place."

Straightening his posture, Lick stroked the paunch of his belly and leaned against the back of the bench.

Wordlessly, he reached his hand inside the grocery sack, pulled out a large plastic bag, and held it up for her to see.

Dilla read the label on the outside of the packaging and gasped.

"Osca—" she whispered before swallowing her surprise.

The description read: "Compacted fish pellets, specially formulated for domesticated alligator consumption."

Chapter 26

THE BEST OF FRIENDS

AT ITS SURFACE, downtown San Francisco was a puzzling network of narrow, often congested streets, many of them designated for one-way traffic—although drivers frequently failed to obey those instructions.

Cable cars trundled up the center medians of roads that crested so steeply, it was almost impossible to clear the summit's intersecting lanes. Bike messengers weaved deftly in and out of a sea of moving bumpers, while impatient pedestrians risked life and limb darting through crosswalks against the light.

Even the most routine of journeys required a certain amount of faith, hope, and reckless daring. It was the organized chaos typical of many a thriving metropolis, underlaid with San Francisco's peculiar brand of West Coast whimsy.

Few people understood just how far beneath the surface that whimsy went.

WHEN THE GOLD Rush tsunami of Forty-Niners hit Northern California's isolated backwater, the surging wave of population triggered decades' worth of frenetic construction. The city that resulted from this hasty, haphazard growth hid the shadowed skeleton of its past deep within its architectural footings.

Below the layers of asphalt and concrete, intertwined with the subway lines and half incorporated into the sewage system, lay a series of tunnels whose framework traced back to the late 1800s. Dirt paths that had once skirted the shoreline had become underground passageways that threaded through the base of the modern-day city.

One tunnel, in particular, roughly followed the line of a downtown alley marked with a street sign reading "Leidesdorff." This secret passage ran beneath the financial district, connecting the lower levels of the Palace Hotel, on one end, to Jackson Square—specifically the basement of the Green Vase antiques shop—at the other.

THE TUNNEL WAS a dark, clammy place filled with insects, rodents, and other rank undesirables. A permanent dampness seeped into every available surface, the combined result of the surrounding water table and the constant drip of leaking sewage pipes.

Many San Franciscans might have found this odorous environment off-putting, but the two residents navigating the tunnel that morning were happily enjoying the experience.

They were an unlikely pair: one large and lumbering with a ruddy face and broad shoulders, the other toothy, brutish, and positioned low to the ground.

Despite their intimidating size and bulky physique, both characters were likable, sympathetic types. Together they proceeded down the slime-walled corridor, enjoying its dank, musty smell as they conversed, albeit one-sidedly, in the darkness.

THE TALLER OF the duo reached into his pocket and pulled out a round pellet shaped like a hockey puck.

"And so, I gave up my job as a janitor at City Hall to become a frog expert," Sam said affably. "Changed my life. Best decision I ever made."

His short-statured partner lumbered along in companionable silence as a rodent scampered across the path.

"Myself, I actually prefer to travel below ground," Sam said jovially as he tossed the pellet through the air to his partner. "Fewer hassles. A lot less traffic."

As if on cue, the blare of a car horn echoed down from the street, causing several insects to scurry into their holes.

"It's far more discreet," Sam added with a wink as his albino friend snapped at the treat. "You don't have to worry about drawing attention to yourself."

UPSTAIRS FROM THE Jackson Square entrance to the tunnel, in the apartment above the Green Vase showroom, Isabella perched atop a pile of books—one of many arranged on the floor in front of the bedroom bookcase.

Her person sat in the middle of the piles, studying the alligator lamp under the beam of her uncle's heavy-duty, broad-beamed flashlight.

With each pass of the light over the globe's ceramic surface, the niece picked up new details of the images embedded within. Every so often, she let out an excited "Ooh" or a thoughtful "Ah." Each exclamation was followed by a diligent search through the reference books surrounding her on the floor as she sought to compare the revelation against the descriptions in the texts.

Isabella knew there was little to be gained from this effort, but she indulged her person anyway. It was early yet, and there was plenty of time to guide the woman to the next clue in her hunt.

Besides, Rupert was still in the kitchen finishing his breakfast.

"ISSY," THE NIECE said, interrupting the cat's internal musings. "I need to check something in the book you're sitting on. The one about the aquarium."

Despite Isabella's peeved expression, she was soon unceremoniously dislodged from her chosen pile. After giving her person a meaningful stare, Isabella strutted a slow circle through the books, trying to decide on her next perch.

"Check this out, Issy," the woman exclaimed as she adjusted her glasses to read the fine print beneath one of the book's black-and-white photos. "The same architect designed both the Bohemian Club's San Francisco headquarters and the original Steinhart Aquarium. There's definitely something going on here."

"Mrao," Isabella replied encouragingly as she continued to survey the piles.

The cat had just settled onto a new stack when she heard a slight grating, several floors below.

Practically inaudible to human ears, it was the type of sound that, even if her person had noticed, she probably would have dismissed. Humans, in Isabella's opinion, filtered out a great deal of important information.

Isabella concentrated on the bedroom floor, listening intently.

The hair along the center of her back formed a narrow spike as a second barely perceptible shuffling floated up from the basement.

Noiselessly, Isabella hopped down from the books. Leaving the niece to ponder the connections between the Bohemian Club and the Steinhart Aquarium, Isabella trotted silently out of the bedroom.

Moments later, she passed Rupert bent over his food bowl beneath the kitchen table. Her tail swished back and forth as she hurried down the stairs to the showroom.

When she reached the first floor, she proceeded immediately to the closed hatch that covered the drop-down stairs leading to the basement.

Isabella's whiskers twitched as she sniffed the wooden floorboards. The scents below confirmed her suspicions.

Someone—or some*thing*—had just come through the tunnel entrance.

Chapter 27
JACKSON SQUARE ASSIGNMENT

SPIDER JONES CRUISED his bike along Columbus Avenue, standing on his pedals as he coasted down the road's gentle slope. He still wore the coveralls from his fake-janitor session on City Hall's second floor earlier that morning. The loose leggings flapped against his knees as he threaded his bike through traffic.

The stoplight ahead flashed yellow, and an exhilarated thrill coursed through his body. With a youth's brazen daring, he switched to a higher gear and vigorously pumped his legs. After the extra kick of energy, the bike swung into the wide turn for Jackson Square at its highest speed.

Brakes screeching, Spider sliced through the intersection, dodging, at the last second, a handful of pedestrians and a swerving taxicab, the latter of which blasted him with a frustrated honk.

Spider simply grinned good-naturedly and waved as he pedaled away.

THE YOUNG MAN'S cheeks were still flushed with adrenaline when he reached Jackson's quiet, tree-lined lane. Panting, he pulled up in front of a row of two- and three-story redbrick buildings.

He stopped his bike next to a small antiques shop whose storefront was framed by a pair of crenellated iron columns. A row of square windows faced the street; every other one of the glass panes was embedded with green-tinted glass formed in the shape of a vase. A sign reading "CLOSED" hung on the inside of the shop's iron-framed door.

Dropping his feet to the sidewalk, Spider lifted his baseball cap and wiped his brow. After adjusting the cap's brim, he returned it to his head and removed a small notepad from the front pocket of his coveralls. He had to dig a little deeper to find the short pencil he'd stashed in the same compartment.

Pad and pencil at the ready, Spider began taking notes about the person the Previous Mayor had instructed him to follow during his brief tutorial session at the French restaurant the previous evening.

According to the PM, the man would be spending his morning in Jackson Square—not at the antiques shop where Spider had parked his bike, but inside the art studio across the street.

Spider had given his next assignment a nickname while riding across town that morning. As he stood on the sidewalk, glancing up every so often at the art studio, he wrote the words across the front of the notepad in bold block print: "OPERATION CARMICHAEL."

Chapter 28
A BUSY SCHEDULE

THREE FLOORS UP from the sidewalk where Spider stood scribbling in his notebook, a fluffy orange and white cat emerged from a dome-shaped litter box in the apartment above the Green Vase showroom.

The litter box had lost some of its shiny red luster over the course of its past year and a half of use, but the hard plastic container still retained all of its functionality. This was a testament to its quality of manufacture—given the daily rigors of Rupert's energetic digging.

The white ruff of hair on Rupert's chest puffed out as he stepped onto the bathroom mat. This morning's litter box dance routine had been a particularly sublime performance, even by his standards. He noted with pride the scattering of litter he'd managed to spray across the floor outside the dome's curving walls, admiring the trajectory like a golfer studying the arc of a completed putt.

This day was off to a splendid start, Rupert thought as he gave himself a good overall shake to knock loose any particulates that might still be clinging to his fur.

Once he was satisfied that he had dislodged the

largest clumps, he waddled into the bedroom, ready to begin his day.

Contorting his body into a stiff arching stretch, he gazed happily across the sunlit space. He was ready to get down to business.

He issued a wide yawn and headed for the bed.

RUPERT STROLLED PAST his person, who was sitting on the bedroom floor in front of the bookcase. He paused briefly to study the books, the brass lamp, and the flashlight gathered around her.

"I think it's got something to do with the aquarium," the niece murmured.

Rupert cocked a furry eyebrow, momentarily intrigued.

"The Steinhart Aquarium," she clarified, seeing his questioning look. "The treasure has to be related in some way to the aquarium."

At the word *treasure,* Rupert drifted off into a second yawn. Sleepily, he hopped onto the covers and began searching for a morning nap spot.

He had almost settled on the perfect cushioned location when his person stood up, pushed her heavy brown hair away from her face, and put her hands on her hips.

"It's time to hit the basement," she announced as she stepped toward the stairs beyond the bedroom door. "There must be something down there that will show me the connection."

Snuggling determinedly into his spot on the bed, Rupert cracked open one eye as if to issue a correction.

It's *time* for a nap, he thought drowsily.

THERE WERE FEW places Rupert disliked more than the basement. It was a dark, dusty place—and more than a little bit creepy. If his person felt like she needed to dig around down there in all of Oscar's junk, so be it. He had no intention of accompanying her.

His sister, however, had other ideas.

AFTER SPENDING HALF an hour hovering over the showroom's closed hatch to the basement, listening to the mysterious intruder tromping around below, Isabella had reluctantly left her post.

Being an independent-minded cat, she hated to admit there was anything she couldn't do. She considered herself just as capable as any human—if not more so.

Try as she might, however, she had been unable to lift the cover from the recessed compartment in the flooring that contained the hatch's handle. She had attacked the flat piece of wood from every possible angle, but it had refused to budge. After much frustration, she had finally reached an uncomfortable conclusion: she needed assistance.

She proceeded upstairs to fetch her person.

ISABELLA ARRIVED ON the third floor just as Oscar's niece finished her study of the alligator lamp.

"Hey, Issy," the woman said as she marched purposefully toward the steps. "You up for a trip to the basement?"

You're so well trained, Isabella thought, gazing fondly at her person.

Isabella turned to follow the niece down the stairs, but, with one foot hanging over the top step, she stopped short. Considering the potential size of the creature lurking in the basement, they might need reinforcements.

She looked back toward the bedroom, her eyes narrowing on the orange and white heap snoring on the covers.

Trotting quickly around to the opposite side of the bed, Isabella issued a sharp, commanding *"Mrao."*

Rupert curled his body into a tight ball and covered his face with his front paws. He began to wheeze out a loud snore—which transformed into a startled *snort* as Isabella pounced on his fluffy back end, her claws fully extended.

MIDWAY DOWN THE stairs to the second floor, Oscar's niece nearly lost her footing as a white blur zoomed past her on the steps.

Chapter 29
A SCALY VISITOR

ACCOMPANIED BY AN enthusiastic Isabella and an extremely reluctant Rupert, Oscar's niece traipsed down the stairwell to the Green Vase showroom.

Thunking the flashlight against the palm of her hand, she continued to ponder the image of the albino alligator she'd studied on the brass lamp's ceramic globe.

"The aquarium," she mused out loud, as she shifted her reflections to the wording on the fried-chicken flyer she'd slid into her back pocket. "It's the Steinharts again."

Halfway down the steps, she ducked her head to avoid a low-hanging beam. Then, with another *thunk* of the flashlight, she said optimistically, "Maybe I'll find something in the basement that will help me figure this out."

At the foot of the stairs, Isabella turned to look up at her person. The cat's furry expression appeared to give confirmation to the niece's basement speculation.

"Mrao."

A MOMENT LATER, the woman stepped onto the showroom's wooden floor. Blinking, she waited for her eyes to adjust to the bright sun streaming in through the front windows.

A slender vase rested on a counter near the front door, its green color a match for that of the similarly shaped images embedded in the windows overlooking the street.

Throughout the room, rows of bookcases and display tables held a wide collection of Gold Rush–era antiques. After several months of the shop being closed to the public, a fine layer of dust had begun to accumulate on many of the items.

Fighting off a sneeze, the woman reached out to the headrest of a worn leather dentist recliner. Clumps of white hair covered the recliner's seat, an indication that it had become one of Rupert's preferred sleeping spots.

Rupert yawned sleepily at the recliner as his person set the flashlight on its seat. Kneeling on the floor near the bottom of the stairs, she slid a pinky finger into a tiny hole in the paneling that had been fashioned to look like a knot in the wood. With a slight tug, she pulled off an oval-shaped cover, exposing a recessed cavity that housed a small handle.

Isabella shook her head with disgust, annoyed by the limits of feline dexterity.

Flicking a lever, the niece extended the handle. She squinted to discern the outline of the trap door, which had been disguised in the pattern of the floorboards; then she braced her feet on either side of the hatch, took a firm grip on the handle, and pulled upward.

A loud clapping sound signaled the release of a set of rickety drop-down stairs unfolding into the basement below.

Picking up the flashlight, the woman switched the beam to its highest setting and shone it into the unlit basement. Isabella led the way as her person tromped down the stair's loose slats.

Rupert lingered on the showroom floor near the hatch, nervously pacing back and forth, reluctant to join the other two. But after a barking *chirp* from his sister, he began a slow descent.

AT THE BOTTOM of the steps, the niece tugged on a string hanging from a bare lightbulb mounted against the ceiling. The light came on, but added little in the way of useful illumination.

Maneuvering around the stiff figure of a stuffed kangaroo, the woman panned her flashlight across the crowded basement, angling the beam toward the far end of the room. The light bounced over several large pieces of furniture covered with drop cloths and then skimmed over the redbrick walls.

It had been several months since the underground tunnel leading into the basement had been used—at least as far as the niece was aware—and she gave the bricks that concealed the tunnel's entrance only a cursory review before turning her attention to the jumbled collection of boxes and crates that took up the majority of the floor space.

"Steinhart . . . Steinhart . . . Steinhart . . ." she repeated softly to herself as she selected a box and began thumbing through its contents.

Losing no time, Isabella immediately set off in search of the creature she had detected earlier. She lifted her head, trying to see over the boxes and crates, as her ears widened, her sonar on high alert. Gracefully, she leapt through the air, clearing several rows in a single leap, before disappearing from view.

Rupert took a few apprehensive steps to follow his sister, pushing his way into the dark spaces between the boxes and crates.

A moment later, Oscar's niece looked up from her box and wrinkled her nose.

"Do you two smell something funny?" she asked, perplexed.

Her question was met with a hissing response.

Spinning the flashlight toward the rear of the basement, the woman caught a brief flash of Isabella slinking across the concrete floor, clearly engaged in a concentrated stalking mode.

"I thought we finally got rid of the mice." She sighed in frustration.

She stepped around the box to see what Isabella was hunting—and almost got run over by Rupert's barreling white figure. He narrowly avoided plowing into his person on his headlong sprint for the stairs.

"What's going on?" she demanded, hurrying to see what kind of animal Isabella had cornered in the rear of the basement.

Continued hissing led the woman to a drop cloth–covered wardrobe leaning up against the back wall.

Isabella crouched in front of the wardrobe, a line of hackles clearly visible along her spine. She let loose a vicious, teeth-baring snarl as the bottom of the cloth rustled with movement.

Nervously wielding the flashlight, the woman pinched a piece of the cloth between her fingers, lifted it up—and froze at the sight of the ghoulish white alligator sprawled across the concrete floor.

The alligator turned toward the niece, his gray eyes blinking in the glare of her flashlight.

His sharp jaws snapped at the air.

Chomp.

Chapter 30

EVERYONE LIKES CHICKEN

THE FLASHLIGHT WENT flying as the niece scooped up Isabella. Desperately trying to keep hold of her protesting cat, who was still hissing and spitting at the scaly intruder, the woman ran pell-mell to the hatch, wildly hurdling over boxes and crates.

The moment she cleared the top of the stairs, she

turned and kicked the trap door closed. The stairs folded back into the ceiling—even as another grinding *chomp* echoed up from the basement.

Breathing heavily, she stared down at the wood paneling, trying to process what she'd seen.

She might have begun to second-guess what had just happened had Isabella not continued to growl at the floor.

"Good grief," the woman sputtered, instinctively jumping away from the hatch as the floor shook from the crash of a crate toppling over in the room below.

THERE ARE SEVERAL potential courses of action a person might take in response to a reptilian invasion of her basement. A telephone call to the emergency operator probably ranks high on the list.

But as Oscar's niece stood in the Green Vase antiques shop, listening to the ongoing bumping beneath her feet, she decided against this approach—at least for the time being.

Perhaps in some southern swampy regions of the country, animal-control officers have set up hotlines specifically dedicated to this type of emergency.

That was not the case, however, in San Francisco.

After careful consideration, the niece headed for the upstairs kitchen. Isabella closely followed and watched as her person reached for the receiver of the old handset-style telephone mounted onto the wall near the sink.

"Wrao," Isabella concurred, her sharp eyes conveying a wise expression.

The woman's trembling fingers began to dial a private line to a business located a few blocks away. It was a phone number she had committed to memory several months earlier, only to be used for emergency purposes.

Of all the possible contingencies that might have arisen, however, this was not one she had contemplated.

Anxiously, she waited for the phone to ring through to James Lick's Homestyle Chicken. She could think of but one albino alligator known to reside within the city limits. The current occupant of the Steinhart Aquarium's signature Swamp Exhibit had been featured regularly in the news over the last year.

"I guess I've found my connection," the niece muttered, recalling the image from the brass lamp.

She brushed her hair back from her forehead and sighed testily.

It would have been nice if she had been warned before the alligator landed in her basement.

HAROLD WOMBLER STOOD at the counter in the steaming-hot kitchen of the North Beach fried-chicken restaurant, a potato peeler in one hand, a half-peeled spud in the other. His greasy black hair was tucked under a hairnet, on top of which rested a green paper hat with the restaurant's gold logo printed on the side.

After finishing off the potato, he plunked it into an iced bucket of salt water. Dropping the peeling implement onto the counter, he stepped back and rubbed the small of his back. A three-foot high pile of unskinned russets awaited his attention.

Harold squinted at the heap of potatoes; then he glanced down at the bin where he'd been collecting the shavings. It had been a long morning's work, and he wasn't anywhere near completion.

"Don't know how I got talked into this job," he grumbled bitterly.

HAROLD WAS ABOUT to resume the task when the telephone on the opposite end of the kitchen let off a jarring ring. His bleary, bloodshot eyes stared accusingly at the device's imposition, but by the third ring he began to move toward it.

"All right, already. I'm coming."

Harold's stilting, limping gait wasn't designed for speed. By the time he reached the receiver and picked it up, he could sense the desperation on the other end of the line.

"What?" he answered crankily.

He didn't bother to identify himself or the restaurant. The number for this phone was only known to a few individuals—and none of them would have used the line to order food.

He heard the woman from the Green Vase antiques shop draw in her breath.

"Are you, by any chance, missing an alligator?" she asked tensely.

After a moment's hesitation, she cleared her throat and added, "An albino one?"

As if the clarification would make a difference to his answer, Harold thought with a grimace.

He pursed his thin lips before formulating an answer.

"Alligator?" He coughed out an intrigued grunt. "Hmm. You don't say."

Harold's eyebrows knitted together as he turned to look at the walk-in freezer located behind the wall where the phone was mounted.

"What have you got in your fridge over there?" he asked cryptically.

"My *fridge?*" the woman replied in an exasperated tone.

Harold gummed his dentures thoughtfully. "I hear dem gators like chicken."

Chapter 31
SPINNING THE STORY

WEDNESDAY MORNING ACROSS San Francisco, local television and radio stations interrupted their regularly scheduled programming with a breaking-news bulletin. An incident of great importance had taken place overnight, and the story was far too time-sensitive to wait for the evening news broadcast.

Surprisingly, the matter didn't have anything to do with the upcoming board of supervisors' vote to select the next mayor or any of the recent political wrangling at City Hall—at least it didn't appear to.

No, all of this attention was focused on the brazen abduction of one of the city's most famous residents.

The news media quickly converged on Golden Gate Park, the scene of the horrendous crime. Large vehicles with satellite dishes and obstructive antennae packed the park's winding streets as reporters and their camera crews filled the lawn outside the California Academy of Sciences.

Most of the television channels had opted for a split-screen view. One side featured a live picture of the chaotic scene outside the Academy's grass-roofed complex. The other half of the screen carried stock footage of the kidnapped celebrity surrounded by his adoring young fans.

Across the bottom, a line of text read out the breaking news: "Clive the albino alligator MISSING from his Swamp Exhibit at the CAS."

HOXTON FIN WAITED impatiently as his cameraman tried in vain to get an unobstructed shot of the Academy of Sciences' front entrance. Rolling his eyes, the reporter turned to look at the surrounding circus.

The entire facility had been temporarily shut down so that the Academy's scientists, security personnel, and insurance specialists—not to mention representatives from the San Francisco Police Department—could determine how the albino alligator had been stolen from his exhibit.

Helicopters churned the air above the building, their propellers swinging dangerously close to the redwoods that ringed the clearing. Beyond the throngs of media, curious onlookers crowded a taped-off perimeter, where groups of observers anxiously speculated about what could have happened to the city's beloved alligator.

HOX TUGGED AT the tie cinched around his neck. He'd begun to sweat profusely in the humid heat, and the new leather shoes the station's stylist had forced him to wear were pinching his left foot.

But these discomforts paled in comparison to

the pounding pain inside his head. The inane subject matter of his next report had given him an intense migraine.

The cameraman finished his background shot and repositioned his gear to frame his lens around the reporter. With a sour, self-loathing expression, Hox focused his gaze on the video camera and raised his microphone.

Best to get this over with, he thought with a groan.

"This is Hoxton Fin, reporting under protest."

"Cut!"

THE FRAZZLED WOMAN standing beside the cameraman threw her hands up and walked toward the street. It was all the producer could do to keep from hurling her clipboard at Hoxton Fin. She'd drawn the short straw on this assignment.

She rubbed her temple with her free hand as she stared at the melee of media concentrated on the Academy's front lawn. Every other news crew in Northern California was here on the scene, shooting clips for their respective anchors. Her channel would be the last to get the story on the air.

It was embarrassing, the producer thought miserably. The station manager was going to flip his lid.

CONSTANCE GRYNCHE—SHE had married her husband despite his last name—was a working mother of four. After finally seeing her youngest child off to first grade, she had resumed her long-delayed career in television news.

It was a struggle, juggling her complicated child-care schedule with the unpredictable working hours required by her job, but, for the most part, she was enjoying the challenge. The adult interaction was a welcome change from her years in relative isolation as a stay-at-home mom, and it was empowering to once more see her name on an income-earning check.

Connie got on well with most of the station's reporting staff. They could share a joke, a cup of coffee, and the common goal of efficiently filming a story and rushing it into editing.

With Hoxton Fin, however, there had been no such rapport.

She blew out a heavy sigh of frustration. She'd take the most petulant toddler any day over *this* prima donna.

Sucking in a deep breath, she summoned the deep well of patience she'd developed during her years of child rearing. Then she returned to the camera crew and pleaded coaxingly with the reporter.

"Come on, Hox. We're about to go live with this."

AS HOX GLOWERED at his producer, a slender, wispy man set a step stool on the ground beside him. The stylist jiggled the stool to level its metal feet on the uneven grass. Then he scampered up the three short steps and bent over the reporter's head.

"Back off, Humphrey," Hox growled as the stylist's delicate fingers splayed out to tease the center spike on his scalp.

"Just let me . . ." Humphrey murmured, licking his fingertips as he hovered above the faux-hawk hairdo, oblivious to the menacing stare on the face beneath.

After fiddling with the reporter's hair, the stylist reached for a canister connected to a tool belt strapped around his slim waist and aimed its nozzle at Hox's head.

Hox hunched his shoulders, his face red with humiliation as Humphrey pumped the bottle of hair spray at him. Finally, at the prompting of the agitated producer, the stylist stepped back and retracted his stool.

With a look of capitulation, Hox shrugged, cleared his throat, and addressed the camera.

"THIS IS HOXTON Fin, reporting from the California Academy of Sciences in Golden Gate Park, where Clive, the Academy's most recent celebrity albino alligator, was discovered missing in the early hours this morning."

Connie smiled with relief. At last, they were under way. If Hox could get through his spiel in

198

one take, they could send the film back to the studio in time for the next half-hour update. There was still a chance she might avoid getting chewed out by the station manager.

"Details are sketchy," Hox continued. "But it appears the alligator left his Swamp Exhibit in the Steinhart Aquarium sometime in the middle of the night. Security cameras were somehow disabled, disguising the identity of the accomplice who assisted in the alligator's escape."

The producer felt the nerves in her shoulders tighten. This was a deviation from the theft-of-alligator script they had discussed. Hox wore the overall expression of a serious professional, but she thought she detected an impish twitch at the corner of his mouth.

Connie gripped her clipboard as Hox proceeded with his report.

"Police are currently treating the disappearance as a kidnapping—er, *gator*-napping—although, technically, we're still within the first twenty-four-hour period, and, at last check, no ransom or other demands have been received."

Connie thumped the clipboard against her forehead. With her free hand, she made a slicing motion across her neck.

Hox pressed on, his voice deep with sincerity.

"Given Clive's adolescent age—he turned thirteen last May—it's still possible this is all just a juvenile prank and he'll turn up for the next feeding, apologetic for his thoughtless and reckless behavior."

Shaking her head, the producer turned and began walking toward the news crew's van.

"Clive is missing one of the digits on his right front paw, so he might have difficulty thumbing a ride . . ."

The cameraman grinned behind the lens, letting his machine run. Hox showed no signs of letting up.

"Please keep an eye out for him on Muni and other modes of public transportation. We'll post his picture at the bottom of the screen along with a hotline number you can call if you should see him."

Chapter 32

A GATOR'S GOTTA EAT

OSCAR'S NIECE HUNG up the phone, exasperated by her conversation with Harold Wombler.

"Do I have chicken?" she muttered, repeating the gist of the query Harold had put to her after hearing that an albino alligator had taken up residence in her basement. "What kind of a response is that?"

As the woman prepared to leave for the North Beach restaurant to discuss the matter in person, Rupert emerged from his alligator hiding spot beneath the living room couch. He stepped tentatively into the kitchen looking like a prickly marshmallow, every fluffy white hair extended in caution.

Rupert gave his person a concerned stare.

"It's safe to come out," she said reassuringly. Then she paused, hesitating as she glanced down at the floor. "At least, I think it is." She bit her lower lip nervously. "Best to stay up here until I get back."

As the niece moved toward the stairs to the showroom, she shook her head in frustration, still mulling over the phone conversation.

"Not everything revolves around fried chicken . . ."

From the feeding station beneath the kitchen table, Rupert issued a disagreeing grunt.

TEN MINUTES LATER, Oscar's niece arrived at Lick's Homestyle Chicken. She pushed open the grimy front door and stepped into the empty dining room.

The restaurant had recently cut back its hours and was no longer serving lunch, but even the reduced schedule was more than Harold Wombler could keep up with. He spent most of each day in the kitchen, working on the preparations for that night's meal.

The niece found Harold at his regular station, standing by the kitchen counter next to a pile of potatoes. He didn't appear to notice the woman as she approached. He simply picked up a large spud from the top of the heap and began mechanically running his peeler over the lumpy brown skin.

Tapping her fingers against the counter, the niece glanced up at a small television set mounted in a corner near the ceiling.

Hoxton Fin's familiar image filled the screen. The television's volume had been muted, but she could guess the story line based on the text scrolling across the bottom of the frame.

"Did he get a haircut?" she asked, momentarily distracted by the reporter's closely cropped head and the odd center-combed styling of his hair.

The video switched to a shot of the Academy of Sciences' Swamp Exhibit. A floodlight reflected off the brass detailing of the seahorse balcony as it shone down onto the empty pond and its unoccupied heated rock.

The niece issued a stern sigh.

"Do you mind telling me what that alligator is doing in my basement?"

Wordlessly, Harold finished peeling the potato and tossed it into a nearby bucket. After waving a wrinkled hand over the pile, he selected another one and began running the blade over its surface.

Gripping the metal edge of the counter, the woman leaned over the potatoes.

"And what does this have to do with the Steinharts?" she demanded.

Harold's eyes remained fixed on the spud.

"Don't you reckon you'd better feed him?"

"Feed who? The alligator?" she sputtered. "Do you know that *I* was almost his next meal?"

Harold shrugged unsympathetically. "A gator's gotta eat."

The niece looked as if she were about to grab a tuber and lob it at Harold's head.

With a wry grin, he chucked the skinned potato into the bucket and nodded toward the rear of the kitchen.

"Come along with me."

Chapter 33
PORTRAIT OF A MAYOR

SPIDER JONES SPENT the first few minutes of Operation Carmichael standing on the sidewalk outside the Green Vase, studiously observing the art studio across the street.

It was more modern than the rest of the buildings on the block; its exterior was made of concrete instead of brick. The glass front exposed an open interior filled with paintings and other artwork hung from the walls and propped up on several easels. A small desk was positioned near the center of the room, its surface clean except for a neat pile of paperwork.

Spider's pulse quickened as his target appeared from around the corner, crossed the intersection, and strolled down the opposite sidewalk toward the studio. He watched, mesmerized, as the tall, skinny man unlocked the studio's front door and walked inside.

Spider tucked his pad and pencil into his front pocket and reached for his handlebars. It was definitely time to move in for a better look.

SPIDER PUSHED HIS bike, as casually as possible, across the quiet street.

Pausing behind a row of parked cars, he tried to come up with a cover story that would allow him to loiter outside the studio's front windows.

After a quick brainstorming session, he rolled his bike to a spot beneath one of the slender elm trees planted along the curb and removed a small tool kit from his backpack.

Thinking of how proud the Previous Mayor would be at his ingenuity, he knelt on the ground beside the bike's chain and began fitting a wrench over the nearest sockets.

As Spider fussed over the perfectly functional gear assembly, he pulled his baseball cap down low over his eyes and peeked over his left shoulder at the man who had entered the studio.

Propping his notepad on his knee, he began jotting down his observations.

MONTGOMERY CARMICHAEL HUNG his suit jacket on a coatrack by the door, exchanging it for a painter's smock that he slipped on over his collared shirt and dark suit slacks.

Slowly, he circled around a sheet-covered easel positioned in the middle of the room near his desk. The flick of a wall switch caused a light to illuminate the cloaked painting.

Nodding his approval of the setup, Monty strode to the side of the room where a plastic case held a rack of vinyl records. He flipped through a collection of big-band hits, perusing the titles. Midway through the stack, he stopped and pulled out a worn cardboard sleeve.

"Ah, yes, that's it. That's the one."

Gently tilting the sleeve, he slid out the selected album. Holding the edges of the record with his fingertips, he carefully blew across the grooved surface before placing the disc on a turntable and rotating the power switch to its "on" position. As the record began to spin, he carefully lifted the needle from its holder and set the point on the record's rim.

With a trill of trumpets, a stirring intro blasted from the sound system. But just as Frank Sinatra's deep, crooning voice started in on one of his famous melodies, Monty scooped up the needle.

"Please, before we get started," he said to his imaginary audience, "I'd like to thank the board of supervisors for their unanimous vote. This moment wouldn't have been possible without their support."

He dropped the needle once more, let it play another stanza, and then, with a slight scratching sound, removed it to add another comment.

"Together, I know we can take San Francisco forward into a new era of peace and prosperity."

Applause roared in Monty's head as he returned the needle to the record, finally letting Sinatra get on with his song.

"I've got the world on a string . . ."

Monty slid across the floor on the flat soles of his dress shoes. Bouncing his shoulders to the swinging beat, he spun an invisible top hat at the end of an imaginary cane.

After making several turns around the room, he stopped in front of the covered easel. Dramatically lifting the bottom of the sheet, he waited for an uptick in the music to throw the cover clear of the painting that had been hidden beneath.

The picture depicted a man in a dark navy suit and a matching narrow-width tie. The subject's curly brown hair had been straightened and combed back from his forehead. His thin lips were pursed into a regal, smirking smile.

The figure stood in front of a wide wooden desk, whose polished surface reflected a small pool of light from a decorative lamp sitting on its corner. It was a stately pose, similar to one struck by a man in a much smaller framed poster hanging by the art studio's front door.

The primary difference between the two images was that the man in the framed poster had twice been elected to the mayor's office of San Francisco. The man depicted in the larger painting was still waiting for his chance.

Monty held a brush over the canvas, studying the details with his experienced artist's eye. His hand hovered in the air for several seconds; then he dropped the brush into a jar of cleaning solution. He could find nothing to improve upon. There wasn't anything he would change—about the man in the picture, that is.

"What a world, what a life, what a . . ."

The needle skipped again as Monty ripped it from the record.

"What a fortuitous circumstance," he said as he spied a woman with long brown hair and bifocal glasses emerging from the Green Vase showroom across the street. He watched, a gleam in his eye as she turned and locked the door.

"Hold tight, Frank," Monty said to the record player as he stripped off the smock and hurried to the studio's front entrance. He reached inside a glass canister filled with keys that rested on a small table by the coatrack.

"I'll be back in a few."

Chapter 34
AN ATTRACTIVE NUISANCE

SPIDER PAUSED, MID-SCRIBBLE, as the object of his surveillance suddenly stopped his bizarre dance-step maneuver and peered out the art studio's front door.

Following the direction of Mr. Carmichael's gaze, Spider spied a woman with long brown hair and glasses leaving the Green Vase antiques shop across the street.

With panic, he realized that he had ventured several feet from his bike. He'd been so focused on Mr. Carmichael's curious behavior that he'd dropped his gear-repair routine and strayed several feet from the curb. There was no time to inconspicuously resume his cover.

Fearing he was about to be exposed, Spider dove behind the nearest parked vehicle, skidded across the asphalt, and slid beneath the under-carriage near the front wheel.

HEART POUNDING, SPIDER looked up from his hiding position, certain that he'd been spotted by either the Mayor's Life Coach or the woman from the antiques shop—or worse, he thought with a gulp, both.

He watched with disbelief as the woman jogged

down the sidewalk to the next corner, never once looking back.

A moment later, Mr. Carmichael strode purposefully out of the art studio and traipsed across the street to the entrance of the Green Vase showroom. He, too, was oblivious to the young man hiding beneath the vehicle.

"Huh," Spider said, once more amazed at the general populace's poor skills of perception.

He began scrupulously detailing the encounter in his notepad.

"I'm starting to feel invisible."

MONTY STOOD IN front of the door to the Green Vase antiques shop, keeping a close eye on the corner where Oscar's niece had disappeared just a few moments earlier. With a last glance up the block, he wrapped his hand around the wrought iron handle. His narrow fingers ran over the image of the tulip engraved in the knob as he tried to rotate it.

"Locked," he surmised with a wry grin after the handle refused to turn.

"Not a problem," he said smoothly, holding up the key he'd grabbed from the glass canister in the art studio. It was one of several duplicates he'd had tooled for just this sort of occasion. "At least not for me."

The key had a long metal stem. One end had been tooled with jagged teeth, the type of fittings used to engage with a typical lock's interior.

The opposite end was more unique. Here, the iron had been cast into the shape of a three-petaled tulip.

Monty fed the regular end of the key into the slot in the door's facing and twisted the stem. The lock released with a satisfying *click*.

Grinning triumphantly, he swung open the door. With a last glance at the apparently empty street, he pulled his key from the lock and goose-stepped inside the showroom.

ABOUT A MONTH earlier, the woman who now owned the Green Vase had hired a locksmith to retool the lock to the shop's front door.

It had taken Monty a little over a week to cast a new set of keys—his only impediment had been picking an appropriate time when he could use his special laser tool kit to measure the spacing between the lock's interior tumblers. After a few tinkering improvements, he had created a suitable mold. From there, it had been a simple process to start cranking out keys.

He had made about fifty copies—all of which he would need when Oscar's niece figured out he was once more gaining unauthorized access to the Green Vase. She had a nasty habit of trying to confiscate his lock-defeating devices.

As Monty lingered in the front entrance, congratulating himself on the success of his key-pirating operation, he paused, considering. Then he reached back to the door and reset the lock. The longer he could keep his neighbor in the dark about his clandestine visits, the better.

THERE WAS NO fooling the shop's resident felines, however. A few seconds later, the cats poked their heads out of the stairwell leading to the second-floor apartment.

Rupert took a few hesitant steps before rushing across the room to greet his fellow fried-chicken enthusiast. He circled Monty's feet, hopefully sniffing the air.

"Hey, buddy," Monty said with a grin. "Sorry, I'm fresh out of treats."

Isabella was decidedly less welcoming in her approach. After sauntering to the front door, she hopped onto the cashier counter and leveled her frosty gaze at the man she clearly considered an intruder.

"Come on, Isabella," Monty said reproachfully. "Where's your sense of humor?"

Her blue eyes stared back, a stern, unblinking response.

UNFAZED, MONTY MEANDERED into the store, stopping at several display cases to fiddle with an antique or two, before eventually making his way to the dentist's recliner at the back of the room.

"Someone's been sitting in my chair," he called out as he brushed off the layer of Rupert fur.

He dropped onto the recliner's leather cushions and pulled a lever beneath the seat so that the chair swung down to its horizontal position.

"Ahhhh." Monty sighed, propping up his feet. "Perfect."

"You know," he said as Rupert padded over to the recliner. "When I'm mayor, I'm going to have one of these in my office. Just think of it . . ."

Monty's eyelids fluttered shut as his shoulders relaxed into the chair's cushioned comfort. They soon snapped back open, however, at a thudding *bump* from the room below.

"Hello?" he called out as Rupert sprung into the air and sprinted for the stairs.

A second *whomp* brought the recliner whizzing back to its upright position.

Monty stared first at the floor, then at Isabella, who had crept up to the basement's closed hatch. A growl rising in her throat, she began to scratch at the surface of the wood.

"What do we have here?" Monty asked, more curious than concerned.

Quietly lifting himself off the chair, he tiptoed across the floor to the hatch. He knelt beside Isabella, quickly removed the small panel covering the recessed handle, and wrapped his hand around the handle's metal bar.

"Brace yourself," he cautioned Isabella as he

lifted the hatch, triggering the drop-down stairs to unfold loudly against the basement's concrete floor.

Holding a finger to his lips, he listened for another indication of movement in the room below.

After a long moment of silence, he started stealthily down the steps.

Isabella watched his descent, cynically pondering what might happen next.

Then, figuring she could run much faster than her spindly-legged neighbor, she cautiously followed him into the basement.

Chapter 35
FEEDING THE BEAST

HAROLD WOMBLER GIMPED across the length of the chicken restaurant's kitchen, motioning for Oscar's niece to follow him. At the far end of the room, he pulled open the heavy stainless steel door to a walk-in freezer and hobbled inside.

"You're not serious about the chicken," the woman said as she shivered in the freezer entrance.

She watched, brow furrowed, as Harold stood in front of a tall metal rack, slowly scanning the rows of shelving.

"This ought to do it," he grunted after selecting a package on the rack's top shelf. He pulled down a large bundle wrapped in white butcher paper.

Giving the woman a sideways glance, he tossed it through the air to her.

"What am I supposed to do with *this?*" she asked, juggling the heavy frozen block to keep it from freezing her fingers. "You don't expect me to give it to the alligator?"

Harold wiped his hands on his apron and grimaced. "You came here for help, didn't you?"

After a long, apprehensive stare, she finally nodded.

"Well, first things first, you've got to feed the beast," he said in a matter-of-fact manner.

"But how do I . . . ?" Her voice trailed off as she gestured with the pack of frozen chicken.

Harold rolled his eyes. He flicked his wrist as if demonstrating a toss. "Walk down to the basement and chuck it to him, I imagine."

"You want *me* to feed him?" she asked warily.

He slapped a bony hand on his hip. "Well, it's *your* basement, isn't it?"

Her face crimped into a clearly unpersuaded expression.

Finally, he threw his hands up. "How hard can it be?" he grumbled as he grabbed a set of keys from a hook behind the kitchen counter. He locked the back door and headed for the front of the diner.

The woman trailed behind him as he continued to mutter.

"It's not like you need scientific training."

Chapter 36
THE SCENE OF THE CRIME

AS THE LUNCH hour approached, the front lawn outside the California Academy of Sciences began to empty out. The media crews had filmed an hour or so of footage of the building's exterior, but with no new developments in the missing-alligator case, they were shifting their focus back to the story at City Hall.

This time tomorrow, the supervisors would begin their special session to select the interim mayor, and it was still anyone's guess as to who would be filling the slot. The city's political pundits had talked themselves silly, debating the likely candidates, but there appeared to be no consensus, even among the board members themselves, as to who would gain a majority of the vote.

On top of all this, a rumor had begun to circulate that the Current Mayor was sequestered in his office after suffering yet another amphibian-related breakdown. After the morning's gator-mania, the newspeople were gearing up for a late-afternoon round of ninja frog jokes.

But as most of the reporters packed up their gear and headed for the parking lot, one could be seen marching toward the Academy's front steps.

Despite his misgivings about the less-than-serious nature of the Clive headline, Hoxton Fin had an inside source to consult on the alligator investigation.

That was something his ingrained reporter's instincts couldn't walk away from—even if it required him to revisit an unpleasant chapter in his personal history.

OUTSIDE THE ACADEMY'S front doors, Hox pulled out his cell phone and scrolled through the names catalogued in his contact list.

With a slight grimace, he selected the number for his former sister-in-law.

He hadn't spoken to his ex-wife or anyone from her family since the divorce, but he kept close track of their whereabouts—if for no other reason than to ensure he didn't inadvertently run into the movie star or, worse, her new fiancé.

It was because of this diligent research that Hox knew his ex-wife's younger sister was likely sequestered inside the otherwise off-limits aquarium.

Little Kimmee Kline was now all grown up, but he still thought of her as the tiny girl in pigtails who had served as the flower girl at his wedding—she was a good twenty years junior to her famous older sibling.

Last spring, Kimmee had received a doctoral degree in the life sciences. Soon after graduation, she had taken a position at the Academy of Sciences in her field of expertise, herpetology.

"Dr. Kline," Hox muttered as the telephone line began to ring. He was going to have a hard time remembering to call her that.

DR. KIMBERLY KLINE set the phone down onto its receiver and threaded her fingers through her thick blond bob. She'd just received a call from her former brother-in-law, Hoxton Fin, who was outside the building waiting for her to let him in. Groaning, she bent her head over her cluttered desk in the Academy's basement.

As if this day could get any worse.

Sighing tensely, Kimberly glanced at a small photo in a metal frame propped on the desk's corner. The picture was of her and her big sister, who, given their sizable age gap, had always been more like an aunt. They'd been close when she was younger and her sister less famous. Nowadays, they only spoke once or twice a year, during the holidays or at rare family get-togethers.

Kimberly wasn't sure what had caused the breakdown in her sister's marriage to Hox, but everything had gone downhill quickly after the infamous komodo dragon incident at the Los Angeles Zoo.

Like the previous divorce, Kimberly had first received news of her sister's recent engagement from the gossip magazines. Her sister's e-mail

217

announcing the event had come several days later.

She frowned, remembering. The magazine article had provided far more details than the e-mail.

KIMBERLY BRUSHED HER hair back from her forehead and tried to assume a confident expression.

So far, she'd managed to hide the fact that she'd lost her set of keys to the Academy's main exterior doors in the hours prior to Clive's disappearance. She'd been searching high and low throughout the exhibits for the last several hours, to no avail. It seemed less and less likely that they had simply fallen off her key chain.

A crushing wave of guilt had risen in her chest as she'd realized that she might be responsible for the alligator's disappearance.

Biting her lower lip, she shoved the key chain into her pocket.

With his probing stare and dogged questioning, an encounter with Hoxton Fin was the last thing she needed right now.

THE BROODING MAN standing impatiently outside the Academy's glass walls looked a little grayer than Kimberly remembered—and a great deal more grumpy.

She nodded to the security guard, who

reluctantly opened the door. Hox brushed past the man and stalked into the atrium.

"Hello there, Kimmee . . . er, ah . . . Dr. Kline." He meted out the fractured greeting as he joined her beneath the dinosaur skeleton. He fiddled with a strap on his backpack before adding, "Well, it's been a while."

"Mmm," she replied, feeling much smaller and shorter than usual.

Hox waited through an awkward silence and then cleared his throat. He might as well get the inevitable pleasantries over with.

"How's Gloria?" he asked gruffly.

"She's fine," Kimberly said, lifting her face toward the ceiling as she tried to avoid eye contact with the surly reporter. She tugged at the hem of her blue Academy T-shirt.

"You heard about . . . ?" Her voice trailed off, as if she were afraid to speak the name of her sister's new beau.

Hox cut in gruffly. "I wish them the best." He shifted his weight, alleviating pressure from his sore foot. "Or *him* anyway. That guy's going to need all the help he can get."

There was another long silence. Even the dinosaur began to feel uncomfortable.

"How about you?" Kimberly asked, struggling to be conversational. "Are you seeing anyone?"

Hox responded with a withering glare. "I'm here about the stolen gator," he said curtly. He thwacked his notebook against the side of his leg with a loud snapping *pop* that caused the scientist to jump.

"That's not really my department," she demurred, trying to maintain her composure. Her gaze now shifted to Hox's lame left foot. "I'm in herpetology."

"You mean frogs," he translated, flipping the notebook open to a clean page. He pulled a pencil from his shirt pocket and eyed her suspiciously. "Surely, there's not much separation between the two."

She opened her mouth to protest, but he cut in again.

"Can you take me to the Swamp Exhibit?"

Chapter 37

SPIDER MAN

SPIDER SLOWLY EASED himself from under the parked car outside the art studio. Straightening his lanky frame, he dusted off the janitor's coveralls and reset his baseball cap.

A few minutes earlier, he had watched the Mayor's Life Coach plug a strange-shaped key into the store's front door and surreptitiously step inside. He had been able to follow Mr. Carmichael's movements as the man wandered around the front of the showroom, but Spider had lost track of his target when he moved to the back of the store.

Fetching his bike from the curb, Spider steered it as nonchalantly as possible across the street toward the Green Vase antiques shop. He peeked into the windowpanes as he approached, but his vision to the showroom's far corners was blocked by a row of bookcases.

He leaned his bike against the nearest tree and sidled up to one of the crenellated iron columns at the edge of the building. Still trying to look like a casual pedestrian, Spider inched out from behind the column and gradually shuffled in front of the glass.

As his eyes focused on the rear of the room, he caught a glimpse of Mr. Carmichael jumping up from a large recliner before the man's slender shadow moved once more out of view.

Frustrated, Spider pressed his nose up against one of the green vase shapes embedded in the front windows. He cupped his hands over his forehead, blocking the glare from the street, just in time to see Mr. Carmichael disappear down an opening that had appeared in the floor.

Pulling back to the cover of the column, Spider glanced up and down the block. Not another soul stirred. It was an oddly unsettling but, he thought, convenient circumstance.

He rushed to the shop's front door, ready to slip inside. Heart racing, he wrapped his hand around the tulip-embossed knob, but despite his forceful twist, it refused to budge.

Puffing out a disappointed sigh, Spider stared through the door's glass panels at the open hatch—so close and yet so far. He'd lost his mark. He might as well get back on his bike and return to City Hall.

But as he gripped the handlebars and prepared to shove off, he noticed an opening for an alley just past the next shop down.

Maybe, he thought with renewed optimism, there's another way inside.

SPIDER ROLLED HIS bike down the sidewalk, past the papered-up windows of the store adjacent to the Green Vase, and nosed his front wheel around the corner into the alley.

On the lookout for a rear access point to the showroom, he pedaled slowly along the narrow passageway. About a hundred yards later, the corridor's steep brick walls opened for a somewhat wider easement that ran behind the backside of the antiques shop.

Taking a right turn down the easement, he quickly arrived at the space behind the building that housed the Green Vase. There he found a small cloth-covered car parked beside a metal Dumpster.

The trash bin saw more frequent use than the vehicle, Spider surmised, after peeking beneath the cover and seeing that the car's battery leads had been disconnected.

He switched his attention to the redbrick building. There didn't appear to be a street-level door on this side, he noticed with chagrin . . . but there was a window one floor up.

He took a few steps back and estimated the distance between the Dumpster and the window. It was a stretch, but he just might be able to swing it.

Glancing up and down the empty alley, he parked his bike and shoved his notepad into the front pocket of his coveralls. Then, latching onto the Dumpster's top rim, he pulled himself up onto its lid. The rubber soles of his high-top sneakers dug into the sides of the bin as he scrambled onto the dented metal roof.

"Who-wee," he muttered to himself as he took in a whiff of the fumes from the refuse in the container beneath his feet.

The Dumpster creaked as Spider eased his weight toward the building's brick wall. Cautiously, he crept to the edge of the metal lid. His eyes firmly fixed on the window's bottom ledge, he slapped his hands together and bent his knees in preparation for the jump.

"Here goes nothing," he said as he leapt into the air.

IT TOOK MORE of a stretch than Spider had anticipated, but his flailing fingers managed to catch the ledge as his body slammed against the brick wall. Straining to keep from falling, he lifted his chin to peek in through the second-story window.

"It's a kitchen," he squeaked as the muscles in his arms and hands began to burn.

Craning his neck, he could see a small but functional cooking area with a worn wooden table on one side, a countertop sink and a dishwasher on the other.

He spied a book laying on the table. "*The History of the Steinhart Aquarium,*" he noted painfully. He wouldn't last much longer; his fingers were about to give out.

Looking down, he grimaced at the brick—windowless—wall that made up the rear of the building's first floor. He'd gleaned all he could from this vantage point. He might as well go back around to Jackson Street. Maybe by now Mr. Carmichael had emerged from the basement.

Resigned to the ten-foot fall, Spider was just about to release the ledge when he realized that the kitchen window was slightly loose in its frame.

"Hold on a minute . . . ," he said, tamping down the screaming pain in his fingers.

Grunting from the effort, he lifted himself up onto his right elbow. Then he reached with his left hand for the seam between the glass and the frame. A hard shove caused the window to creak open about two inches. Gritting his teeth, he pushed again, but the window refused to budge any further.

Spider's body swung precariously back and forth as he tried to gain leverage. His knees dug into the brick wall, and he hefted his weight higher up on the ledge. The window groaned, giving another inch, as he thrust his arm upward.

"Just one more . . ."

Grating as if it had been years since its last movement, the pane finally slid open.

"Aha!" he shouted with relief.

AS SPIDER DANGLED from the ledge outside the open kitchen window, he was suddenly overcome by a rush of caution. He was about to cross the line from mere observation and harmless impersonation to something a bit more delicate in nature. He could get into serious trouble if he were caught breaking and entering a private residence.

The concern left him as quickly as it had arrived. He was working for one of the most powerful men in San Francisco. Surely, the Previous Mayor could bail him out if anything like that happened.

"Nothing ventured, nothing . . ."

With a heave, he pulled his body up onto the ledge. Tumbling through the open window, he landed head and hands first on the kitchen's tile floor.

"Gained," he completed with a wince.

GINGERLY, SPIDER ROLLED himself into an upright position and looked around the room. Luckily, no one appeared to have noticed his scrambling entry.

Straightening his baseball cap, he stood and turned to face the stairwell leading to the first floor.

He took a few steps toward it and then stopped.

There was another potential consequence to this risky behavior that he hadn't considered. The image of his mother's stern expression flashed before him. What would she say if he were arrested? His face contorted as he imagined the high-pitched tirade that would ensue. The police, he realized, would be the least of his problems— and there was nothing the Previous Mayor could do to mitigate that complication.

Spider glanced at the open window. There was still time to retreat down the alley.

But as he once more weighed the wisdom of his actions, a slight *bump* echoed from the room below, a muffled, mysterious sound. What was Mr. Carmichael doing down there?

Spider couldn't help himself. He had to find out.

Nervously, he swiveled back toward the stairs and, treading as lightly as possible, started down the steps to the first floor.

Chapter 38
HELLO, HELLO

SPIDER CREPT CAUTIOUSLY down the stairs toward the showroom. Despite his best efforts, the wood squeaked beneath his feet with every step. And if that noise wasn't enough to announce his presence, he accidentally slammed his forehead against a low-hanging beam, sliding down a few steps before he regained his footing.

He covered his face as he turned the corner at the bottom of the stairs, fully expecting to find a squadron of police officers waiting to make his arrest.

The shop was, instead, eerily quiet. The dentist's recliner was still empty, just as he'd last seen it. In the wood flooring nearby he spied the open hatch where Mr. Carmichael had disappeared.

Cautiously, Spider approached the opening and peered into the hole. His nose crinkled at the smell that seeped up from the area below. The air was damp and moldy, like a school locker room toward the end of basketball season.

Leaning back from the hatch, Spider flipped to a new page in his notebook. He drew a crude sketch of the shaky, unstable-looking stairs leading to the lower level—a sign of diligence, he told himself, not one of delay. Nonetheless, he continued his nervous scribbling. Even the upstairs showroom, with its shelves full of dusty relics, was starting to feel a bit creepy.

Spider's pencil jumped on the page as a loud *bump* vibrated beneath his feet. He took a wide step away from the hatch, gulped apprehensively, and pulled down on the brim of his cap. Tentatively, he eased his body back toward the opening.

As he peeked over the ledge, a man's voice whispered up from the level below.

"Hello?"

Spider scrambled away from the hole, his dark face paling. His mouth went dry as his lips opened and closed, trying to form a response. His notepad trembling in his fingers, he croaked out a hoarse reply.

"Hello?"

Just then a man and a woman approached the store's front exterior. There was a grating sound of a key entering the lock, followed by the distinctive *clink* of the internal metal fixtures shifting in their settings.

Spider dove behind the leather dentist recliner as the door opened and the pair walked inside. He lay motionless, afraid to breathe, as he sprawled across the floor, certain that, this time, he was done for.

The woman's voice called out from the front of the store.

Spider's whole body cringed, but he had no idea what to make of the words she spoke.

"I don't care what you say, Harold. I'm not going to throw that hunk of frozen chicken meat down into my basement."

Chapter 39

A DIFFICULT PEST TO ERADICATE

"HELLO?"

The first whispered greeting had just left Monty's lips. He stood by a row of dusty boxes near the back of the room and tilted his head toward the basement ceiling. A moment earlier, he'd listened to footsteps tread down the stairs from the kitchen and tiptoe across the showroom.

"Hello?" A faint reply came down through the hatch.

Monty's brow furrowed. Someone was in the store above him—and it wasn't Oscar's niece. The voice of the upstairs intruder was distinctly male in gender.

"Hellll-looo," Monty repeated, this time in a more suspicious whisper.

Green eyes narrowing, he began to sneak across the concrete floor toward the hatch.

Despite a diligent search, one enthusiastically aided by Isabella, the only out-of-place item

Monty had found in the basement was the niece's heavy-duty flashlight—mysteriously left turned on and resting haphazardly on the concrete floor.

He wasn't sure how to explain the earlier *bump* that he'd heard while sitting in the dentist recliner, but now several strange noises were emanating from the room above. If he'd been a superstitious person, he might have thought a ghost was playing tricks on him.

Monty swung the flashlight's beam toward Rupert, who was perched on the shoulders of the stuffed kangaroo that stood in the corner behind the drop-down stairs. The kangaroo was as far as Rupert had been willing to venture into the basement's dark confines.

"Who is it?" Monty mouthed at the chunky white cat, but he received no discernable response. Rupert glanced briefly up toward the showroom and then returned his fearful gaze to the basement's back wall.

Isabella circled around Monty and leapt gracefully over a teetering cardboard box. Halfway across the room, her furry body dropped into a stalking stance, hugging the ground as she neared the bottom of the steps.

She made a soft clicking sound at Rupert. Apparently, this was a far more effective communication than Monty's verbal mime. Rupert immediately leapt from the kangaroo's shoulders and skittered up the stairs.

"Wait for me," Monty hissed as Isabella followed her brother out of the basement.

Monty scooted toward the exit. A series of footsteps now thumped across the floorboards as more voices entered the showroom.

What was going on up there?

As he neared the stairs, he swung the flashlight's beam at the ceiling and the shadowed figure who had just moved over the opening.

"WHY IS THE hatch open?" Oscar's niece whispered as Harold followed her through the Green Vase's front door carrying the package of frozen meat. "It was closed when I left."

Panic swept over her as the worst-possible scenario flashed before her eyes. She would never forgive herself if either of her cats—or, she couldn't bear to think it, both—had been gobbled up by that alligator.

She raced through the showroom, her feet thundering across the floorboards. She nearly fainted with relief as first Rupert and then Isabella bounded out of the basement.

"What were you two doing down there?" she demanded. "That thing could have swallowed you both in one gulp."

"*Now,* do you want to feed the beast?" Harold asked, holding the package out to her.

Grimacing, she took the still frozen parcel from him and stepped up to the hole. She heard a shuffling sound in the basement; then a blinding light turned toward the opening at the top of the stairs.

That alligator was eating her flashlight, she thought with fury.

Channeling the previous moment's fear that the alligator had eaten her cats, she swung her arms back and prepared to heave the package down into the hole.

HALFWAY UP THE basement stairs, Monty squinted at the figure bent over the hatch. Blinking, he caught sight of Oscar's niece standing on the top step, a fierce expression on her face as she leaned over the opening.

A voice on the first floor—one Monty had no trouble recognizing—grumbled loudly. "What are you waiting for? Just toss it in there."

"Wait!" Monty called out, waving the flashlight as the woman's arms swung through the air and lobbed a solid, round object through the hatch.

Her action was so unexpected that it caught him off guard. He wasn't sure if he should rush up the stairs or drop back. It was a costly moment of hesitation.

The frozen package caught him square across his mid-section, knocking him off the steps onto the concrete floor.

"Whug."

• • •

OSCAR'S NIECE LEANED back from the hatch, a troubled expression on her face.

"How did *he* get in here?" she asked, perplexed. She put her hands on her hips as she turned to look at the Green Vase's front door. She'd had the lock rekeyed not more than a month ago. Surely, Monty hadn't managed to undermine it already.

The wrinkled old man standing beside her wore an unusually jubilant expression on his face.

Harold grunted sarcastically as he began to hobble toward the exit.

"You got yourself a pest, all right," he said as he reached for the door's handle. "But this one's goin' to be much tougher to eradicate than any old gator."

Chapter 40

THE FLOWER SHOP

"RIGHT THIS WAY, Clive," Sam said as he ushered his albino companion down the tunnel away from the Green Vase's basement. They'd made a hasty departure after the alligator's impromptu encounter with Oscar's niece and her two cats.

"We've got a busy schedule today," Sam continued. "Places to go, people to see. The Green Vase was meant to be a temporary stop, anyway."

With a nervous chuckle, he added, "Just not *that* temporary."

• • •

IT WAS SLOW going, navigating over the tunnel's uneven ground with an alligator in tow. Clive had extremely short legs, so that even his fastest pace left Sam constantly having to stop and wait for him to catch up.

Plus, Sam found that the gator didn't hurry unless he was chasing after a fish pellet. The plastic bag of treats Sam had brought along with him got lighter with each step. He was starting to worry that his supply would run out before they reached their destination.

And so, it was with great relief a few minutes later that Sam breathed in the strong scent of flowers, indicating that they were nearing Wang's Montgomery Street flower shop.

A few yards further, they reached a ladder formed out of rebar that had been drilled into the tunnel's concrete wall.

"You wait here," Sam instructed, tossing Clive the last of the smelly treats. "I'll be right back."

SAM CLAMBERED UP the ladder, quickly reaching the trap door in the floor of the broom closet at the back of Wang's flower shop. Pushing up on the door's flat surface, he poked his head through the opening to look around.

Other than an old mop and a rusty bucket, the closet was empty. The coast apparently clear, Sam proceeded to squeeze his large frame through the hatch. With difficulty, he raised himself to a standing position and turned to face the broom closet door.

A quick check of the handle confirmed that it was, predictably, locked.

Sam fumbled through his overalls, searching for the key he'd used to open the tunnel entrance to the Green Vase's basement. But after a thorough search through all his pockets, at least as thorough of a search as was possible in the closet's cramped confines, he concluded that the key was lost. He'd probably dropped it during the trip through the tunnel.

He looked down at his feet, thinking of the creature waiting below. The key was likely sitting in the alligator's belly.

After checking the handle once more to be sure, he held his breath and lightly rapped against the facing.

LILY WANG STOOD in front of a large table at the rear of the flower shop, arranging cuttings for a special delivery to Union Square. She had just scooped up a bundle of violet-colored tulips when she heard the first knock.

She paused, her hands wrapped around the long stems, her arms frozen in the air above a slender green vase.

A second knock, this one more persistent, echoed from the broom closet.

Her forehead wrinkled with concern. She wasn't expecting any visitors—at least not anyone from the shop's tunnel entrance. Her father wasn't due back yet from his trip to Pier Seven; his fishing expeditions often lasted several hours.

Lily threaded the stems through the mouth of the vase and then cautiously approached the closet. The knocking sounded a third time as she crept up to the door.

The handle moved as someone jiggled it from the opposite side. The floorboards creaked, indicating a heavy, formidable presence.

"Who's there?" she whispered tensely.

But it was a gravelly voice from inside the flower shop that made her jump.

"I believe that's for me."

Lily spun around to find Harold Wombler standing beside the front rack of flowers. A light sheen of sweat dotted his brow, as if he'd been hobbling at top speed, and he was loaded down with a large box. Panting, he carried his carton across the flower stall.

"I've had to chase them all over town," Harold muttered without explanation as he pushed past Lily to the broom closet.

Setting his box on the floor, Harold released the lock and pulled open the door. Sam smiled apologetically at Lily as Harold bent down to the container.

"You'll be needing more of these," Harold

said, handing Sam a plastic bag of brown pellets.

He reached back into the box and fished out a stack of folded clothing. "This outfit is for you."

As Sam juggled his packages, Harold tossed a red scarf on top of the pile.

"And this one's for your friend."

Chapter 41

A HOLLOW STOMACH

SPIDER HUDDLED BEHIND a bookshelf in a corner of the Green Vase showroom, his heart pounding from his latest close call. He'd managed to scoot out from beneath the dentist recliner and scramble into this hiding spot while the woman with the long brown hair and her elderly companion were bent over the opening to the basement.

Peeking around the corner of the bookcase, he'd watched as the woman tossed a package wrapped in white butcher paper—from the discussion, he gathered it was some sort of frozen meat—down into the hatch. The projectile had apparently caught Mr. Carmichael, socking him in the stomach.

Strange goings-on inside this antiques shop, Spider mused as he pulled back from the edge of the bookcase.

Hunched in the corner, he propped his notebook

on his knee and steadied his pencil. Still listening to the conversation in the rear of the room, he began quietly taking notes.

GRIPPING HIS STOMACH, Monty collapsed onto the dental chair, which had been reextended to its flattest reclining position. Moaning, his narrow face contorted into exaggerated expressions of pain.

"Good thing it hit me in the middle here," he said, pointing feebly at his stomach. "That's all muscle, you know."

The woman appeared unmoved by his physical discomfort. Isabella sat beside her person, similarly unsympathetic. Rupert hovered near the stairs to the second floor, wanting to head up for his long-delayed nap but intrigued by the package lying on the floor next to the hatch.

"I think I broke a rib," Monty said pitifully, gripping his lower chest.

"Would serve you right," the woman replied as she walked to the opening and peered into the hole. "You're lucky that's your only injury," she muttered grimly.

Brow furrowed, she turned her gaze from the hatch to the recliner. How had Monty missed the alligator? Her eyes dropped to her female cat, the hunter who had nearly attacked the beast during their earlier encounter.

Isabella yawned, as if to communicate that her

second trip to the basement had been far less eventful than the first.

The woman returned her attention to the recliner. "What were you doing in my basement?" she asked suspiciously.

Monty let out a pitiful groan. "I heard something bumping around down there. I thought you had an intruder."

The niece shook her head. "Afraid you had competition?"

"You should be thanking me for going to check it out," Monty insisted. "I'm a hero in this situation, you see."

The woman held out her hand, palm turned upward.

"I don't know how you got a copy of the key, but hand it over."

Monty lifted his head from the recliner's top cushion. Wincing, he raised his left hand to point a bony finger at the front door.

"You left it unlocked," he said, his voice pitching despite his attempt at a sincere expression. "You're lucky it was me who came inside. *Anyone* could have sneaked in here off the street."

Monty swung his head back and forth as he searched the room for signs of the other intruder—the one he had exchanged hellos with before being ambushed on the basement stairs.

Oscar's niece sighed, taking his antics as

mockery, but the young man hiding behind the bookshelf gulped nervously.

"Key," she demanded testily.

"I just have one question," Monty replied as he reached into his pocket.

"Fire away," she said, exasperated.

"What did you just throw at me?" he asked, this time his expression truly perplexed. "What's wrapped up in that butcher paper? A cannonball?"

The woman turned away from the recliner. She would have tried to come up with a false answer to Monty's question, but the label that had been affixed to the butcher paper clearly identified its contents.

Monty's gaze followed hers. Squinting, he read the printing.

"Boneless breast meat?" he exclaimed, jumping up from the recliner, instantly recovered from his sore stomach. He bent over the package, rereading the description.

"Why would you be throwing a ten-pound pack of frozen chicken into the basement?"

The woman pursed her lips. She didn't have a ready explanation—at least not one that didn't involve a rogue albino alligator on the loose in the sewer system beneath downtown San Francisco.

"New tenderizing technique," she responded with a shrug, but her nosy neighbor was not one to be put off from such odd behavior.

Predictably, he ignored the woman's last

comment. Stepping over Rupert, who was inching closer to the package, Monty speared his finger into the air.

"If you *were* looking to scare off a burglar," he proclaimed confidently, "there were other weapons at your disposal." He pointed to a display case containing an antique cutlass. ". . . ones that were easier to wield than a lump of frozen chicken."

"*Did* the frozen chicken intimidate my burglar?" the woman asked curiously. If so, she would have to start stocking it in much greater quantities.

"Nope," he replied with a sharp wag of his finger.

"Just checking." She sighed ruefully.

Monty began to pace a slow circle around the woman, wrapping his arms around the back of his waist as he made contemplative humming sounds. At the completion of two rounds, he announced his conclusion.

"You're on the hunt for something."

It was no use, the niece knew, trying to dissuade him. Capitulating, she pulled the green flyer from her jeans pocket and held it out to him.

Snatching the piece of paper from her grasp, Monty waved it under his nose. After a deep sniff, he arched his eyebrows knowingly.

"Something from dear old Uncle Oscar by the smell of it."

Monty slid across the floor toward the open hatch. "Something in the basement . . ."

The woman reflected on Monty's line of questioning. She couldn't imagine the alligator climbing up the steps to the showroom. There was only one way it could have entered—and exited—the basement, and that was through the underground passageway.

Monty's eyes lit up as if he had read her thoughts.

"No! It's the tunnel!"

"All right, all right," the niece relented. "You can come along."

She pointed at the frozen package. "But you're carrying the chicken."

SPIDER HUDDLED BEHIND the bookcase, his feet going numb from lack of circulation while he furiously took notes on the conversation between Mr. Carmichael and the woman with the long brown hair.

As the pair departed, accompanied by one of the cats, Spider rubbed his forehead, puzzling over what he had heard. His pages were littered with questions.

Mr. Carmichael hadn't mentioned their exchange of whispered hellos—although he'd given Spider quite a fright with his reference to intruders. Why hadn't he told the woman someone else was in the Green Vase? And why, Spider pondered, had Mr. Carmichael sneaked into the store in the first place?

Tugging on his baseball cap, Spider shifted his queries to the woman with the long brown hair. Who was this Uncle Oscar? What was she "on the hunt" for? And where was the tunnel she was presumably heading toward?

It was all very suspicious, Spider summed up as he crept cautiously out from behind the bookcase, and well worth his earlier climb onto the Dumpster to squeeze through the kitchen window—although, he thought with a sniff, he still smelled like garbage.

Grinning nervously at the plump orange and white cat sitting by the stairs, Spider tentatively approached the hatch. He leaned over the hole, hesitating for only a moment as he waited for his eyes to adjust to the dimmer light below.

Then, tightly gripping his notepad and pencil, he tiptoed down the steps into the basement.

RUPERT HAD WATCHED the proceedings between Monty and his person with guarded interest, but when they set off for the basement tunnel, he decided to remain behind in the Green Vase showroom. He, for one, was unwilling to risk another encounter with the alligator. That, and it was long past time for his morning nap.

As Rupert stretched his mouth into a sleepy yawn, a young dark-skinned man in janitor's coveralls stepped out from behind a bookcase in the corner of the room. After a quick look around, he started down the steps to the basement.

Rupert gave the mysterious man a curious stare, but the cat didn't budge from his spot by the stairs. He was pondering an issue of far greater importance than the Green Vase's multiple intruders.

Rupert considered himself an expert on all things chicken: roasted chicken, chicken soup, chicken à la king, and, of course, fried chicken.

He'd had a chance to thoroughly inspect the outside of the butcher paper–wrapped package before Monty carried it down to the basement.

Of this Rupert was certain: whatever its previous existence prior to being frozen, the contents inside that white wrapping had never once clucked or borne feathers.

Chapter 42

A LONG WHITE TAIL

ISABELLA LED THE way as her person and Monty clomped down the steps to the basement.

Picking up the flashlight from the floor, where Monty had dropped it, the woman set off through the piles of boxes and crates. By the time she made her way to the wardrobe on the opposite side of the room, Isabella had already checked beneath the cover, but the woman aimed her light under the cloth anyway, just to be sure.

"Explain to me again why I'm carrying a package of frozen chicken?" Monty asked as he tossed the bundle into the air, catching it like a basketball. "And what does this have to do with the flyer from the chicken restaurant?"

"If you see anything moving toward you," she replied as she swept the light in an arc across the floor, "throw the chicken at it."

"What?" he exclaimed, now gripping the frozen package with somewhat greater urgency.

But the niece had turned her attention to finding the secret doorway in the basement's back wall.

"I think it's over here somewhere," she murmured as she searched for the keyhole that was hidden in the wall between two bricks.

"What, exactly, might be moving toward me?" Monty asked apprehensively.

"Just keep a close eye on the ground, and I'm sure you'll be fine," the woman said as she ran her hand over the wall, waiting to feel the slight current of air from the tunnel.

"There it is," she said as she found the narrow crevice that hid the keyhole.

From her pocket, she pulled out the metal key to the store's front door. While the toothed portion had been retooled with the changing of the upstairs lock, the three-petaled tulips on the opposite end remained in the same configuration.

Angling her light at the keyhole, she fed the key's petal points into the opening. She rocked the rod back and forth until the shapes lined up; then, with a twist of the handle, an interior mechanism released, and a four-foot section of the wall slid backward. Placing her hands against the wall, she pushed open the door to the passageway.

As she shone her light into the dank tunnel on the opposite side, the niece couldn't suppress a shudder. Somewhere in the darkness, a rogue alligator potentially lay in wait. But, with it, she hoped she would find the next clue to the Steinhart treasure.

Juggling the flashlight, the niece scooped up Isabella. She had no intention of letting her cat become gator-food. With respect to her interminably nosy neighbor, however, she was less concerned.

The woman nodded to Monty.

"After you."

THE GROUP PROCEEDED into the tunnel, Monty leading the way with the frozen chicken, the niece struggling to balance Isabella and the flashlight. The beam bounced wildly against the walls as Isabella squirmed, trying to look over Monty's head.

"Can you keep the light steady?" Monty protested. "I'm having a hard time seeing where I'm going."

"Just keep walking," the woman replied tensely.

• • •

IT HAD BEEN well over a year since the niece's last journey through the passageway, but the tunnel had changed little during her absence. She quickly remembered why she hadn't returned sooner.

The damp, oozing walls reeked of mold, fungus, and, she suspected, raw sewage. The constant chattering of insects filled the dark corridor, wreaking havoc with her imagination. She felt as if bugs were crawling over every inch of her skin.

On top of the aesthetic unpleasantness of the place, she couldn't help wondering how some of the less stable sections of the tunnel had withstood San Francisco's frequent earthquakes—and whether they might give way if the next shake hit the right fault line.

AFTER ABOUT FIFTEEN minutes, Isabella chirped out informatively and pawed against her person's arm. They were passing the ladder leading to Wang's flower shop.

The niece glanced up at the broom closet's trap door. She was sorely tempted to abandon the alligator hunt, exit the tunnel, and head back to Jackson Square, but she pressed on.

Just a little bit further, she told herself. They had to be on the right track.

ABOUT A HUNDRED yards past the flower shop portal, they reached a fork in the passageway.

"Which way, chicken-master?" Monty asked, stopping in front of the intersection.

The niece didn't remember the fork from her previous journeys through the tunnel. One of the pathways must have been blocked off during her earlier visits.

She swung her light back and forth from the left to the right. It was impossible for her to tell which was the main route.

"What do you make of this?" Monty asked, kicking a brown puck-sized pellet with the toe of his shoe. "I've seen a few of these along the path here."

He bent down to pick it up, his nose wrinkling as he gave it a sniff. "It smells strangely . . . fishy."

The niece aimed the flashlight at the pellet, and then shifted it back to the fork. The trail of pellets turned off to the right.

"*Mrao,*" Isabella called out, pawing again at her person's arm.

The niece gritted her teeth and took a firmer grip on her cat.

"To the right," she instructed. After biting her lip, she added, "And Monty?"

He glanced back inquiringly. "Yes?"

"Be ready with that chicken."

A SHORT WALK later, the floor of the tunnel began to slant slightly upward. The noise from the street-level traffic grew louder.

As the trio rounded a corner, they could see a pair of shadowed figures in the distance. The duo appeared to be standing outside an elevator, waiting for its car to arrive so they could walk inside and ride it up to the street.

"Who's that?" Monty whispered as the niece angled her light around his shoulders to shine it toward the elevator.

The beam revealed a broad-shouldered hulk of a man dressed in a flashy suit, tie, and cufflinks.

The woman quickly panned the flashlight toward the ground, illuminating a short-statured creature with a long, loglike body, four crooked legs, and an intimidating snout.

The niece returned her light to the man's reddish orange hair.

"Is that Sam?" she asked, incredulous.

But she was drowned out by the comment of her skinny partner, who, in his surprise, dropped the package of frozen chicken.

"Is that an *alligator?*" Monty sputtered.

Isabella offered a one-word answer.

"Mrao."

Chapter 43
FASHION CLIVE

A SHARP, PULSING tweet whistled through the air outside the St. Francis hotel as a bellman flagged a passing taxi. The guests climbed into the cab's backseat, and the car sped off down Powell, its worn tires punching through a pothole with a spring-squeaking *whomp*. All the while, the cable running beneath the street's center median hummed with movement as it dragged trolleys over the city's steep hills.

San Francisco's Union Square graced a pleasant lunchtime scene. The line of flags hanging above the hotel's front steps fluttered expectantly, the rising breeze signaling a coming shift in the weather. The slightest expression of relief creased the stone face of the Atlas figure holding a clock above the entrance to a nearby jewelry store.

The square had been the center of the city's high-end shopping for the better part of a century. The elaborately tooled masonry on the surrounding buildings reflected the square's historic roots, while the underground parking garage constructed beneath the center pedestrian space highlighted its modern-day functionality.

Massive billboards mounted on the nearby rooftops advertised the latest in fashion, jewelry, and theatrical releases. One of the largest placards overlooking the square promoted an upcoming box-office thriller featuring a famous actress who was once married to a local newspaperman.

As the noon hour approached, the square's flat platform began to fill with shoppers, eaters, and those out for a midday walk. Men in flashy suits with colorful ties and polished leather shoes strode briskly through intersections. Women in impossible heels and skirted business attire stood in line for lattes, their bare legs vintage California casual.

The occasional eccentric stood on a street corner, proclaiming opinions that went unheard or, at best, ignored. The most prominent provocateur was a hairy-chested man wearing tennis shoes, a sandwich placard, and nothing else, who had commandeered a portable microphone and speaker. He stood on a small box in the middle of the sidewalk, shouting out his alleged qualifications for becoming the city's interim mayor.

The antics generated a few raised eyebrows but nothing more. On any given day, the average San Franciscan came across a great deal in the way of flamboyant spectacle. Even the most outlandish behavior often evoked nothing more than a yawn. It took a lot to capture the attention of these citizens.

The man who emerged from a vacant storefront at the far corner of the square, however, immediately drew interest—not for his dapper suit, shiny silver cufflinks, or incongruous rumpled red hair—but for the creature attached to the leash he held in his hand.

It was a sight at which even the city's most jaded residents had to stop and stare. Gone were all thoughts of the political turmoil over the pending mayoral vacancy. The subject matter of important afternoon meetings immediately vanished from consideration. Even the restaurant selection for that afternoon's lunch—for many, the most important decision of their day—fled from consciousness as they gawked at the animal attached to the leash.

Strolling down the sidewalk, heading toward the underground parking garage, the tip end of its long tail tilted slightly upward, was an albino alligator with a red scarf tied fashionably around his neck.

Chapter 44
A DISTINCTIVE ACCESSORY

KIMBERLY KLINE WATCHED uncomfortably as Hoxton Fin leaned over the Swamp Exhibit's brass seahorse balcony. The reporter stared down at the alligator-less pond, studiously taking notes on the details of the service door near the rear of the tank, the likely point of access for Clive's abductor.

Several security guards and members of the local police ringed the tank's upper-floor perimeter, squawking into radios, conferring among themselves, and documenting the scene with flash photography.

Extra lighting equipment had been brought in to illuminate the area. Gangly metal poles had been clamped to the balcony's railings, positioned so that their high-wattage bulbs shone down on the water below.

Academy scientists clad in plastic jumpsuits and hip-high rubber boots waded through the tank, closely examining every inch of the exhibit. One of the workers propped open a small plastic case on Clive's heated rock, removed several small vials, and began collecting water samples. Another, wearing a full wet suit and snorkel mask, floated beneath the water's surface inspecting the tank's turtles, who, for their part, appeared bemused by the extra attention.

Hox glanced up from his notepad. Craning his neck, he looked past the seahorse balcony to the multi-story rain forest exhibit in the building's adjacent wing. Then he shifted his steely gaze to the planetarium, the sign pointing toward the penguin area, and the stairwell leading to the aquarium's basement level.

"Academy of Sciences," Kimberly heard Hox

mutter under his breath. "Place is a glorified zoo."

She cringed at the glowering expression on his face as he shifted his weight off his left foot.

"I hate zoos."

WITH A GRUNT, Hox returned to his notes. He had interviewed the female detective who had been assigned to Clive's case a few minutes earlier. While the woman had been intentionally vague about the status of the investigation, it had been clear to Hox that the police had yet to develop any serious leads. There was no telling what had become of the poor creature or where he had been taken.

As to the means of the alligator's departure, however, both the scientists and the detective had reached the same conclusion. Clive had apparently been lured from his lair by a trail of fish pellets.

Hox flipped the notepad closed and thwacked it against his left thigh.

Dr. Kline flinched at the noise. She was beginning to hate that notepad.

"You're sure you didn't notice anything odd yesterday?" Hox asked sternly. He couldn't put his finger on it, but his instincts told him she was hiding something.

Before she could respond with yet another meek denial, a static-filled *squawk* issued from the nearest policeman's hip-holstered radio.

"Unconfirmed sighting . . . suspect has been reported at Union Square . . ."

Hox immediately switched his attention to the policemen as the radio-transmitted voice wavered, seemingly unsure of the accuracy of the information being relayed.

"Albino alligator accompanied by a burly man with red hair."

The policeman yanked his radio from his holster and held it to his ear, motioning to the detective as he muted the transmission. A second later, the pair sprinted toward the atrium and the Academy's front entrance.

"I'm off," Hox said curtly, suspending Dr. Kline's interrogation, at least for the time being. He gave her a stringent stare. "I'll be in touch."

"Red hair . . ." Kimberly murmured to herself. Then she turned and ran after the reporter.

"Wait, Hox. I'm coming with you."

HOXTON FIN LEAPED from a taxi at the corner of Post and Powell, his dark eyes quickly scanning the scene at Union Square. It had taken just under fifteen minutes to get there—they'd been lucky to catch a cab passing through Golden Gate Park—but they were too late. Several people milled about the area, but the alligator was nowhere to be seen.

Kimberly Kline joined Hox on the sidewalk. Bracing herself for yet another loud *pop* from the notebook, she nervously handed him the change for the fare and the cabdriver's receipt.

Hox stuffed the money in his pocket and stamped his left foot against the concrete, as much out of frustration as for the throbbing at the spot of his amputated toe. His gaze traveled grimly to the rooftops on the opposite side of the open pedestrian area, and he let out a spitting *pfft*.

The largest billboard flanking the square was for his ex-wife's next movie.

THE FULL RESOURCES of the local news media quickly converged on Union Square, joining a melee of squad cars, ambulances, and fire trucks—the latter two categories having been called to the scene as a precaution. No one knew what kind of casualties might be generated from an alligator roaming the streets of San Francisco.

As the brightly painted news vans began pulling up along the curb, Hox commandeered a pair of witnesses, eager to get their statements before they started embellishing their stories under the glare of the television cameras.

The two women were well-dressed lawyer types who had taken an early lunch to do some shopping. They'd just visited a clothing store run by a famous haberdasher, who had been honored with a commemorative table at a French bistro a few streets over.

Dr. Kline stood patiently to the side as Hox flipped open his notepad, licked his pencil lead, and began his questioning.

"SO, LADIES, CAN you tell me what happened?"

"We were walking along the sidewalk," the first woman explained. She pointed to a vacant storefront at the corner of the square. "Right over there. That's where we saw him." She sighed longingly. "It was the scarf, really, that caught my attention. We'd just been looking at a similar one in the store, but I'd told myself I couldn't afford it. I bought new shoes yesterday and a blouse the day before . . ."

Hox looked up from his notepad. His brow furrowed quizzically. "I'm sorry. Did you say *scarf?*"

"Clive was wearing a beautiful red scarf," the woman confirmed wistfully. "It was a perfect contrast to his white coloring. It was quite stunning really."

The reporter's gray-flecked eyebrows knitted together. He cleared his throat skeptically.

"Hermès," the second woman added with an informative nod. "Silk and cashmere blend. From their fall collection. You couldn't miss it. It was a very distinctive scarf."

The first woman tugged self-consciously at her sweater. "It's kind of sad really. That alligator's dressed better than I am."

"There, there, dear," her friend said, wrapping a comforting arm around her shoulders.

Hox's jaw stiffened as if he were biting back a snide comment. From the expression on his face, it was clear he wished he'd selected a different pair of witnesses. Taking in a deep breath, he resumed the interview.

"The man who was with Clive," he asked crisply. "Can you describe him?"

"Mmm," the first woman paused, remembering. "He had on a nice suit, but it wasn't very well sized to his figure. The cut in the shoulders was all wrong. He really could have done with some fitting and adjustments. You know, they're running a special at Mario's, around the corner from here. Their tailor has a great eye for those things."

Hox gripped his pencil, his irritation building.

Dr. Kline peeked timidly over Hox's shoulder. "Did he have red hair?" she asked tentatively. "The man who was with Clive?"

As the second woman nodded affirmatively, the first tilted her head and tapped her chin, as if remembering an additional detail. Hox sighed testily, waiting for her to speak.

"I thought he was kind of cute," she said dreamily.

"The man with the red hair?" Hox probed gruffly.

"No," she replied, looking at him as if the reference had been obvious. "Clive."

With a grunt, Hox shoved his notepad in his

back pocket. He handed each woman a business card.

"Call me if you think of anything else," he said with a suppressed eye roll as he turned to scour the square for additional witnesses.

Chapter 45
A CONVINCING CLIVE

SPIDER CROUCHED IN the tunnel, trying not to touch the wall as he peered down the dark passageway. A few moments earlier, he'd watched Mr. Carmichael and his party enter an elevator carriage and apparently return to ground level.

This was a welcome development for the young City Hall staffer. He was ready to get out of this damp, forbidding place.

"Note to self," Spider murmured as he cautiously approached the elevator shaft. "Never leave home without a flashlight."

Trying to ignore the insects rustling on the walls and ceiling, he ran his hands along the elevator's side fronting, his fingers desperately searching for the call button.

He finally found a circular depression that seemed to have the right dimensions. Holding his breath, he punched in on it.

"Oh, thank goodness," he said with relief as the button lit up.

· · ·

THE GROUND SHOOK beneath Spider's feet as the elevator's rusted, rickety cage began bumping down toward the tunnel. With a loud grinding of gears, the cage settled into its scaffolding, and a metal door slid open—revealing an interior empty of its previous passengers.

Spider pushed open the grating and stepped inside. A dim bulb hanging from the ceiling provided a meager, but much appreciated, light.

It was a grimy, grungy space. Scattered across the floor, he saw upturned roach carcasses, trails of rodent droppings, and a mysterious brown puck-shaped object.

"What's this?" he asked, bending down toward the brown lump. Gingerly, he picked it up and brought it toward his face. His senses were immediately overwhelmed by the smell of stale fish.

"Ew," he whispered, quickly dropping it and wiping his hand on the back of his coveralls.

Straightening his baseball cap, Spider pulled the grate shut and selected a button on the elevator's inner wall. There was no label, so he could only hope that it would take him the right direction: up. He glanced one last time at the tunnel's black corridor. He had no desire to travel farther down into the earth.

After an interminable twenty seconds, the metal door clanked shut and the elevator began a slow, shaky ascent.

• • •

AT THE TOP of the bone-rattling climb, Spider slid open the front grating and gratefully stepped out of the elevator.

He found himself inside an empty storefront. He assumed he was still in San Francisco, but given the twists and turns he'd taken while down in the tunnel, he would have been hard-pressed to speculate exactly where.

He was in a much brighter, if similarly repulsive, location as the elevator and the tunnel. The store's front windows had been covered up with brown kraft paper, but the sunlight from the street still permeated through the sheets, casting a dim glow about the room. Broken and discarded bottles were strewn across the floor. Piles of faded newspapers commingled with dirty heaps of clothing and a worn-out shoe that had somehow become separated from its mate.

Gripping his notepad and pencil, Spider carefully picked his way through the debris, following a trail of fishy brown pellets to the front door.

ON THE SIDEWALK outside the building, Spider stood awestruck, staring at the chaotic scene in Union Square. He turned a half circle, scratching his head in confusion.

What had happened while he'd been down in the tunnel?

A flood of reporters and other media types had gathered about the area. Their bulky vans were parked up every available side street; some were even blocking the perimeter of the square—to the immense frustration of the taxi drivers attempting to navigate through the madness. Spider winced as a belligerent horn blast sounded in his ear.

Throughout the square, reporters posed in front of camera crews, performing monologues and conducting man-on-the-street interviews.

Twirling his pencil, Spider edged up to one of the television news teams so he could listen in on a conversation with an apparent eyewitness as it was being videotaped.

The reporter finished his opening spiel and turned toward his interviewee, a hairy-chested man Spider recognized as one of the fringe mayoral candidates from the Castro.

The cameraman strategically aimed his lens at the upper portion of the man's body, taking care to crop out his unclothed lower half.

"Sir, can you tell us what you saw?"

The nudist stroked his chin thoughtfully.

"Well, they were walking right down this sidewalk here . . . the man and his, uh, pet."

The reporter cut in. "The alligator?"

"Yes." The man shrugged. "I figured it had to be a joke; I mean, who ever heard of such a thing? Really strange, if you ask me."

The reporter blinked his eyes, struggling to keep a straight face.

"And could you tell if it was the alligator that went missing earlier this morning?"

The naked man paused, as if reflecting, before assuming a serious, mayoral expression.

"I've been to the Academy of Sciences many times, and I've seen the gator's photo on the news. I have to say, it sure looked like Clive to me."

Chapter 46
THE GOLDEN GATOR

OSCAR'S NIECE STOOD on the northeast corner of Union Square, both arms tightly wrapped around Isabella, while Monty, still carrying the package of frozen chicken, waved the flashlight in the air, trying to hail a cab.

A colorful sea of news media, police, and pedestrian onlookers whirled around them. Honks, whistles, cell-phone ringtones, and the chatter of human voices filled the air. In the midst of this overwhelming scene, only Isabella noticed the young man in a blue baseball cap and janitor's coveralls exiting the vacant storefront that held the tunnel's elevator entrance.

A TAXI BRAKED at the corner, due more to the impediment of a news crew crossing the street than in response to Monty's flailing flashlight.

The driver leaned out his open window, warily eying Monty's dripping package.

"Where to?" he hollered as Monty tucked the flashlight under his arm and wrapped his hand around the rear door handle.

"Jackson Square," Monty replied, motioning for the niece to join him.

"Hold on a minute," the man said, clicking his rear doors locked. "What's that you're carrying? I don't want it dripping all over my seats."

Then he caught sight of the woman and her cat.

"No way, pal," the driver yelled. Shaking his head, he rolled up the window.

Fumbling with the package and the flashlight, Monty reached into his pocket for his wallet. With difficulty, he flipped it open and pulled out his City Hall identification card.

Rapping his knuckles on the glass, Monty held up the card to the window, flashing his Life Coach credentials as if they afforded him special privileges.

The driver read the inscription, laughed, and drove off.

"COME ON, MONTY," the woman called out as she set off in the direction of Jackson Square. She wanted to get Isabella back home before she managed to escape her grip. This was no place for a cat to be on the loose.

"I'll have that man's license when I'm mayor of this town," Monty fumed at the cab's departing bumper.

Skeptically rolling her eyes, the woman continued across the street. "Don't forget to bring my flashlight."

Reluctantly, he fell in line behind her.

Isabella propped her front paws on the woman's shoulders. As they left Union Square, her blue eyes focused on the young man who had followed them through the tunnel.

RUPERT MET HIS person, Isabella, and Monty at the front door to the Green Vase, his blue eyes eagerly searching for his regular afternoon fried-chicken package. After such a long absence, his stomach had high expectations—no matter that his person had left through the basement instead of the showroom.

He stared with disappointment at the drippy package Monty held in the front doorway.

Chicken imposter, he sniffed sulkily.

WITH A WEARY sigh, the niece set Isabella and the flashlight on the front cashier counter. She quickly crossed to the basement's open hatch and slammed the door shut before returning to the front door to take the soggy butcher paper–wrapped bundle from Monty.

Sending Monty on his way, she climbed the

stairs to the kitchen, holding the package at arm's length as she reflected on the journey through the tunnel, the chaos at Union Square, and the sight of Sam and Clive getting into the elevator.

"I've missed something," she said, her forehead wrinkling as she replayed the images once more in her mind.

Still contemplative, she slid the melting package into a large garbage bag and propped it upright in the freezer compartment of her refrigerator.

Much as she wanted to throw the wet heap into the trash bin behind the building, there was no telling when she might need it again, she thought with exasperation—either for feeding a wayward alligator or for throwing it at Monty's stomach.

AFTER A THOROUGH hand washing, the niece put a kettle on the stove for a cup of hot tea. A crisp breeze had begun to blow through San Francisco. Even with Isabella pressed up against her chest, the woman had felt chilled by the time she returned to the Green Vase.

Rubbing her arms, which were sore from over an hour's worth of carrying her cat, the niece wandered into the living room.

At the far end of the couch, she bent down in front of the end table and turned on the switch for the brass lamp.

"How did Sam get involved in this?" the niece pondered as the bulb began to glow, illuminating the exterior scene of the Steinhart Aquarium. The last she'd heard, Sam had been working up in the Sierras with a team of frog researchers.

Slowly, the niece rotated the lamp to the image on the globe's opposite side. The albino alligator sat on his heated rock inside the Swamp Exhibit, a golden glow surrounding his pale body.

"And what's it all got to do with Clive?"

STILL PERPLEXED, THE woman glanced out the front window to see Monty leaving his art studio. He had changed into a fresh suit and tie, and he had slicked his hair back with a thick layer of gel. Given his allergies to the stiffening hair product, she reasoned, he must be heading to a special meeting. Most likely, Monty had an appointment with the Mayor.

Clive's disappearance had temporarily bumped the interim-mayor discussion from the top of the news feed, but with the board of supervisors scheduled to vote on the matter the following afternoon, the topic would soon retake the headlines—unless, of course, the alligator made another surprise appearance.

As the niece considered the conspicuous overlap in the news stories, she began to wonder whether her uncle's current caper was about something more than hidden treasure. It wouldn't be the first time he had meddled with city politics. Given the magnitude of the interim-mayor decision, she reflected, it wouldn't be surprising if he were trying to influence the outcome.

The kettle whistled from the kitchen, and the woman flicked off the lamp. After a rejuvenating cup of hot tea, she would head over to the Academy of Sciences to see for herself.

Chapter 47

THE MAN IN THE MIRROR

BY MID-AFTERNOON, THE marble corridors at City Hall had started to empty out. Many of the building's government workers had left their offices a few hours early in preparation for the following night's festivities.

Thursday's board of supervisors' meeting promised to be a long, drawn-out affair. It was expected to last late into the evening. Most of City Hall's regulars planned on camping out in the supervisors' chambers until the decision on the mayor's replacement was finalized, so a preparatory good night's rest was in order—curled up in front of the television set watching the latest peculiar news on the Academy of Sciences' missing albino alligator.

But on the east side of City Hall's second floor, important business was being conducted. The lights were still on in the Current Mayor's office suite.

MABEL CARTER, THE Mayor's long-serving administrative assistant, switched off her computer and reached into the bottom desk drawer for her purse.

After spritzing a squirt of lemony perfume against the sides of her neck, she stood from her chair and turned to stare apprehensively at the heavy wooden door leading to the Mayor's office.

She really should be clocking out. She was meeting a friend at a restaurant across town, and it would take forever to get there if she got caught in rush-hour traffic.

Mabel glanced down at her watch and then back to the door. She was afraid to leave the reception area without first checking on the Mayor. He had been acting strangely lately— more so than usual.

With a sigh, she tiptoed across the room and leaned against the door for a discreet listen. The Mayor's even voice resonated through the wood, a steady, reassuring sound. She smiled and gently patted the door with the palm of her hand.

Gripping her purse handle, she took one more note of the time and turned for the exit.

The sooner the Mayor completed his transfer to Sacramento, the better, she thought as she headed down the second-floor hallway, the heels on her sensible dress shoes smartly clicking against the marble.

At the top of the central staircase, she paused and shook her head.

That poor man was still convinced the building was infested with frogs.

ON THE OPPOSITE side of the heavy wooden door, the Mayor sat at his wide desk, gazing thoughtfully at a mirror mounted onto a nearby wall.

The board of supervisors would be meeting the following day to select his successor. He had a weighty decision to make, and he could delay it no longer.

He had one last card to play, a minute piece of leverage that might just be enough to swing the vote. Earlier that week, the supervisor from the Marina district had approached him about getting his nephew a paid internship in Sacramento. With the current statewide budget crisis, such spots were hard to come by, but the Mayor had managed to find room in his lieutenant governor's payroll to squeeze in the slot.

Thoughtfully, the Mayor ran a hand over the top of his sculpted hair. He had been subjected to the board's petty machinations for the last seven years. He knew its members well, and he had learned how to manipulate them.

He had a sneaking suspicion that, if timed correctly, the endorsement by one of the supervisors to just the right kind of candidate might cause the rest to fall in line—if for no other reason than to bring the haggling process to a close.

The Mayor folded his long fingers together contemplatively. After everything he'd been through during his tenure at City Hall, the prospect of going out on such a triumphant note was certainly tantalizing.

The only question now was which interim candidate the Mayor would use the Sacramento internship to support.

THE MAYOR STARED pensively into the mirror. This was one of the most important decisions of his political career—given his inauspicious future as lieutenant governor, it might be the last important governmental decision he would ever make. He needed to ensure he made the right choice.

He took in a deep breath and then slowly released it.

"Well, there's Jim Hernandez," the Mayor suggested to his reflection. "He *was* helpful the other day after the alligator incident."

"Eh," the reflection replied. Both images grimaced with displeasure.

"I think we can eliminate that option," the Mayor concluded as the mirrored Mayor nodded in agreement.

"What about the Previous Mayor?" the

reflection proposed. "He was, in many ways, your mentor."

"Yes," the Mayor agreed with himself. "But, I think the city needs someone new . . . someone who would bring a fresh perspective to the office . . . someone who would still allow me to have some influence here at home while I'm away in Sacramento."

The reflection paused, stroking his chin with the tip of his finger. "Well, that leaves us just one option."

"It's the right selection," the Mayor said confidently. "I sense it's the right pick."

"Shall we tell him together?" the reflection asked.

"Let's not waste another minute," the Mayor replied smugly.

THE MAYOR TURNED to the slender, slick-haired man in a suit, tie, and whimsical cufflinks sitting on the opposite side of his desk.

"What do you say, Carmichael? Are you up for this?"

"It would be my honor, sir," Monty squeaked with excitement, jumping up from his seat to shake the Mayor's hand.

SPIDER JONES LAY flat on his stomach on the wide balcony outside the Mayor's office. Propping himself up on his elbows, he diligently began taking notes on the meeting he'd just watched on the opposite side of the glass. The open windows above Spider's head had provided ample audio to the conversation between the Mayor, the Mayor's reflection, and Mr. Carmichael.

Still amazed at what he had heard and observed, Spider once more peered through the glass as the Mayor picked up the phone and began dialing a number for a residence located in San Francisco's Marina district.

"Hello, Supervisor? This is the Mayor . . ."

Chapter 48
MORE THAN FROGS

AFTER A SHORT walk through the financial district, Oscar's niece skipped down a public staircase into one of Market Street's underground mass-transit hubs, quickly falling in among the jostling crowds of commuters.

The cavernous concrete bunker sank several levels below the street, a network of multiple platforms connected with crisscrossing diagonals of escalators and stairs.

The niece found what she hoped to be the right landing and waited for the N Judah to arrive. A moment later, she took in a deep breath, as if preparing to dive underwater, and squeezed into a standing-room-only Muni car bound for the Sunset district.

The Muni train rolled slowly along, stopping every couple of blocks to let off passengers. As the car began to empty out, the niece took a spot on a plastic bench seat. Slipping her backpack from her shoulders, she pulled out the aquarium book and opened it on her lap.

She flipped through the pages to a black-and-white photograph of the Steinhart Aquarium's original building, a less colorful rendition of the image than the one she'd discovered embedded in the ceramic shade of the brass lamp.

The Muni car swayed back and forth, weaving around a sharp corner as the woman shifted her attention to a second image on the page. Her fingers ran across the slick paper, tapping on the picture of the Steinhart's first alligator Swamp Exhibit and the standing seahorse balcony framing its upper rim.

A WIND WHISTLED through the Sunset's flat, empty streets as the niece exited the Muni train and set off on the short walk to Golden Gate Park. The blue had begun to drain from the sky, and the air carried the wet scent of a looming fog.

With a shiver, she zipped up her jacket. Hurrying across a busy intersection to the edge of the park, she removed a map from her backpack and unfolded it to show the western half of the city. She was determined, for once, not to get disoriented beneath the park's thick redwood canopy.

About a hundred yards later, she gave up on the map. She'd always had a poor sense of direction, and this instance was no exception—she had already lost her bearings. She would just have to follow the posted signs to the Academy of Sciences.

AS THE WOODS closed in around her, the woman tried to imagine the coastal forest where the Bohemian Club had held their secretive meetings.

The campsite where the elder Steinhart brother had found his inspiration for the aquarium would have looked much like the area where she now walked, the ground covered in sound-muffling needles, the air pungent with a musky redwood scent.

Reaching a fork in the trail, the niece stopped and glanced back and forth, trying to choose a direction. A scattered light filtered down through the trees, playing tricks with her mind, changing the scenery from one moment to the next.

It was the perfect setting, she thought as she threw up her hands and set off down the right-hand path, for pitching such a daunting plan. The mercurial landscape would have provided the optimal stage for the writer Mark Twain to conjure up the most fantastic challenge his vibrant imagination could divine—an elaborately designed aquarium, expansive in scale and stocked with fishes from all over the world—and lay it temptingly at Steinhart's well-funded feet.

The woman sighed, reflecting as she stared skyward at the treetops' identical spikes.

This same mystical outdoor arena was also tailor-made for the theatrical skills of her elusive Uncle Oscar.

WHEN AT LAST the niece emerged from the trees and stepped into the clearing that held the Academy of Sciences, she found the building—which had been much photographed and videotaped earlier that day—now devoid of activity. Large placards affixed to the front windows advised that the Academy was closed until further notice. A single figure manned the ticket station near the entrance. Otherwise, the exterior was unusually deserted.

The woman wandered halfway up the concrete walkway leading toward the glass-walled atrium and then veered off onto the grass. She placed the history book on the ground and opened it to the photograph of the original aquarium.

Stepping back from the picture, she gazed across the lawn. In her mind's eye, she placed the wading pools filled with chubby sea lions, the concrete paths packed with meandering pedestrians, and the square stone facade ringed with stately Corinthian columns.

Beyond, just past the building's entrance, she envisioned a seahorse balcony surrounding a large tank and, splashing in the water on his heated rock . . . an albino alligator.

A GUST OF wind swept across the yard, flapping the pages of the book. As the niece bent to the grass to close it, a taxi pulled up to the curb near the bicycle racks along the Academy's front drive. Hearing the passenger door swing open and then quickly slam shut, the woman turned to see a broad-shouldered man with a slight limp charging up the walkway.

"Hoxton Fin," she murmured with a small smile. He gave her a curious nod as he strode past. He wasn't near as imposing in real life as he appeared on the television screen.

Scooping up her pack, she watched as the reporter approached the ticket booth. He was there about Clive, she realized. By now, the whole of San Francisco would be on the lookout for the missing gator.

She didn't have much time left to inspect the Swamp Exhibit without the hindrance of its wide-mouthed occupant.

"I've got to figure out a way to get inside," she concluded.

She thought back to her earlier experience in the tunnel. She could think of only one way to break into the locked-down building.

Turning, she set off through the woods, only getting lost a couple of times as she retraced her steps to the Muni stop on the opposite side of the park. Waiting on the corner for the streetcar to arrive, she pursed her lips resolutely.

"I've got to find Sam."

HOX MARCHED UP to the ticket booth by the Academy's front doors and nodded authoritatively at the man seated inside.

Pushing a speaker button, the attendant bent his head to a microphone.

"Sorry, sir. The Academy's closed."

Hox replied with a sharp-eyed look. He pulled out his press badge and slapped it against the window.

"Got a quick question, if you don't mind," Hox said as the attendant leaned toward the glass.

"What's up?"

Hox pushed a button on his cell phone and held it to the glass for the attendant to see.

"Do you recognize this man?" he asked. The phone displayed a picture taken during Clive's brief Union Square appearance. Though blurry, the photo captured the head and shoulders of the red-haired handler who had led Clive through the square. The news station's tip hotline had received the image from an on-scene witness half an hour earlier.

The attendant squinted through the glass.

Hox held his breath, waiting to see if his hunch would pan out.

"Oh, yeah. Yeah, yeah," the man said, his face flashing with recognition. "I've seen that guy before. It was . . . let's see, Monday afternoon. He came to see Dr. Kline."

"Dr. Kline?" Hox repeated. "Are you sure?"

"Hold on a second; I'll get you his name." The attendant turned to his keyboard. After tapping through a few menu screens, he looked back up again.

"There he is. Sam Eckles. He's a frog consultant. Kimberly brought him in to advise on a problem with the new amphibian exhibit." The attendant let out a short chuckle. "They call him the Frog Whisperer—he's got a badge and everything."

As Hox scribbled the information into his notebook, he arched his thick eyebrows and huffed out a cynical grunt.

"It seems he's got an expertise in more than just frogs."

Chapter 49
THE BEARD IS WEIRD

HOX FLIPPED TO a clean page in his notebook. He looked over his shoulder at the dinosaur skeleton mounted inside the Academy's front atrium before returning his gaze to the attendant manning the ticket window.

279

"What else can you tell me about this Eckles character?" he asked, leaning in toward the glass.

Before the attendant could answer, Hox's cell phone began to buzz. He held up an apologetic hand and glanced at the incoming number.

"Just a minute," he said as he saw the digits for the newspaper's dispatcher. "I have to take this."

Stepping back from the guard station, he brought the phone to his ear.

"What do ya' got?"

He listened for less than ten seconds before clicking off the phone and ramming it into his shirt pocket.

"I'm going to have to get back to you on this," Hox called out to the ticket booth attendant before rushing back to the street.

Panting heavily, he climbed into the waiting taxicab.

"Ballpark," he barked hoarsely. "And step on it."

TEN MINUTES LATER, Hox sat impatiently in the taxi's rear passenger seat as the vehicle idled in place. The street ahead was clogged by rush-hour traffic. There was no way he would get to the ballpark in time.

The notepad made a snapping *pop* against his thigh. He was about to be outmaneuvered by an alligator—again.

He reached for his phone and dialed back the station's dispatcher.

"Tell the van to meet me there," he said tersely. He leaned forward in his seat to check his reflection in the rearview mirror and then added with a grunt, "They'd better bring Humphrey."

SAN FRANCISCO'S REDBRICK waterfront ballpark was just over ten years old, but the facility still gleamed with newness, the cornerstone of a redevelopment effort that had completely transformed the South of Market neighborhood of Mission Bay.

In the not-too-distant past, the area had been a wasteland of abandoned warehouses, empty lots, and flagrant criminal activity. But with the ballpark's installation, the once sketchy streets were soon paved over with new construction. The neighborhood now featured sky-rises of multi-million-dollar glass-walled condos, high-end restaurants, a life-sciences technology center, and one of the city's largest grocery stores.

The local baseball team's success on the field had further buoyed the redevelopment venture. Every home game, San Francisco's rabid baseball fans flocked to the park. Hox, a season ticket-holder, was one of many who enjoyed the venue's stinky garlic fries and handcrafted bratwurst sausages.

The intrepid reporter did not, however, participate in the waterborne antics in McCovey

Cove, an inlet off the bay that encircled the south side of the park.

No matter how gruesome the game-time weather, the cove routinely filled with all manner of improvised watercraft, precariously stacked with fans waiting for home runs and, more frequently, foul balls, to soar over the wall and plunk into the water.

In addition to making unplanned swims, the McCovey faithful were known for their elaborate costumes. One of the local favorites was a masked Batman and Robin duo who sped around the park's perimeter on a makeshift raft powered by an outboard motor.

Although Hox wouldn't have been caught dead in a superhero outfit, much less out on the water in an inflated air mattress, he did often join in the tradition of wearing a loose-hanging black beard to the game.

The beards were a tribute to one of the team's closers, an eccentric man—even by San Francisco standards—who had both a wicked fastball and bizarre tastes in dress and demeanor. The pitcher was known throughout the city by his signature beard, a rough, overgrown mat of hair dyed jet-black that covered the lower half of his face.

At any given baseball game, a number of men, women, young children, and babies could be seen at the park sporting enormous black beards.

To Hox's recollection, however, he had never

seen a beard wearer quite like the one in the image that had been forwarded to his phone by the newspaper's dispatcher. The time stamp at the bottom of the photo indicated it had been taken about a half hour earlier. As the taxi struggled through traffic, Hox shook his head, staring at the picture.

It wasn't the burly man with reddish orange hair wearing the team's signature orange and black jersey that struck Hox as unique—although he was keen to learn more about that odd fellow. Dr. Kimberly Kline, he mused, would have some explaining to do about her frog-expert friend.

Hox rubbed the scruff of his mustache as he shifted the phone's image toward the big man's feet and the albino beard wearer standing on the sidewalk beside him.

"How in the heck did he get a beard on that alligator?"

Chapter 50
POWERED BY PELLETS

THE NIECE HOPPED off the Muni train at the first return stop inside the financial district and climbed the steps to the Montgomery Street exit.

A cold blast hit her at the top of the concrete stairs. She zipped up the collar of her jacket and pulled the cloth over her nose, but the effort did more to block her vision than the arctic air.

Thinking of the warm apartment above the Green Vase antiques shop, the woman hurried down the block toward Jackson Square. Between her rush to get home and the impediment of her collar, she almost missed the white cargo van pulling up to the curb outside Wang's flower stall. But as the van's rear doors swung open and a burly man with ruffled red hair hopped out onto the pavement, she momentarily forgot the cold.

"What's going on here?" she murmured as she watched from a corner about a hundred yards away.

"Sam!" she called out, but the wind caught her words.

The niece began jogging across the intersection as Sam turned back toward the van's cargo area, scooped up a long, tarp-covered object, and eased it out the rear doors. After taking care to clear both ends of his log-shaped bundle from the van, Sam carried it into the flower shop, where Mr. Wang's daughter, Lily, helped him through the entrance.

The niece ran the rest of the way down the block, but by the time she reached Wang's, she found the front door had been locked. With a quick glance at the stall's exterior, she saw that sheets of plywood had been secured over the windows, sealing off the interior. The place was closed up as if the business would be shut down for the rest of the day.

She cupped her hands against the glass portion of the front door, trying to see inside, but a rack of flowers had been rolled in front of the entranceway, strategically blocking her view into the stall.

Puzzled, the woman knocked on the door.

There was the slight scraping sound of a cane against the floor. Then Mr. Wang's crippled form hobbled around the rack.

"Hello," he said with a cryptic smile as he unlocked the latch. "We've been expecting you."

THE NIECE FOLLOWED Mr. Wang past the flower rack and into the shop, trying not to breathe in the room's high concentration of pollen.

The rest of the display shelves had been pushed to the sides of the room, creating an open space in the middle for the tarp-covered object Sam had just set on the floor.

Suspiciously eyeing the tarp, the woman circled to the small area at the rear of the stall. On the table beside the broom closet, she spied a bag of brown alligator pellets—next to a red Hermès scarf and a scraggly black beard.

She turned back toward the main room, her eyes widening with realization.

"What's under the tarp?" she asked warily as her nose began to tingle with a coming sneeze.

Gray eyes glittering, Mr. Wang nodded at the floor. "See for yourself," he replied.

As the niece bent toward the tarp, her sinuses swelled and her eyes began to water. She put her hand over her mouth to try to stifle the coming sneeze.

"Ach-oo!"

She jumped back as the tarp started to wiggle from the creature hidden underneath.

Chuckling, Sam lifted the edge of the heavy fabric, revealing a scaly white foot that was missing its right pinky digit. Even in the flower stall's dim light, the woman recognized the leathery texture of the albino alligator's skin.

Cautiously, she stepped toward the tarp. "Surely, that's not . . ."

With a flourish, Sam flipped off the rest of the cover. After a brief moment of panic, the niece sighed with rueful relief. She couldn't believe she'd been duped.

Though incredibly lifelike, the alligator was in actuality a robot whose metal frame had been encased in a spongy synthetic material.

Wang stroked his long spindly beard; then his thin voice rasped hoarsely, "I believe you've already met our friend Clive."

SHOW ME HOW this thing works," the niece said after a close inspection of the robot.

"It's quite simple really," Sam replied. He walked over to the table in the back room and returned with the bag of fish pellets.

"There's a motion sensor in Clive's head. He's been programmed to follow the pellets—it's just like how the scientists at the Academy lead around the real alligator."

"The robotic version is a bit safer for the general public," Wang added with a wry grin.

"So *this* is the alligator that was in my basement," the niece said as she watched the demonstration.

Sam tossed the pellet through the air in front of the robot. Its internal motor made a barely perceptible hum as the lizardlike legs powered forward.

"Then . . . where's Clive?" the woman demanded.

Mr. Wang arched his thin eyebrows and nodded toward the robot.

"No," the niece said, trying to keep a straight face as Sam tossed another pellet. "I mean the real one."

The robot's mouth opened wide, catching the brown lump.

Chomp.

Chapter 51
A SECRET PROJECT

AS NIGHT FELL across a shuttered San Francisco, the wind retreated into the Pacific, releasing a damp fog that squeezed its thickening mass through the Golden Gate and slowly oozed out

287

onto the bay. Seeping inland, the pillowing invader swept across the city's steep hills, erasing huge tracts of land with a single swallowing gulp.

Gliding through the disappearing streets, the smooth shadow of a pearl-colored Bentley motored toward the Civic Center's open plaza of government buildings. The driver parked his stylish ride in an underground parking garage, killed the purring engine, and stepped from the front seat.

The Previous Mayor stood beside the car, shaking out the tailored folds of his black trench coat. He straightened the gray felt bowler perched on his balding head and tugged at the cuffs of his hand-sewn leather gloves. Then he reached into the passenger seat and picked up a small paper bag.

Carrying his package, he rode an elevator to the surface and strolled off into the darkening mist.

AFTER A SHORT walk, the PM strode briskly up City Hall's stone steps. With a confident tap on the gilded glass doorway and a wave to the security guards manning the front entrance, he held up his bag, which was filled with hot donuts, fresh from a local bakery.

The door was quickly buzzed open by the chubby night-shift guard seated behind the security desk.

"Evening, Mayor," the guard said, hungrily reaching for the bag as the PM slid it across the counter.

A SINGLE LIGHT burned at the end of a darkened corridor in the far corner of City Hall's basement. The vacant area was quiet and still, save for the occasional belching burps from the building's boiler, which had recently been cranked up to its highest setting.

Spider Jones bent studiously over his desk, seemingly unbothered by the solitude or isolation.

Teetering piles of papers, news clippings, and folders were stacked on either side of his workspace. An additional heap towered up from the floor beside his chair. Almost all of the papers bore sticky flags and Post-it notes, but it was the contents of the yellowed file laid open on the desk that held Spider's full attention.

After months of research, he had finally closed in on his prize. The secret he had only speculated he might find was now sitting before him, plainly written on the file's faded sheets.

The only question that remained, he pondered, was what he would do with this unearthed information.

As Spider contemplated his discovery, a dark figure crept down the narrow hallway toward his desk. The young staffer failed to notice the approaching intruder; the gurgling boiler masked the man's footsteps.

The shadow paused, tilting his head as he tried to discern the contents of the file spread open on the staffer's desk. The man's hand reached up to the curved brim of his bowler and then thoughtfully drifted down to his neatly trimmed mustache.

Earlier that day, the Previous Mayor had confirmed his suspicions about the young man's research. Whatever project Spider had been working on all these late nights down in the basement, it wasn't one officially sanctioned by the Current Mayor. The PM's years of practical experience told him there was something odd going on here.

After a long moment staring at the papers on the desk, the PM cleared his throat, announcing his presence.

"Spider, I thought I might find you here."

SPIDER LOOKED UP from the file, noticeably startled.

"Mayor," he said, quickly slapping the folder shut. "Good to see you."

"What's got you working so late?" the PM asked casually, trying to hide his keen interest.

"Oh, it's just a little project I'm working on for the Mayor," Spider replied, patting his hand on the closed file. It was a casual gesture, but, the PM noticed, one that blocked the writing on the outside label.

Stroking his chin, the PM ambled over to the red-painted bike propped up against the edge of the cubicle, watching out of the corner of his eye as Spider shoved the file beneath a stack of papers.

The PM tapped the shiny helmet hanging from the handlebars.

"That's my mom's idea," Spider offered with an embarrassed grin. "She's always nagging me about wearing it."

The PM smiled knowingly. He'd once had a protective mother, too. He shifted his gaze back to the young staffer.

"How did you get on with the Mayor's Life Coach?" the PM asked casually.

"It's as you suspected," Spider replied, eager to change the subject. He pulled the notepad from his pants pocket and began flipping through the pages. "The Current Mayor's definitely throwing his support behind Mr. Carmichael." He looked earnestly up at the PM. "I'd stake my life on it."

"There's no need to go that far," the PM replied with a laugh. He placed a gloved hand on the staffer's shoulder. "We should meet for dinner tomorrow night after the vote."

He gave Spider a stern smile and nodded at the pile of papers where the young man had hidden the file. "Then you can tell me about your other little project."

"All right, sir," Spider replied sheepishly. He had known that eventually he would have to share his findings with the elder statesman. The implications were too politically sensitive for him to handle on his own.

With an impish grin, Spider added firmly, "But this time, *I'm* picking the restaurant."

Chapter 52
INTO THE SWAMP

OSCAR'S NIECE STOOD in the Green Vase showroom, watching the evening fog drift across Jackson Square as she waited for her ride to arrive.

Sam was returning to the Academy that night for a second unauthorized visit—to take care of some "unfinished frog business," as he put it—and he had agreed to bring her along with him so that she could search the Swamp Exhibit for whatever Steinhart treasure or valuable memorabilia might be hidden there.

The woman nervously tapped her fingers against the cashier counter as she thought about the task that lay ahead. In the hours since she'd left the flower shop and started preparing for her upcoming trip, the realization that she might have to explore the area in the bottom of the tank's exhibit had begun to sink in.

"Water," she muttered anxiously. "Why did it have to be water?"

Twice in the past year and a half, she had been exposed to a rare spider-venom toxin that her uncle had unearthed during his Gold Rush research. The toxin caused intense delusions of drowning, eventually followed, if the antidote was not rapidly administered, by paralysis.

The experiences had left the niece with a strong aversion to any body of water. Swimming in an unoccupied alligator tank was not an activity for which she would have otherwise volunteered.

She glanced down at the tote bag near her feet, where she'd stuffed a pair of goggles, a towel, and her flashlight. It was a rudimentary collection of tools, but there was no piece of equipment that could have quashed the tension building in her stomach. She was feeling rather ill-equipped for this challenge.

AS THE BURLY Frog Whisperer drove up in the white cargo van, Isabella circled the tote bag with one last certifying sniff. She had given her person as much help as was felinely possible. It was up to the woman to put together the last pieces of the puzzle on her own.

Isabella looked up and waved an instructive paw

in the air. With a warbling *"Mraw-wow,"* she issued her last piece of advice.

"I'll try to remember that," the woman replied as she swung the tote up to her shoulder and pulled open the door.

Rupert gazed hopefully out the window as the woman circled the van and climbed into its front passenger seat.

Don't forget to bring back some chicken, he thought as he propped his front feet against the glass.

THE NIECE HAD little time to worry about the potential perils of the Swamp Exhibit during the drive through the city to Golden Gate Park. Drowning was soon the least of her safety concerns.

Sam was a well-intentioned but easily distracted driver. Eager to get to the Academy to check on his frog conspirators, his attention was now dangerously diverted.

"My guys played their part perfectly," Sam said as he drove down Jackson Street to the first corner past the Green Vase. He glanced over at his passenger.

"I slipped a little something in their water before they got to the Academy," he explained as he motored through the stop sign without the slightest decrease in speed. "That's what turned their skin a different color."

"Sam," the woman sputtered, clenching the armrest. "Did you see that . . ."

"Poor Dr. Kline was totally fooled," Sam continued, grinning at the success of his covert operation.

The van squealed through two more heart-stopping turns.

"Uh, Sam," the niece tried again as they approached the busy thoroughfare of Columbus Avenue.

"Don't get me wrong—I like Dr. Kline," Sam added, oblivious to the looming cross traffic. "She's a nice lady, all right."

The woman paled as the van careened into the wide intersection, drawing the ire of multiple car horns.

"She just doesn't know much about frogs."

Gulping, the niece nodded at a bobblehead figure of the Current Mayor stuck onto the van's dashboard.

"Does Monty know you've been borrowing his vehicle?"

Sam winked mischievously.

"He thinks it's parked in the alley behind the chicken restaurant."

Gripping the handle above her window, the woman double-checked her seat belt.

"He really should be more careful about where he leaves his keys."

AFTER SEVERAL NEAR misses that the niece wasn't sure how the van managed to escape unscathed, she and Sam finally arrived at Golden Gate Park's east entrance. With few traffic impediments to avoid within the park's boundaries, Sam guided the van without incident down a curving road and parked near a forested area a couple hundred yards behind the Academy of Sciences complex.

A streetlamp wrapped in fog dripped a small puddle of light onto the pavement. Otherwise, the area was completely dark.

Grabbing her tote, the woman climbed gratefully out of the front passenger seat. She met Sam at the van's rear doors and waited as he leaned into the cargo area.

He pulled out a ventilated glass carrier with a handle on its lid.

"I'll be laying low for a while after tonight's caper," he said, gesturing with the carrier as he locked the van. His tone and expression suggested he was looking forward to his banishment.

"Where will you go?" the niece asked as they turned and walked through the trees toward the Academy's rear entrance.

"Oh, someplace deep in the woods," Sam replied vaguely. He pointed at the green logo sewn onto his vest. "Someplace good for frogs."

A FEW MINUTES later, Sam clomped up to the Academy's back door and removed a set of keys from a pocket in his vest.

"What about the guards?" the woman whispered as he held the set up to a security light mounted over the door, selected a key, and fed it into the lock.

"We've got about twenty minutes until the security team passes back this way," Sam replied, glancing at his watch.

He pulled open the door and stealthily stepped inside. Gripping her flashlight, the niece slipped through after him.

Sam paused before heading for the stairwell entrance marked "Steinhart Aquarium." Bending toward her ear, he whispered, "I'll meet up with you in a few."

He nodded toward the Swamp Exhibit. "Good luck."

THE NIECE SET her flashlight to its dimmest setting and took a quick glance around the Swamp Exhibit's darkened perimeter, circling the beam of her flashlight over the artificial banyan tree, the moss dangling from its branches, and then down to the brass seahorse balcony.

The seahorses had been depicted in sharp detail on the picture embedded in the brass lamp's ceramic shade. Maybe, she thought hopefully, she could avoid a dip in the tank after all.

The woman bent to her knees and began working her way around the exhibit's upper rim, testing each brass seahorse, searching for some slit or crack in the casting. They were remarkably well crafted, and each one was stamped with the date of the Steinhart's original opening: 1923. But she reached the end of the circuit without finding anything of note.

The seahorses, the niece had to concede, were far too exposed to the visiting public to contain whatever Steinhart treasure had been hidden in the Swamp. Besides, there would have been no need for her uncle and his team to remove Clive from the exhibit if the treasure were that easy to access.

"If it's not up here," she mused, pushing her hair back from her eyes, "it has to be . . ."

She aimed the flashlight's beam down into the tank. The turtles' dark, boulderlike shadows moved through the water, swimming slow circles around the heated rock. Several large catfish snaked along the bottom.

She gulped, hesitating. Then she closed her eyes and took in a deep breath.

If the treasure was hidden down inside the Swamp Exhibit, there was only one way to find out.

She whipped off her eyeglasses, quickly exchanging them for a pair of goggles from her tote bag.

She had to move fast. She was running out of time.

THE NIECE WRAPPED her hands around the balcony's top railing and swung a leg over the bar. As she teetered back and forth, trying to regain her balance, she glanced down at the tank. It suddenly seemed like a much farther drop than she had envisioned while studying the image on the lamp.

"Starting to wish I'd thought to ask Sam how he got in there to remove Clive," she muttered. Pursing her lips, she slid her second leg over the railing. It was too late now for regrets.

Carefully, she rotated her body so that she faced the balcony. Then she slowly dropped her feet down until they met the tank's upper wall. Easing herself off the top railing, she shifted her hands to the brass seahorse brackets.

After swinging from this halfway point for a long moment, she dropped her grip a little farther, adjusting her hold so that she was hanging from the balcony's bottom railing. The row of decorative tile ringing the tank's upper rim ran directly in front of her face; her legs dangled about ten feet above the water.

Just as she was about to release the bar, she tilted her head to make one last check of the area directly beneath.

"Oh, come on, buddy," she moaned as a turtle meandered into her drop zone.

Despite the niece's urgent hissing sounds, the turtle took his time wading toward his next destination.

"Okay," she said when at last the space below

had cleared. She took in a deep breath. "This is it."

She kicked back from the wall and fell into the tank.

"HERE YOU GO, little fellas," Sam cooed as he leaned through the rear opening of the terrarium holding the special-exhibit frogs from South America. Cupping his hands, he gently lifted the pale-looking trio into the ventilated glass carrier.

"You're going to love the place where I'm taking you next," he said as replaced the exhibit's back cover. "Best frog accommodations *ever,*" he assured the carrier's occupants. "I promise."

After tiptoeing down the long corridor behind the exhibits, Sam peeked out the black-painted doorway at its end. Hunched down, he crept into the aquarium's main foyer. He was about to head for the stairwell leading up to the Academy's main floor when he heard a loud splash.

He turned toward the glass-ceilinged tunnel and squinted through to the opposite end.

In the lower-level view window for the Swamp Exhibit, he spied Oscar's niece, her hands and feet treading through the water, her long hair swirling around her face—accompanied by a large turtle, who was curiously inspecting the tank's new specimen.

Chapter 53
THE OBSERVERS

A GROUP OF four gathered in the trees near the Academy of Sciences' rear entrance, watching the goings-on at the Swamp Exhibit through the building's back wall of windows. All eyes focused on the building's interior as, after a moment's hesitation, the niece began crawling around the seahorse balcony on her hands and knees.

At one end of the line, Mr. Wang sat in his wheelchair, thoughtfully stroking his chin. Dilla stood behind him, nervously gripping the chair's handles.

When the woman slung her legs over the balcony's top railing and began easing herself down toward the tank, Dilla pulled off her flowered hat and used it to cover her face.

"Oh, I'm afraid to watch," she said with a shudder.

Beside her, Harold Wombler let out a disapproving snort as the niece's body dropped from the balcony and splashed into the water. "Why didn't she just use the service door at the bottom of the tank?"

The fourth member of the group silently rubbed the scruff of his chin.

"I think we're done here," James Lick said, a smile creasing his worn face as he turned and walked toward the road, pleased at the evening's result.

Chapter 54
THE MARCHING HORSES

THE NIECE PLUNGED into the water, sinking several feet into the tank. The Swamp Exhibit was far deeper than she had expected, and her feet floundered, searching for the bottom.

Trying not to panic, she pushed her body upward. Unlike her previous drowning delusions with the spider toxin, this time the water did little to resist her efforts. With a great deal of relief, her head broke the surface, and she gasped in a deep breath of the swamp's moist, fishy-smelling air.

Treading water, the woman tilted her goggles away from her face to clear their interior compartments. Then she slowly spun herself in a circle, studying her surroundings.

"See now this isn't so bad . . ." she assured herself—before stifling a scream as a turtle bumped his head against her knees.

PUSHING HERSELF AWAY from the turtle, the niece tried to think back to the image on the lamp and the glowing white alligator lying on its rock.

But then she stopped and reconsidered.

Was the glow from the alligator or the rock underneath?

Quickly, she paddled toward the center of the tank. Taking in another deep breath, she ducked her head beneath the water and scanned the heated rock's lower support structure. Other than a half-eaten post, she didn't notice anything out of the ordinary.

Resurfacing, the woman hoisted herself up onto the rock. She paused for a moment, appreciating the radiant heat, as she pulled off the goggles and wrung some of the water from her shirt. Then, she bent to inspect the surface.

At first glance, the rock appeared to be solid, but as she felt her hands around the base, she realized there was a small cache located just beneath. She leaned over the edge, trying to see into the hole, but darkness and water blocked her view.

"There's something in here," the niece said, straining to reach her arm into the space.

The service door at the far edge of the tank grated open, and Sam leaned out into the Swamp Exhibit.

"Psst. Are you about done?" he whispered.

Before she could reply, a piercing siren blasted through the air.

"Time to go," he yelled over the noise. He waved his hand, motioning for her to swim toward the service door.

The woman looked back at the rock. Grimacing, she thrust her hand through the water and into the crevice. Her fingers wrapped around a small cloth-wrapped package, and with a slight tug, she yanked it out.

There wasn't time to inspect the package. She hopped back into the tank, crossed to the service door, and followed Sam through an interior stairwell to the first floor.

FORTY-FIVE SECONDS LATER, the niece scooped up her flashlight and tote bag from the floor beside the seahorse balcony. Leaving a trail of wet footsteps, she chased after Sam, who had tucked the glass carrier under his arm like a football as he chugged out the Academy's rear door.

The woman looked over her shoulder at the Swamp Exhibit as she sprinted away.

A cloud shifted in the sky above the exhibit's translucent ceiling, sending a dim glow down onto the artificial banyan tree with its clinging strings of moss. The brass seahorses glinted in the dim moonlight as they marched across the balcony.

But as the niece squinted at the water below, it seemed to her that the flat surface of the heated rock had lost a little bit of its glow.

Chapter 55

THE STEINHART REWARD

ABOUT A HALF hour later, the niece placed the soggy package from the Swamp Exhibit on the table in the kitchen above the Green Vase showroom. The woman stood on the kitchen's tile floor, a damp towel wrapped over her wet clothes, while Rupert and Isabella occupied the chairs on either side of her.

All three were intensely focused on the package—Isabella and her person wondering what treasure might be hidden inside, Rupert holding out hope for a chicken-related reveal.

USING A PAIR of scissors, the niece carefully began cutting off the package's outer layer. The fishy-smelling fabric soon fell away from a small plastic box.

The niece bent over the container's modern design, perplexed. Given its pristine condition, it couldn't have been submerged in the water for very long, perhaps no more than a few days. The box's plastic construction certainly wasn't anywhere close to an early 1900s-era vintage.

Both cats leaned over the table as the woman wedged open the box and lifted out a sealed plastic bag.

"Oh, Issy." The niece sighed. "I think we've been had."

"*Mrao,*" Isabella concurred.

Rupert, however, began sniffing energetically at the bag's contents. It was filled with a scent he had tracked down before—in the mattress springs beneath the bed, in the crevice behind the clothes dryer, and, most recently, in a tissue box on the living room end table.

The niece unzipped the bag and pulled out a wad of cash. Each bill contained a heavy fried-chicken scent.

It was a reward from her uncle for following his clues, more than enough to pay the bills for the next several months, but an indication, in her mind at least, that he didn't yet trust her with one of his valuable antique treasures.

As Rupert hopped up on the table and began rooting through the money, the niece unfolded a single sheet of paper that had been included with the pile.

Her uncle's familiar handwriting scrawled out a location and the following message: "Make sure Clive gets home safely."

Chapter 56
A STRANGE DUCK

THURSDAY MORNING, SAN FRANCISCO awoke drenched in fog, its once bright sun now demoted to a translucent disc in an otherwise empty sky.

The city shouldered up and soldiered on, slogging through the wet commute. The sluggish pulse of traffic coursed along the main thoroughfares, drawing influx from the outlying neighborhoods.

The inbound rush across the Golden Gate split at the foot of the bridge, with one portion of the transit curving along the shoreline, the other half slicing through the Presidio and passing by the northern edge of Mountain Lake.

Despite close proximity to all this hustle, the lake existed in a quiet, isolated bubble, nestled beneath the hill of the Presidio's challenging golf course.

A feathery breeze creaked through the trees surrounding the water, bending the reeds that grew up along the lake's southeast corner. The occasional muttered curse floated down through the mist from the golfers on the hillside above. Every so often, a small child shrieked on the jungle gym near the parking lot. Otherwise, there was little to disturb the lake's inhabitants.

It was a swampy, secluded area, the perfect

hideaway for an albino alligator seeking a little R & R from his duties as the Academy of Sciences' most prominent public ambassador.

A LITTLE-USED PATH circled the lower half of the lake, leading to a worn wooden bench positioned in front of an opening in the reeds. The few pedestrians that routinely traveled the path were typically either running or riding a bike, headed toward the Presidio's extensive trail system, and didn't stop long enough to search the water for the telltale ripple of an alligator's snout. Consequently, Clive's presence in the lake had gone unnoticed since his late-night arrival a few days earlier.

On that particular Thursday morning, however, a slow-moving woman in a jogging suit and sneakers rounded the south corner of the lake. She was perhaps not as energetic as most, her pace hampered by her own physical limitations as well as the small lapdog attached to the leash she held in her right hand.

"Now, now, Fluffy," the woman said sternly as the dog began yapping furiously at the water. "You know you're not allowed to chase the ducks."

The woman stopped near the bench and looked out across the water.

"That's strange," she thought. "I don't *see* any ducks out there in the lake."

She glanced down at her dog, who was emphatically pulling against his leash, and then returned her gaze to the water, where a trail of bubbles had begun moving toward the shoreline.

Something was swimming beneath the surface . . . something large and white . . .

"Fluffy," the woman screamed, yanking the dog's leash. She scooped up her pet just as a large jagged mouth emerged from the water.

Chomp.

A HOBO LYING in the grass about fifty yards from the bench raised himself up on his elbow and whispered into a receiver tucked into his tattered sleeve.

"Wang, this is Lick," he said, watching the woman fleeing toward the gravel parking lot in a far more expeditious manner than she had left it minutes earlier.

"It's time for another distraction."

Chapter 57
AN ANONYMOUS TIP

HOXTON FIN STRODE briskly up Market Street, heading toward City Hall, where the board of supervisors' meeting was about to get under way.

The selection of San Francisco's interim mayor was a serious matter, one in which he would ordinarily have been deeply vested, particularly since he still had no idea who the board would eventually choose. He had dismissed the Previous Mayor's suggestion of Montgomery Carmichael as pure lunacy, and yet, no other sources had been able to provide a credible alternative.

Despite all this, he couldn't help himself. His thoughts were fixated on the missing alligator.

"How does this guy walk around town with an alligator—a *white* alligator no less—without anyone catching him?" he muttered under his breath.

A pulsing *beep* buzzed in his shirt pocket.

Hox whipped out his cell phone and read the display. After a quick glance at the incoming number, he let out a groan and sent a pleading look up at the sky.

He was sorely tempted to let the call ring through to his voice mail, but after a few more persistent beeps, he reluctantly pushed the phone's talk button.

"This is Hox."

THE PREVIOUS MAYOR sat at a lunch table in a restaurant located at the far end of Fisherman's Wharf. A window near his seat looked out across the foggy bay. A waiter stood a discreet ten feet away, closely monitoring the PM's dining progress.

The PM wiped the corners of his mouth with his

napkin as the reporter's deep voice growled through his wireless earpiece.

"Hoxton, how are you?" the PM asked pleasantly, ignoring the bitter tone of the man on the other end of the line.

"What's up, Mayor?" Hox replied tersely. "I'm on my way to City Hall."

"I've just finished an amazing appetizer at a place here on the Wharf," the PM said smoothly. "It was a phenomenal concoction of raw fish, a refreshing ceviche. The citrus in the marinade had a nice tang to it. The perfect palate cleanser . . ."

"I haven't got all day," the reporter cut in harshly. "You didn't call me to talk about seafood."

The PM paused for a moment, intentionally drawing out the silence, letting his listener's impatience build.

"Seafood . . . No, no, not exactly . . . As a matter of fact, I had in mind a discussion about a freshwater creature. I believe certain members of the species can tolerate a moderate amount of salt, but they're definitely not your traditional ocean inhabitants."

The PM stopped, letting a sly smile break across his face. He could hear Hox grinding his teeth in frustration.

After a sip from a glass of ice water and an unnecessary napkin dab at his mouth, the PM continued. "I thought you might be interested in a little anonymous tip."

Hox breathed heavily into the phone. "I'm listening."

"On my way to the restaurant—did I mention I have a lovely table? There's a delightful view of Alcatraz. You can barely see it poking through the fog . . ."

"I'm hanging up, Mayor."

"As I was saying," the PM continued breezily. "On my way to the restaurant, I passed the most intriguing sight on the pier. An unpigmented swamp denizen, a bit scaly in texture . . . with a rather fearsome-looking mouth."

The curt response came back immediately.

"I'll be right there."

Chapter 58

THE LAST CHICKEN

THE NIECE WALKED up Columbus Avenue toward Lick's Homestyle Chicken, a determined expression on her face.

She had stayed up late the previous evening, sitting at the kitchen table, staring at the plastic box from the Swamp Exhibit and the pile of money she'd rescued from Rupert's rooting. She'd tossed and turned most of the night, thinking about the package. After she finally fell asleep, it had been the first thing on her mind when she awoke that morning.

"Enough is enough," she'd decided over breakfast.

It wasn't that she didn't need the money—she was very nearly broke. But she was tired of being led around by her uncle's games.

"Make sure Clive gets home safely?" she said, repeating the message she'd found in the box. "As if I'm supposed to go tromping around Mountain Lake looking for him."

She stuffed the money into the box. "I'm done with this alligator," she announced, putting the box into her tote bag. "I'm giving the money back."

THE NIECE COULD tell something had changed a few blocks before she reached the empty shell that had once been James Lick's Homestyle Chicken. The faded green awning that had stretched across the storefront was gone, and the windows were even dustier than before. It was now almost impossible to see inside.

The front door swung open at her touch.

"Harold?" she called out as she stepped cautiously inside, but she immediately sensed that she would receive no response.

The room was empty. The portrait of the original Lick had been stripped from the wall. The tables and chairs in the dining area had all been removed.

Nothing remained but a stack of discarded green paper flyers sitting on the cashier counter. She slipped the pile into her coat pocket on her way to the kitchen.

The back of the restaurant was nearly pitch-black. Reaching into her tote, she pulled out her flashlight. Even with the help of its wide beam, she still tripped on the steps leading to the second floor.

She reached the open upstairs room to find it similarly cleaned out. The terrarium and its amphibian occupants had disappeared. Missing, too, were the mouse cage and its many spinning wheels.

Trying to stifle the deflated feeling in her stomach, the niece returned to the first floor and wandered into the kitchen.

The pots and pans had vanished, along with the other cooking implements. The woman peeked briefly inside the walk-in freezer, whose heavy metal door was propped open with a small wooden wedge. The storage room was still slightly cold, but the racks that had been filled with all of those white butcher paper–wrapped packages were now completely empty.

Slowly, the niece approached Harold's workstation. His lonely stool was all that remained. Sitting on its seat, she found the restaurant's last green paper sack.

The bottom of the sack was warm to her touch. She unfolded the top of the bag and looked inside to find two green paper boxes.

On the top of each box, her uncle's scrawled handwriting had printed the name of the cat for whom the contents were intended.

Chapter 59
A DISCORDANT GROUP

THE PRESIDENT OF the Board of Supervisors glanced up from his notes and looked woefully out over the cavernous meeting chamber. From his seat in the middle of the wide rostrum at the center of the chamber's sunken stage, Jim Hernandez had a view of the cordoned-off supervisors' area and the expansive audience gallery beyond.

The scene was enough to dampen even his habitually cheerful disposition.

As ornately decorated as the rest of the building, a light-colored wood paneling of rare Manchurian oak covered almost every surface of the room. Two long desks positioned perpendicular to the president's rostrum provided seating for the rest of the supervisors. Each of his ten colleagues sat next to a powered-up laptop. Cell phones accompanied each supervisor, their ringers set to silent, their screens angled to provide constant text updates.

The enormous room took up a substantial portion of the west wing of City Hall's second floor, and the gallery had seating capacity for several hundred audience members. Today, it was filled to capacity.

• • •

SO FAR, THE meeting had gone remarkably well, considering. There had been a few protesting amendments—which Hernandez had adroitly handled—and quite a bit of individual posturing, but the process for selecting the next mayor was at last moving forward. That was all he could have asked for.

However, there was one more item yet to be completed before they moved on to nominations.

Reluctantly, the president shifted his gaze past the carved wooden balustrade that separated the supervisors' desk area and up toward the stadium-style public seating. As he surveyed the audience, his inner dread deepened.

Hernandez pushed back the floppy bangs from his forehead and pounded his gavel against the rostrum.

"We'll now begin the public-comment period. I would like to remind all of the speakers that they are limited to just two minutes at the mike." He cleared his throat for emphasis. "*Two* minutes."

THE FIRST GENTLEMAN approached the lectern set up at the front of the gallery area, and Hernandez said a silent prayer of appreciation for the lectern's thick wooden construction. It was clear, even from his vantage point fifty yards away, that the man was completely nude.

"I would like the board to consider my application to be San Francisco's next mayor," the

316

man began. "If selected, I would bring honesty and transparency to City Hall."

Hernandez put his hands over his eyes as the man stepped to the side of the lectern and swung his arms wide.

"What you see is what you get."

Chapter 60
BUSKER CLIVE

HOXTON FIN STOOD beside a wooden sun-bleached pier at Fisherman's Wharf, trying to ignore the raucous, deep-throated whelping of the sea lions clustered on the floating platforms behind him.

A number of gawkers had gathered on the pier, curiously watching the arriving news vans. It was a mixed crowd, the locals being easily distinguishable from the out-of-towners. Most of San Francisco's permanent residents were well acclimated to the city's regular foggy fifty degrees; they wore light jackets and the occasional scarf. Tourists, on the other hand, huddled in recently purchased sweatshirts, many bearing some version of the city's logo or initials.

Word of Clive's most recent appearance had circulated quickly. More and more people pushed against the nearby barrier, craning to see the reporters who were filming on the pier.

Hox huffed out a resentful grunt. He wasn't the only one who had been tipped off by the Previous Mayor.

HOX TURNED TOWARD his producer, who had arrived with the rest of the crew not long after Hox jumped out of his taxi. The news team had failed to get a shot of the elusive alligator, but the tourists who had been on the pier at the time of his arrival had provided plenty of cell-phone footage. The photos were already being uploaded to the station's main studios.

Constance Grynche nodded her approval, indicating they were ready to begin. Hox swatted off the stylist, who had climbed onto his ever-present stool to fiddle with the reporter's hair; then he squared his shoulders toward the camera.

Trying not to think about the absurdity of the report he was about to give, Hox brought a portable microphone to his mouth.

"This is Hoxton Fin reporting from Fisherman's Wharf."

AS HOX BEGAN filming his segment, one of the many buskers who performed for the tourists at the Wharf breached the crowd barriers and crept up behind the reporter, trying to squeeze into the camera's shot. Like many of the Wharf's street artists, the man was dressed in a shiny aluminum suit, hat, and shoes; every inch of exposed skin, including that on his face and hands, was covered in silver paint.

"Less than thirty minutes ago," Hox intoned, unaware of the busker's antics, "witnesses here at the Wharf reported yet another sighting of the missing albino alligator from the California Academy of Sciences."

As the busker assumed more and more comical poses behind the reporter's back, the cameraman glanced questioningly at the producer, but she merely nodded serenely, signaling him to continue filming.

"Although it remains unclear how Clive is being transported around the city, he appears to be on a sightseeing tour, of sorts. This is his third appearance in a highly trafficked area."

A second silver-painted busker joined the first, lifting his friend a few feet into the air so that the man could make swooping arm movements on either side of the spike in Hox's hair.

"I believe we have a picture of the latest sighting to show you on our screen," Hox continued, pausing for the image to be spliced into the feed.

The cameraman blinked back tears as the busker mimed disapproval of Hox's hairstyle, removed his own silver-painted hat, and gently set it on the reporter's head.

Grimacing, Hox wrapped up his spiel.

"As you can see, both Clive and the man accompanying him were wearing tinfoil accessories."

Chapter 61
THE ALLIGATOR LINE

THE NIECE TURNED the corner onto Jackson Street, discouraged and depleted. Her uncle had once more disappeared without warning, leaving her to muddle through on her own. Her tote bag hung heavily from her shoulder, the packet of money inside it weighing down her thoughts.

"Make sure Clive gets home." She muttered her uncle's last message as she approached the Green Vase's front door. "How am I supposed to do that?"

Then she glanced down at the green paper sack from the fried-chicken restaurant. She suspected her uncle already had a plan in place to wrap up that detail. Likely, it wouldn't be long before she found out what predetermined role she had been assigned. With a frustrated sigh, she slid her key into the front door's lock and turned the tulip-embossed handle.

AS SOON AS the niece stepped inside the Green Vase, she sensed that something was out of place.

Rupert was front and center, of course, eagerly bouncing up and down, his wobbly blue eyes glued to the paper sack she held in her hand.

Isabella, however, was putting out a clear warning. The cat trotted urgently from behind one of the back bookcases, vigorously chirping with her voice as her tail swung stiffly through the air.

The niece quickly scanned the showroom. The display cases appeared to be undisturbed, and the hatch to the basement, she noted with relief, was firmly shut.

Eyes narrowing, she focused on the rear of the store, where Isabella continued to circle.

"You can come out, Monty."

As her skinny neighbor stepped from behind the bookcase, the woman glanced toward the ceiling. The frozen hunk of chicken was in the freezer section of the upstairs refrigerator—too far away to be of use on this occasion.

"Tattletale," Monty hissed at Isabella. She arched her back, the hair along her back bristling in response.

"What are you doing in here?" the niece demanded.

Monty dropped down onto the leather dentist recliner and kicked back the lever. He crossed his bony legs one over the other.

"I need your help," he said with a lazy yawn.

The niece didn't hesitate in her response. "No."

"Aht, aht, aht," he replied, wagging his finger in the air. His thin mouth stretched into a jubilant smile. Then he meted out the sentences he knew would have the desired effect.

"I've got a line on the alligator. I need you to help me return him to his rightful home."

Chapter 62
THE NOMINATIONS

THE BOARD OF supervisors' meeting was well under way by the time Hoxton Fin wrapped up his report from Fisherman's Wharf and hopped a cab to City Hall. He slipped through the back doors of the meeting chambers and found an open seat next to an individual dressed in a chicken costume.

"What'd I miss?" he whispered, leaning toward his neighbor's feather-covered shoulder.

The clucking response was uninformative, but Hox soon pieced together what had happened during the early proceedings. After a lengthy public-comment period, Jim Hernandez had opened the floor to nominations. Motions supporting Hernandez for mayor had already been defeated three times by five-to-six vote counts. They were now moving on to alternative candidates.

Hox yawned as a motion was raised to nominate the Previous Mayor. He could tell from the supervisors' faces that this, too, would fail. It might be another couple of hours before the board moved to a meaningful vote.

A scribe from a competing paper waved at Hox from a seat ten feet away, pointed at his head, and gave Hox a mocking thumbs-up. Hox grumbled a reply, halfheartedly accompanied by a rude gesture in rebuke.

He would never admit it to Humphrey, but despite all the negative feedback—or perhaps because of it—the new hairstyle was starting to grow on him.

JIM HERNANDEZ SIGHED and tabulated the results of the most recent motion. The Hail Mary pass to nominate the Previous Mayor had been doomed before the voting on the motion even began.

He leaned into his microphone and announced wearily, "By a count of four to seven, the motion fails."

A cloud of speculating whispers rose from the audience as the supervisors looked at their laptops, cell-phone texts, and, finally, across the table at one another, each one sizing up their next move.

Hernandez surveyed the scene. All of the board members, himself included, were still holding out hope for his or her own nomination. He took a sip from a stale cup of coffee, his third of the meeting. It was going to be a long night.

There was a stirring on the left row of supervisors' desks. Hernandez cleared his throat as one of the supervisors raised her hand.

"Do we have a nomination?"

The woman nodded affirmatively.

"The floor recognizes the Supervisor from Twin Peaks."

"Thank you, Supervisor Hernandez. I would like to nominate . . ."

A ripple of murmurs swept through the audience, momentarily distracting the speaker. She glanced down at her cell phone as it vibrated on her desk and gasped with surprise.

"Clive!"

Hernandez jerked forward toward his mike. "Excuse me?"

The supervisor smiled apologetically.

"I'm sorry, sir. There's been another sighting."

HOX'S EYELIDS HAD begun to droop as he fought off the urge to doze off into a nap. The upper seating area had grown uncomfortably warm, particularly next to the feathered chicken costume.

But his head snapped to attention at the exclamation from the floor of the chambers. As he shifted his weight forward, a woman on the row ahead of him held up her cell phone. Reaching over the back of the woman's seat, Hox grabbed the phone from her hand and turned its display so that he could see the image she had just uploaded.

"What in the . . ." the person in the chicken costume sputtered at the picture.

Instantly awake, Hox tossed the phone back to its owner and scooped up his backpack. The rest of the reporters were still gathering their gear when the heavy wooden doors to the supervisors' chambers swung shut behind him.

Chapter 63
COMMUTER CLIVE

A CAVERNOUS REDBRICK building at the corner of Washington and Mason housed the massive iron gears that powered San Francisco's cable car lines. The enormous round rims took up most of the building's basement, where they spun, day in and day out, with ceaseless humming unity.

From a small museum on the powerhouse's second floor, the public could look down on this churning feat of engineering. For those wanting to take a more hands-on approach, several refurbished cable cars were also on display.

The city was proud of its long history with the hill-climbing carts. Several groups were actively dedicated to the preservation of this somewhat antiquated mode of transportation. A number of local craftsmen worked to rehab the cars that had been decommissioned over the years.

It was one of these that creaked out of a storage barn next to the powerhouse and teetered around a sharp corner headed toward the financial district.

THE BRAKEMAN AT the helm of the cable car was an elderly Asian fellow. Despite his crippled limbs, Mr. Wang proved to be surprisingly nimble at maneuvering the heavy metal hooking mechanism along the car's center shaft. He grinned beneath a red cap with a wide front brim, ringing a brass bell mounted to the brakeman's station as the old cart lumbered up a steep incline.

Wang slowed the cable car at a hilltop intersection, braking for traffic to clear. Then he steered the rig down California's dramatic slope. As the car made the turn, several drivers stopped to stare at the two passengers seated on the outer left bench.

Sam Eckles wrapped one hand around a safety pole to keep from falling out onto the pavement; with the other, he gently patted the neck of the large albino alligator sprawled across his lap.

Wearing his own red cap, Clive grinned out at a foggy San Francisco.

ABOUT A HUNDRED yards behind the cable car, a red-faced reporter with a faux-hawk hairdo chased as fast as his ampu-toed foot would allow.

Chapter 64
HIS BEST CHANCE

THE NIECE SAT on the living room couch in the apartment above the Green Vase showroom, staring at the brass alligator lamp as she waited for her ride to Mountain Lake. A few minutes earlier, Monty had set out on foot to recover his van from the alley behind the now-defunct fried-chicken restaurant. Any second now, he would drive by to pick her up.

She had at first refused to participate in Monty's ill-conceived rescue operation, but the prospect of at least nominally complying with her uncle's parting request—combined with the potential spectacle of her gangly-legged neighbor wrestling a live alligator—had proved too tempting to resist.

A GROGGY BURP croaked up from the opposite side of the couch, interrupting the niece's thoughts.

Rupert lay stretched across the couch's firmer cushions while his distended stomach struggled to digest the large chicken meal he'd just scarfed down.

The niece sighed as he let out a satisfied wheeze and rolled over onto his side. She hadn't had the heart to tell him that the dinner was likely the last of Oscar's chicken—at least for the foreseeable future.

A HONK ECHOED up from the street outside. The niece grabbed her tote bag and hurried through the kitchen to the stairs leading to the first floor.

The bag bumped against her hip as she skipped down the steps. In it, she'd stashed her flashlight and a first-aid kit—both of which she suspected she might need before the night's escapade was over.

A moment later, she stepped out onto the sidewalk and turned to lock the front door. The van, this time driven by its rightful owner, idled on the street as she trotted around to the front passenger-side door.

"What about the cats?" Monty demanded as she climbed in.

"They're inside," she replied, pointing up at the second-floor apartment, where Isabella's tiny head peeked through the binds. "Come on. Let's get going."

Monty looked perplexed. "But we always travel with the cats."

The niece sighed tensely. "*We've* only traveled together once," she corrected him. "On the trip to Nevada City."

Once had been more than enough, she thought with a grimace.

Monty turned the key in the ignition, killing the motor.

"My instructions were very clear," he said officiously. "For this alligator extraction to be successful, it's essential that I bring both you *and* the cats."

"Whose instructions?" she demanded, although she knew the answer. "Look, Monty, there's no reason to drag the cats into this."

The driver was unpersuaded. He shook his head in vehement disapproval. "No cats, no deal. It's bad luck to try it without them."

The niece unbuckled her seat belt and pushed open her door.

"Oh good grief."

OKAY, THIS IS it," the niece called out as she hefted the second carrier into the van's rear cargo hold. She pushed the crates up against the floor brackets so they wouldn't slide around during the drive. Rupert yawned sleepily inside his carrier, while Isabella stared alertly out of hers.

Monty waved from the driver's seat and cheerfully restarted the engine.

Dusting her hands on her pants legs, the woman stepped away from the bumper so she could secure the back door. But as she grabbed the handle and prepared to swing the door shut, she noticed a small round lump on the floor between the cat carriers and a black canvas bag filled with Monty's gear.

Leaning back inside the van, she peered down at the brown fish pellet.

"I've got a bad feeling about this."

MONTY SWITCHED ON the radio as the van left Jackson Square. It was tuned to a local government-access station that was broadcasting the board of supervisors' meeting.

The president's voice crackled desperately through the speakers, "Does anyone have a nomination? Anyone? Anyone?"

"I'm surprised you're not there," the niece said. She pointed at the Current Mayor's bobblehead jiggling on the van's dashboard. "What with your various political interests and all."

"Oh, I offered to go," Monty replied quickly. "But the Mayor thought there was a better chance of success if I stayed away."

The niece glanced over at him skeptically. "Success of what?"

Chapter 65
THE VOTE

THE PRESIDENT OF the Board of Supervisors stared wearily across the supervisors' chambers. Everyone in the room was exhausted, board members and audience alike, but having seen the process play out this far, no one was willing to leave until the final vote was completed.

Supervisor Hernandez drained his sixth paper coffee cup and added it to a growing pyramid tower on a side table beside the center dais.

After all these many hours, they were about to vote on the most ridiculous nominee of the night. In his opinion, this was a complete waste of time, but the rules of procedure dictated he go through the motions.

With a glance at the upper section of the

audience, where the person in the chicken costume had been performing the moonwalk, Hernandez pounded his gavel.

"We will proceed to take the vote," he announced dubiously.

"The supervisor from the Marina district?"

"Aye."

Not surprising, Hernandez thought with a shrug. He was the one who'd made this oddball nomination.

"From the Richmond?"

"Aye."

This, too, Hernandez dismissed. The supervisor who had seconded the nomination was practically obliged to carry on with this charade.

"The supervisor from Union Square and the Tenderloin."

"Aye."

Hernandez snorted out a short laugh. Always a comic, that one. He probably thinks of this as one big joke.

"From the Mission?"

"Aye."

Now, Hernandez was starting to get concerned. What was going on here? He stuttered, confused, as he summoned the next vote.

"Uh . . . ah . . . Chinatown?"

"Aye."

Hernandez cleared his throat. This could not be happening. He leaned forward in his chair and issued his sternest, most serious stare at the next representative.

"The supervisor representing the Castro?"

"Aye."

The word echoed through the chamber. That was enough. Six votes made a majority. The rest was merely procedural. Hernandez's face flattened with awe as he completed the tally.

"Aye . . . Aye . . . Aye . . . Aye."

He was down to the last vote—his own. He gulped, tugged at his tie, and hoarsely spoke his name into the microphone.

"Supervisor Hernandez, on behalf of the Excelsior district."

He paused, licked his lips, and with a punch-drunk grin gave his assent.

"Aye."

Chapter 66
A RECOUNT

AS THE BOARD of supervisors cast their final vote of the evening, Monty steered the white cargo van into the dimly lit parking lot for Mountain Lake.

The fog had settled over the landscape, blotting out all but the nearest features: a small jungle gym with peeling paint set up in a sandy playground and a narrow path winding toward the lake's south shore.

The niece looked out through the front passenger-side window, trying to see into the mist. She could sense more than see the lake, which lay, dark and brooding, beyond a row of scrubby trees.

Securing the brake, Monty leaped from the driver's seat and began jogging a victory lap around the van. His high-pitched holler echoed through the foggy night.

"I am the mayor! I am the mayor!"

"I demand a recount," the niece muttered.

From the rear cargo area, Isabella offered her own thoughts on the matter.

"Mrao," she opined dubiously.

Chapter 67
THE NOTE

WITH THE FINAL, stunning vote completed, City Hall quickly emptied out. The supervisors and the audience members spilled down the central marble staircase, through the rotunda, and out onto Civic Center Plaza. Television news crews filmed quick summation clips and then wrapped up their gear and headed home.

Hoxton Fin sat in the chambers long after everyone else had left, still pondering how the supervisors had arrived at this bizarre result, contemplating what it would mean for the city's future, and wondering whether the missing-alligator saga had distracted him from doing his best reporting on the interim-mayor story.

ONE LONE OCCUPANT of City Hall continued to work, his progress unabated by the selection of the new mayor, whose identity he had known for almost twenty-four hours.

A lone lamp was lit in the basement cubicle where Spider Jones sat at his desk, reviewing the documents he planned to present to the Previous Mayor at their late-night dinner meeting.

Spider glanced at his watch. He would need to leave soon if he didn't want to be late. He gathered up the selected pile, tapped the edge of the papers against his desk so that they were neatly aligned, and slid the documents into his backpack. He wanted to have everything perfectly laid out when he presented his discovery to the PM.

He was about to reach for his bike when the night-shift janitor shuffled into the basement office area.

"Hey, Spider," the man said, handing him a piece of paper. "Someone wants to see you upstairs."

Spider read the writing on the paper and grinned. The PM must be trying to get out of the restaurant Spider had selected for their dinner. Leaving his bike propped against the cubicle, he slung his backpack across his shoulders and headed for the stairs.

Chapter 68
ALL THINGS IN MODERATION

THE PREVIOUS MAYOR exited a cab on Columbus Avenue near a busy bistro toward the south end of North Beach's busy restaurant scene. He stood on the sidewalk, wincing as he stared at the black-painted storefront. The kitchen had been cooking at full capacity for several hours now. Even on the street outside the dining area, the scent of roasted garlic was overwhelming his senses.

"Touché, my young friend." The PM sighed as he pulled a water bottle out of his coat pocket, unscrewed the lid, and took a long sip.

Reluctantly, he walked through the entrance and approached the hostess's station for a table. A couple at a nearby booth pointed him out, waved, and clicked his picture with their cell phones.

He would have some explaining to do in his next column, he mused ruefully. The sacrifice was worth it, he told himself. He was becoming more and more worried about what Spider might have gotten himself into.

The hostess hurried up. Her face flashed a mixture of recognition and confusion as she showed the PM to a front-window booth. While she was ushering him to his seat, a waiter walked past carrying a platter of garlic mashed potatoes.

With a smile, the PM pointed at the plate.

"I think my friend would like one of those when he gets here."

Chapter 69

THE CEREMONIAL ROTUNDA

SPIDER JOGGED UP a narrow flight of stairs to City Hall's main floor, his loaded backpack sliding down his shoulders, the note from the janitor clutched in his left hand.

He emerged from the stairwell to find the building's primary lighting system had been switched off. With the completion of the supervisors' meeting, the security staff had resumed their regular after-hours routine. The dimmer secondary lighting reflected off the many polished stone surfaces, throwing shadows across the expansive interior.

Spider continued, unfazed. The rubber soles of his sneakers squeaked as he hurried across the pink marble floor beneath the rotunda. He'd worked late into the night more times than he could count in the last several months. He was accustomed to the building's spooky evening glow.

Halfway up the central staircase, however, the

spring in his step deadened at the sight of a darkened figure—not that of the Previous Mayor—standing on the landing above.

Spider stopped on the stairs and glanced around the rotunda area. Hundreds of feet of open space stretched above him, the hallways that ringed the upper levels were empty, and the floor below was vacant. He was alone with this stranger.

The man crossed through a patch of light and Spider relaxed, breathing out a sigh of relief at the chiseled face of Hoxton Fin. The reporter grunted a greeting as he passed the young staffer on the steps.

LAUGHING AT HIS moment of panic, Spider reached the landing at the top of the staircase. It was silly to have been scared, he thought as he held up the piece of paper and unfolded it to reread the writing.

Yes, he confirmed, scanning the area, this is where the message had instructed him to meet the Previous Mayor. He noted the bust of Harvey Milk positioned off to the side of the smaller ceremonial rotunda.

A second nervous sensation crept over Spider as he looked up at the round balcony right above the rotunda. He must be imagining things, he told himself, shifting his backpack from his shoulders to the ground. He couldn't shake the feeling that someone was hiding in the shadows.

"Hello?" he called out, his voice pitching with anxiety.

In that odd, eerie moment, Spider remembered his previous trips to the second floor. He'd stood in just this spot, wearing the janitor's coveralls, sweeping the mop across the floor, spying on the building's occupants while hiding in plain sight.

Suddenly, he didn't feel quite so invisible.

Chapter 70

CURIOSITY KILLED THE . . .

"EASY BREEZY—THAT'S what this is going to be," Monty called out from behind the van, where he was struggling into his wet suit.

The niece stood a discreet distance away, holding leash handles attached to her two cats. She'd fitted both felines with body harnesses to ensure they didn't inadvertently escape. Isabella had slipped easily into her equipment, but the woman had had to make some widening adjustments to Rupert's.

"So, what is your plan, exactly?" the niece asked skeptically. Charging into the lake in a wet suit didn't appear to be the wisest course of action.

Monty stepped from behind the van's rear doors, his body fully encased in the black rubber wet suit. He carried a snorkel mask in one hand, a pair of flippers in the other.

"Oh, come on," he said, pooh-poohing her concern. "Didn't you see the pictures of Clive riding the cable car earlier today? Sam had his arm wrapped around him like a puppy dog."

Monty bowed, waving his hands through the air as if ushering a guest through a door. "I'll just lead him right out of the water and into the van."

The niece's eyes widened as Monty marched past her and started off down the path toward the lake's south shore. Clearly, Oscar and his gang hadn't told Monty that the alligator roaming the streets of San Francisco had been a robotic imposter.

"Uh, Monty," the niece sputtered, trying to find the right words to correct his misconception, but he was already out of earshot, the wet suit squeaking loudly as he walked.

"Monty!"

Scooping up the two cats, the niece hurried after him.

CLIVE FLOATED IN the murky, muddy water, about fifty feet from the shoreline, contemplating a late-night snack.

Feathers, he thought, gumming his large mouth distastefully as a low hooting honk resonated from across the bay on the opposite side of the Presidio's sweeping hills.

That's my only complaint about this place, he grumbled, eying a pair of plump ducks paddling a short distance away. *Too many feathers in the food.*

His snout sank into the water as he reluctantly assumed a stealth approach on the birds. He was about to move in for the kill when he sensed a disturbance at the edge of the lake.

What's this? Clive mused, immediately intrigued.

THE NIECE SCANNED her flashlight's beam over the water's surface, but the light did little to cut through the dense, soupy fog. She stood beside the lake's southernmost bench, holding onto the leashes for her cats, both of whom sat on its seat.

Turning, she glanced nervously at a short rise behind the bench, where a homeless man slept in the grass, but after a puzzling stare at his snoring heap she quickly returned her attention to her wet suit–clad neighbor.

"Are you sure this is a good idea?" she asked as Monty slipped his snorkel gear over his head. "I don't think you have the right information about Clive . . ."

"You'll see," Monty cut in, his boast a little too confident. "He'll be just like a puppy dog."

"Monty," the woman tried again as he splashed into the reeds. "You don't understand . . ."

"Cllliii-iive," he called out stubbornly. "Over here, *ally-gator, ally-gator.*"

The niece sighed with frustration. Shrugging, she looked down at Isabella.

"I give up."

The cat's face crimped dubiously, but, after a moment's reflection, she pawed the air instructively.

"Mrao."

"I suppose you're right," the woman conceded with a sigh. "The gator might choke on his snorkel."

She hesitated a second longer before calling out again.

"Monty, wait!"

But her voice was drowned out by a pair of squawking ducks. Monty's head dipped below the water as a loud grating sound ricocheted across the lake.

Chomp.

The niece covered her mouth with her hand.

"Oh dear."

Chapter 71
A LIFE CUT SHORT

THE MAN GASPED with painful surprise as the first tearing slice ripped through his body, across his chest, and down his left arm. The second puncture seared his left lung. His breath whistled out of the wound.

It all happened so quickly. His attacker had appeared from out of nowhere. He spun around, trying to defend himself, but his assailant's face was a blur.

"Why?" his voice wheezed in shock and disbelief.

The third blow brought him to his knees.

Blood gushed onto the floor. A gurgling flow filled his mouth, gagging him, choking him.

Disoriented and quickly losing consciousness, he tumbled to the hard marble floor at the foot of the Harvey Milk bust.

Spider reached out with his right arm, struggling to crawl toward the stairs, but the trauma inflicted to his body was too severe. His eyes fluttered; the brown skin on his young face began to pale and stiffen.

His blue baseball cap lay upended, teetering on its rounded crown next to his outstretched hand, where his fingers still grasped the crumpled piece of paper.

AFTER WATCHING THE young man's last writhing breath, a mysterious figure stealthily bent to the marble floor and, with a gloved hand, removed the note that had summoned the young staffer to his death.

Chapter 72

AN EMPTY BELLY

MONTGOMERY CARMICHAEL ABANDONED his flippers as he streaked out of the lake. His bare feet scrambled through the reeds near the shoreline and up the muddy embankment. His skinny legs had never pumped so fast; rarely had his slim body exerted such physical effort.

The newly appointed Mayor of San Francisco never once looked back at the pale white glow of the albino alligator forlornly watching his fleeing dinner.

CLIVE FLOATED DISAPPOINTEDLY in the water, cursing his poor eyesight. He had been so close to capturing the feather-free creature, but it had slipped away from him at the last minute. The meal might have been a bit bony, he reflected, trying to comfort himself as he rotated his long body back toward the center of the lake.

Ducks it is, he thought with a gloomy shiver. His short, stubby legs paddled through the water. He was really starting to miss his heated rock.

JUST AS CLIVE was about to droop off into duck-induced depression, a hobo-dressed figure carrying a large sack appeared at the edge of the lake. With a sharp summoning whistle, the man reached into his bag and pulled out a small brown puck-shaped object.

Clive blinked. He dared not believe what he was seeing.

The puck sailed through the air, skipping across the surface of the water like a rock, until it stopped and began to sink about a foot from Clive's pointed snout. The alligator moved instinctively toward the pellet.

Chomp.

Chapter 73

THE PIED PIPER

HOXTON FIN TROMPED into the Palace Hotel, strode wearily down its lavishly decorated main corridor, and pulled open the heavy wooden doors for the Pied Piper Bar. Sliding into a stool facing the several-foot-long Maxfield Parrish painting that gave the bar its name, he slumped over the mahogany counter and ordered a cocktail. The sharp, brooding angles of his face deepened as he stared at the wall, lost in thought.

The bartender placed a liquor-filled glass in front of the sulking reporter. Hox waved his hand over the glass, blocking the barman from adding a toothpicked cherry or the offered slice of orange.

AS HOX GLARED down the bartender, an elderly woman in a feather-plumed hat slid into the seat beside him. Hox turned to stare at his drinking companion. He'd seen the woman several times at City Hall—she was always there, with her ridiculous hats, lurking around the edges, but he'd never been able to figure out in what capacity. Regardless, his curiosity on matters bizarre was at a low ebb.

"Not now, Dilla," Hox grumbled into his drink.

"I've been following your latest reports on the telly," she replied, not in any way taken aback by his gruff demeanor. "Your investigative journalism on the alligator . . ."

Hox took a swig of his drink. "Should have been paying more attention to the board of supervisors."

"Now, now, dear," she said, a twinkle in her eye. "You were on the right track."

Slowly, Hox set his glass on the bar. He swiveled in his stool, eyeing her suspiciously.

Dilla leaned toward him and whispered conspiratorially, "Clive's ready to come home. Someone just needs to find him."

She winked up at the Pied Piper painting.

"Are you ready to lead the pack to his location?"

Chapter 74
HOW TO TAIL A CAT

"**THIS IS HOXTON** Fin reporting from Mountain Lake, where Clive, the missing alligator from the California Academy of Sciences, was found earlier this evening. Half an hour ago, Academy scientists used compacted fish pellets to lure Clive out of the water and into a truck, which has transported him back to the Swamp Exhibit. Police are still on the hunt for the red-haired man seen accompanying Clive around San Francisco the last couple of days."

Hox turned to allow the cameraman to pan his lens over the still-chaotic scene. News teams surrounded by bright floodlights lit up the lake. A number of police cars along with a handful of fire trucks were crammed into the small gravel parking lot near the playground. Curious residents from a nearby neighborhood walked about the area, pointing at the water.

Grimacing, Hox returned his gaze to the camera.

"In a perplexing addendum to this story, just prior to Clive's rescue, Montgomery Carmichael, the city's new Interim Mayor, was seen fleeing the area in a full-body wet suit. I believe we have some shaky cell-phone video on this that was sent in to the station. Interim Mayor Carmichael will no doubt have some explaining to do at his first press conference, scheduled for tomorrow morning."

Hox paused, his rugged face paling as he transitioned to a second breaking story.

"In other news, a young man was found murdered tonight at City Hall. Just eighteen, the victim was a junior staffer for the Outgoing Mayor. His body was discovered by a member of the janitorial staff at the top of the central marble staircase near the Harvey Milk commemorative bust. We will, of course, keep you up-to-date as more details become available."

JAMES LICK SAT behind the wheel of the large white cargo van, listening to the news update from the vehicle's radio. As Hoxton Fin finished his report, Lick reached a worn, stubby hand for the dial and turned off the radio. Then he returned his grip to the steering wheel and steadied the van as its tires bumped across one of the lower outbound lanes of the Bay Bridge.

Sam Eckles rode in the front passenger seat, holding two ventilated glass carriers in his lap, each one amphibian occupied. On their way out of the city, Sam had introduced the three new frogs to the two older frogs. The two camps stared curiously at each other through the glass walls, googly eyes to googly eyes.

A third carrier rested on the floor of the van near

Sam's feet. This cage held a tiny hairless mouse, who had curled up in a soft handkerchief-sized blanket and dozed off to sleep.

"Take a good look, fellas," Sam whispered to the frogs, holding the carriers up to the window as the van approached the bridge's Treasure Island exit and midpoint tunnel. "We won't be back for a good long while."

The driver flexed his stiff arthritic hands as his rounded shoulders hunched forward in the seat. The sooner they got off the interstate, the better. They would be taking the back roads that night through the Sonoma hills to a reclusive compound near the Bohemian Grove.

Lick glanced in his rearview mirror. The headlamps from a passing semi threw light onto the floor of the back cargo area. Next to a discarded fish pellet lay a crumpled canvas heap. Lick's eyes squinted as the glare lessened, and the image became clearer.

With a sad sigh, he returned his eyes to the road. He couldn't bear to look at the blood-spattered backpack.

Their latest caper had gone horribly awry.

THE NIECE SAT on the cratered-out couch in the living room in the apartment above the Green Vase antiques shop, staring at the lamp on the nearby end table.

On the floor next to the coffee table lay a

souvenir she'd found on her doorstep when she and the cats returned from Mountain Lake earlier that evening. The mechanical alligator tail was a far less convincing imitation when unattached to the rest of the robot's body.

Even Rupert was no longer afraid of the appendage. He crouched next to the end piece, his own tail swirling in the air as he tentatively swatted a paw at the leathery exterior.

"I don't know, Issy," the woman said, turning her gaze from the lamp to the cat perched on the couch's opposite armrest. "I just can't shake the sense that I missed something here."

Isabella let out a sleepy yawn, as if to convey that she'd given up trying to lead her person through Uncle Oscar's obscure clues.

"Unless . . ." the niece said, standing from her seat. Thoughtfully tapping her finger against her chin, she walked into the kitchen.

Crossing the tile floor, the woman reached for the handle to the refrigerator's freezer compartment. She pulled open the door and removed the large plastic bag containing the butcher paper–wrapped package labeled "boneless breast meat"—the bundle that Monty had carried through the basement tunnel to Union Square—the one that Harold Wombler had insisted on giving her during her last visit to the still-operational fried-chicken restaurant.

Brow furrowed, the niece set the package on the

kitchen table. Carefully, she began peeling back the stiff outer layer of the frozen plastic bag. When she'd uncovered a sizable portion of butcher paper, she fetched a knife from a nearby drawer and used it to slice away the paper. After a few minutes' work, she lifted the sheet.

She shook her head at the clear block of ice revealed beneath.

Frozen in the block's center was a large gold object, cast in the shape of a standing seahorse. A date stamped into the design indicated the year the Steinhart Aquarium first opened for business: 1923.

AS THE NIECE stared down at the table, she heard a banging *bump* in the living room. Wiping her hands on a hastily grabbed paper towel, she hurried out of the kitchen.

Rushing to the living room door, she quickly found the source of the noise.

Rupert's furry orange and white body staggered back and forth next to the coffee table, his head encased in the fake alligator tail.

Isabella sat on the armrest, serenely observing his predicament. She looked up at her person as the woman stifled a laugh.

Isabella blinked her blue eyes and assumed a smug expression that clearly transmitted her thoughts.

"I figured out how to tail a cat."